SHACK GIRLS

L.A. Scott

ISBN: 978-1-66783-223-4 (softcover)
ISBN: 978-1-66783-224-1 (eBook)

DEDICATION

To all the wonderful, strong, talented women in my life.

ACKNOWLEDGEMENTS

Special thanks to Susan Bruck, Julie Mianecki, and Robin Locke, for their talent, professionalism and thoughtful assistance during the production of this book.

CHAPTER 1

Winter 2019

IT WAS WINDY and cold as I walked along Michigan Avenue in downtown Chicago. I pulled my hat down over my ears and clutched my coat close. As I did, I glanced up and noticed I was in front of the Art Institute. I stood there for a few seconds and watched as throngs of people, even in this cold weather, climbed the steps and flowed into the entrance. I thought about the thousands of pieces of priceless art, from all around the world displayed inside. I wondered if these people were as excited to see those exhibits as I was to see the pieces of art I was going to see, exhibited in a small private gallery only a block away.

Just a few months ago, I'd seen that art in progress, and now it was on display here in Chicago. I was eager to see the pieces in their final form. Each artist, utilizing her particular medium and area of talent, had created a piece that represented something personal and meaningful to her. It also represented her special connection to the other artists in the collection.

As I neared the entrance to the gallery, the door flew open and I heard, "Lynnie!" as Jo wrapped her arms around me in a big warm hug. "I've been watching for you. I couldn't wait for you to get here. Come on," she said taking me by the hand and pulling me inside.

"She's here," Jo called out as heads turned to see who had just arrived. Suddenly, a group of women came running toward me, quickly engulfing me in hugs and welcomes.

"Hey, let her breathe!" exclaimed, Smitty, attracting even more attention from other gallery visitors. As the arms loosened, and I was let free, I pulled back to get a look at my dear friends.

"I'm so excited to be here and see you all," I said. "It seems like such a long time since I've been with you. I've missed you all, and I can't wait to see how your pieces turned out."

"We're so glad you were able to come," Carrie said. "We've been waiting anxiously for you, and I think the anticipation made us a bit out of control."

"Speak for yourself," Kellan said as she stepped forward, gave me another big hug, and whispered in my ear, "I was willing to wait my turn and not make a scene."

"Well, I wouldn't have missed it for the world, mainly because I get to spend some time with you all, but also because the last time I saw these pieces they were still in process. I'm so excited to see how they turned out."

We walked around the gallery together, one mass of six women, viewing and talking about each piece. It had been months since I had seen these pieces and at that time they were still being created. But now, I was seeing them finished and they were just as beautiful as remembered. I was surprised at how intimate the pieces were and the connection they had to each other. I knew these women well and, while the other people here to see the exhibit did not know them, they would get a glimpse into each artist as they experienced her piece and her unique personal perspective. They would also get a view into the relationships between these artists and their experiences working together in their studio, a place affectionately called the "shack."

CHAPTER 2

Winter 2018

"OH, SMITTY, WAIT. Wait just one second before you close the kiln. Can I run and grab a piece I've been keeping in Callie's studio?"

"How big is it? There's not a lot of room left in here," Smitty said without looking up, and continuing to carefully arrange the pieces inside the kiln.

Lynne stood up, her hands covered in wet clay. "Let me wash my hands and get it so you can see." Rinsing her hands in the sink and drying them on her apron, Lynne headed down the long wide hall of the artists' shack to Callie's studio.

"Hey, Callie, are you here?" Lynne called out as she knocked on the door and peeked in. Spotting Callie she said, "Oh, hi. I wasn't sure you were here today."

"Mike went hunting this morning, so I decided to come in and get some things wrapped up."

"I left a piece in your closet because we ran out of space in our studio. I hope that's okay," Lynne said as she strode past Callie to get to the storage closet.

"That's fine," Callie replied, watching as Lynne emerged with her vase in hand. "I wondered if that was yours. It's beautiful, Lynne, and I find that shape very seductive. You are good! You can use my closet anytime."

"Thank you! I think it looks pretty good too, especially for me," Lynne said smiling. "Smitty is ready to run the kiln, so I need to bring this down to her before she shuts the door and I'm too late for this round. I'm eager to see how the glaze works out."

"Me too," Callie replied. "Don't forget to show it to me when it's done."

Lynne returned to the ceramics studio with her vase. As she entered, she saw Smitty waiting patiently by the kiln.

"That's a great piece, Lynnie. I don't remember seeing you working on it," Smitty said as she removed it from Lynne's hands and placed it carefully into the kiln. "And it fits perfectly."

"Thank you—and thanks for waiting for me. I'm glad it fit!" Lynne said, as she dipped her hands in water and sat down at her workbench to resume working on a massive bowl.

The two women worked along in companionable silence until they were interrupted by the unexpected sound of a male voice.

"Well, Lynne, I finally found you. How are you?"

Without looking up to see who it was, Lynne felt the hairs on the back of her neck stand up. She was struck by an overwhelming wave of anxiety that made her sick to her stomach. She forced herself to look in his direction, her heart pounding uncontrollably. Her panic made it hard to focus her eyes, and even though she knew it was him, she couldn't make out the details of his face. Her body had gone into fight or flight mode. She stood up, and as she did, she felt light-headed.

"Do you remember me?" he asked.

"No," she lied, trying desperately to sound matter-of-fact in her response.

"Now, Lynne," he said, in a sickeningly sweet tone of voice, "of course you do. It's me, David—David Hoffman. We met a few years back at Byron's Bar. Remember? We had such a great time. I'm sure you must remember me. Come on, now—you're hurting my feelings."

He leaned nonchalantly against the door frame, like he was right at home and very comfortable in her space. He watched Lynne with great intensity, reading the fear and shock on her face. She'd never been good at covering up her feelings, and she knew he could see the explosion of dread and anxiety written in her expression and shaking hands.

"What are you doing here?" she asked angrily.

"Now, Lynne, that's not very nice. Is that any way to greet an old friend? You seem almost hostile."

"You are not an old friend, and neither of us is confused as to why I'm being hostile toward you. What are you doing here?" she repeated more forcefully, her anger giving her strength.

"It's taken me a long time to find you. Imagine my surprise and disappointment when I went to your house and found out you'd moved. It took me a while to find out where you'd gone, and when I did, well, I decided I had to come see you. It's been such a long time. Sixteen long years, Lynne. It's been sixteen years," he said with emphasis. "I just wanted to see how you were doing—and I must say you are looking good, Lynne," he said, leering at her. "Time has been good to you."

"Get out or I'll call the police. You are trespassing."

"Actually, I was let in by a lovely lady just down the hall," he said, smiling as he pointed to the front of the shack.

Smitty had been quietly watching the entire interaction. She could see that Lynne was in great distress. "Lynne, if you don't want him here, I will show him out."

Lynne reached out and took Smitty's hand. "Smitty, would you please call the police and tell them we have an intruder?"

Smitty squeezed her hand, and, without saying a word, started toward her workbench.

Immediately, David stepped in front of her and blocked her from reaching her phone. Then, keeping his eyes on Smitty while continuing to speak to Lynne, he said, "Now, Lynne. I just wanted to talk. There's no need to get angry and threatening. We need to catch up. A lot has happened. I want to hear about everything that's happened since the last time I saw you."

Lynne's face was now bright red, her voice was filled with rage. She felt more confident and in control of her emotions. "You are the one who is being threatening. I have nothing to say to you, and I don't want to hear anything about you. Just get out!"

"And get out of my way," Smitty added.

David put his hands up in front of him without touching Smitty. Addressing Lynne, he said, "We have some unfinished business," and he removed something from his shirt pocket. "I want to make it clear that I'm not going to leave town until we talk. I'm leaving my contact information here with your friend," he said, holding the card out to Smitty.

Smitty looked at Lynne and then pulled her hands away, forcing David to put the card on a nearby shelf.

Then, in a low grumble he said, "You call me, and it better be soon. Don't force me to take matters into my own hands."

As he stepped into the hall, his demeanor changed completely. He broke into a smile and said in a calm, pleasant voice, "Sorry to bother you, Smitty." But when he turned to face Lynne, his face became hard again, and he said, "I expect to hear from you soon." He turned and left the studio, striding down the long hall and out the front door.

Smitty looked at Lynne and reached out to take her by the arm. "Sit down, Lynne. You don't look well."

Before Lynne could make it over to her workbench, her knees buckled and her legs went out from under her. She collapsed to the floor taking Smitty with her. She lay with her back on the floor and pulled her knees up in an attempt to get the blood flowing back into her head. Then she put her forearm over her eyes and began to cry, whether from distress or relief, or both, she wasn't sure.

Jo heard footsteps coming down the hallway, and stuck her head out of her studio, just as David walked by, looking very angry. She stood and watched as the front door slammed behind him, then turned and headed to

Smitty's studio. As she entered, seeing Lynne on the floor and the look on her face, she knew that something terrible must have happened. "Are you two okay? What was that about?"

"We're okay," Smitty said, stepping closer to Lynne.

"What happened?" Jo asked.

"I'm not sure," Smitty said quietly; and then looking at Jo, Smitty said in a calm but firm voice, "Would you please lock the front and back doors?"

Still not knowing what had transpired, but picking up on the urgency in Smitty's tone, Jo raced down the hall to lock the doors. As she started to lock the back door, Sam walked in.

"What are you doing?" Sam asked in an irritated voice.

"We have a bit of a situation here, and Smitty asked me to lock the front and back doors."

Hearing this, Sam marched down to Smitty's studio and found Lynne on the floor with Smitty sitting close to her.

"What the hell is going on?" Sam asked.

Ignoring Sam, Smitty leaned forward and gently put her hand on Lynne's forehead. "What just happened, Lynnie?"

Callie came in and asked, "Are you two okay? What the hell just happened? Who was that?"

Lynne said in exasperation, "Oh, nothing happened. I just overreacted. I'll be fine in just a minute. I was just surprised is all. It's nothing." She wiped away the tears from her face with the back of her hand and started to get up.

Smitty patted her arm. "Why don't you stay down here for a minute. The color hasn't come back into your face yet."

Lying down again, Lynne said, "I need to call Betsy. Would one of you hand me my phone? It's on my workbench."

Jo, who'd finished locking the doors, ran over, picked up Lynne's phone and handed it to her.

Lynne's fingers fumbled with the buttons, while Smitty stayed close; Jo and Callie stood over her with expressions of concern and bewilderment, since none of them understood the significance of what had happened. After several attempts, Lynne was finally able to put in the correct numbers, and she waited as the phone rang.

"Please, dear God, let Betsy be home," she said quietly to herself as the phone rang and rang. Finally, Betsy answered.

"Hey, Lynnie."

"Betsy, is Ron home for lunch yet?" she asked as her voice broke.

"Yes. He's here," Betsy said. "What's wrong?"

"David Hoffman was just here."

"Who?"

"David Hoffman."

There was a long pause. "Oh, Lynne, I am so sorry. There was a man who came by the farm this morning asking for you. He was very charming and seemed to know you well. It never dawned on me to ask him who he was. He just said he was an old friend. I'm so sorry! I told him where to find you."

"You should be careful, Betsy. I don't know what he's up to. Tell Ron so he knows to be careful too."

"Ron's here," she said. "I'll tell him and I am sure we'll be fine. But I am worried about you. Are you okay, Lynnie? Do you want us to come and get you?"

"No, I'll be fine. I was just taken by surprise. The shack girls are here with me. I'll be fine," she said again to convince herself. "I'll be home in a little while." Lynne hung up and looked around at everyone's worried faces.

"Lynnie, do you want me to drive you home?" Jo asked.

"No, thank you. I'll be okay in a few minutes, and besides, I have some work I want to finish up." Lynne said, trying to smile and sound confident. "I just need time to pull myself together. You don't need to be concerned. I'm sorry to have taken you all away from your work. I'm going to finish a few things, clean up my workbench and then head out to the farm."

"Lynnie, before you do anything else, we need you to explain to us what just happened. We need to know if we should be concerned either for you or for ourselves," Callie said firmly.

"It's nothing. He's someone I used to know a long time ago; and seeing him appear out of nowhere so suddenly was a bit of a shock."

"It was more than that. You were clearly scared to death—and you just called to warn Ron and Betsy about him. Why are you warning them? Should we be worried too?"

"Just tell us what happened," Sam demanded.

Lynne sat in the middle of the floor for several minutes, while the women stood around her, looking at her intently.

Finally, Callie knelt down and took hold of Lynne's hand. "We're here for you and can help you if you'll let us, but we need to know what this is really about."

Smitty sat down directly across from Lynne, and in her kind, soft voice said, "Tell us what's wrong, Lynnie."

Tears of frustration and anger started running down Lynne's cheeks. Jo knelt beside her, wrapping both arms around her and repeated, "We are here for you Lynne. Let us help you."

It had been sixteen years, and for all that time, Lynne had worked hard to get over what had happened and conceal her story. But today, sixteen years later, she had come face to face with it once again, and so had everyone she cared about.

CHAPTER 3

Summer 2001

IT WAS WEDNESDAY, and every Wednesday after work, a group of us from the office met at Byron's Bar for a drink, to defuse the pressure of the week and spend some downtime together. It was an opportunity to unwind and share stories outside of the office environment. One after another, as the afternoon wore on and anticipation began to build, my colleagues poked their heads into my office to remind me it was "Byron's Wednesday" and to ask if I was coming that night.

I was definitely ready for some downtime and could hardly wait to finish the workday. Finally, even though I was not quite finished with my report, I decided to stop for the day and head over to Byron's. I stuck some papers in my briefcase, planning to review them with fresh eyes later that night after I got home.

I walked out to my car, and as I settled my briefcase in the backseat, I noticed my gym bag on the floor. I'd forgotten that I hadn't made it to the gym that morning. Feeling a bit guilty about that and, noticing that the sun was still out and it was a glorious summer day, I decided to get a few steps in by walking over to Byron's.

I sat down on the front seat of my car, took off my heels, and put on my running shoes. It was only about a mile to Byron's, and it was just six o'clock. In July, it stayed light until about eight-thirty or nine. I would need to remember to leave Byron's a bit early so I could walk back to my car before it got dark. I locked my car and set out.

People from the office honked as they passed me or rolled down their windows to ask if I wanted a ride. I waved and thanked them but explained I preferred to walk. The air felt so refreshing after being cooped up inside my office all day. I felt truly content and at peace. My life was really pretty great. I had a terrific job, wonderful friends, and I was outside on a beautiful evening.

I walked through the city park, where I inhaled the smell of freshly-cut grass and kicked the clippings that were scattered across the sidewalk. There were lots of people in the park. They were out enjoying the summer evening too. I passed people sitting on the park benches talking or reading the paper, a couple of kids kicking a soccer ball, and a man walking his dog. A woman with a small cart smiled at me as she passed, pulling her groceries along behind her on her way home.

It seemed like only minutes until I reached the door to Byron's. Byron's was an institution in town. It was an older bar, but one known for great food. They had plenty of space, so people could move around and talk with each other easily—and it wasn't too dark or too bright inside. Tonight, the door was propped open and, as I approached, I could hear the music and the laughter inside. I could smell the fries and burgers cooking, and they smelled great. My stomach growled.

As soon as I walked through the door, my friend Wendy ran up to me and grabbed me by the arm. Leaning in close, she whispered in my ear, "I have someone I want you to meet." She was grinning from ear to ear as she led me to the end of the bar.

"Dean, this is Lynne. Lynne, meet Dean. I thought you two would hit it off. Dean was just telling me that he likes to bike, too."

"Really?" I said.

Dean stood up as she introduced him to me. He was very tall and very handsome. He had violet-blue eyes, dark curly hair, and a confident smile.

He extended his hand to me and said in a deep sultry voice, "Pleased to meet you, Lynne."

As I extended my hand, he enveloped it with his. I looked up from my hand to his handsome face and said, "Hello, Dean. It's nice meeting you, too."

"May I buy you ladies a drink?" he asked as he pulled a chair out for each of us. I felt my stomach flutter, and I tried to maintain my composure as I smiled back at him and sat down.

"That would be nice. Thank you," I said as I turned to ask Wendy how she and Dean knew each other. But she'd already made her way to the other side of the bar.

"How do you know Wendy?" I asked Dean.

"I just met her. We'd only been talking for about fifteen minutes before you got here."

"Really. So how does she know we'll 'hit it off'?" I asked.

"Well, I'm not sure. We'll have to ask her, or—we could just get to know each other and make our minds up for ourselves," he said with a grin.

We did hit it off. We ended up ordering dinner, and we talked for several hours. I felt comfortable talking to him. He told me all about himself. He did like to bike and, in fact, was looking for a cycling club. He'd just moved to Chicago from Detroit and was working for a small tech consulting firm, working long hours and even weekends, meaning he did not get home to Michigan very often to visit his dad and two brothers.

He told me about his mother and how they had been very close. She had passed away when he was in college after years of struggling with multiple sclerosis, and her loss had been something his father had not gotten over. His brothers lived close to their dad, and they checked on him regularly, but he still felt guilty for not getting home more often. When they were growing up he and his brothers called themselves the "boys band," and he missed them terribly. *He is perfect*, I thought to myself as I listened to him.

Someone bumped into me as they walked past me on their way out of the bar. As they opened the door, I could see it was dark outside. I looked around to see if anyone was still there from my office—but I didn't recognize anyone. They had all gone. I turned back to Dean and said, "I'm not sure where the time has gone, but I have to go. I walked over from my office and need to go back there to get my car."

"Can I offer you a ride? I can drop you off on my way home."

I looked up into his violet-blue eyes and thought how handsome he was and, feeling my face flush, I became immediately embarrassed—hoping he couldn't read my mind.

"Well, thank you. If it's not a bother, I would appreciate that."

"Great, my car is out front," Dean said.

We settled our bill and walked outside to his car. He opened the car door for me, and as he did, I got a whiff of new car smell as I sat down. I love cars, but I wasn't focused on this new car — I was focused on him. I watched him walk around to the other side of the car and open his door. I could feel my heart and stomach begin to flutter. I really liked him.

As he sat down, I looked down and noticed my feet. Oh my God! I had forgotten I was wearing my running shoes with my skirt! I was so embarrassed. I tried to tuck my feet as far under the seat as possible, and when I looked up at him, I could see him looking at me intently with a beautiful smile on his face.

"Okay, how do we get there?" he asked.

"Just go straight down this street until you come to the park, follow it around, then pick up the road again on the other side. It really is just a straight shot from my office to Byron's," I explained as I realized this wonderful evening was about to come to an end.

As we approached the office, I directed him to the parking lot and pointed to where my car was parked. Dean pulled up behind it, got out, and walked around to help me out. I could feel my heart flutter again as he took my hand and then really go crazy as he hung onto my hand as he walked me over to my car. We stopped by the side of the car, and he waited while I fumbled around in my purse to find my keys to unlock the door. As the door lock clicked up, he opened the door for me. *I like him a lot,* I said to myself as I sat down in my car.

Just then, he bent down, gave me a gentle kiss on the cheek and said the words I'd been dying to hear, "I had a great time tonight, Lynne. May I call you?"

"Yes, I'd like that," I said trying not to appear too excited. Then clumsily, I scrounged around in my purse until I found a pen and scribbled my cell phone number on the back of my business card.

As he took it, Dean said, "I had a great time tonight, Lynne. I'll call you so we can arrange to get together soon." Then he carefully closed my car door.

I was so happy. Giddy is really a more accurate description of how I felt. I tried to look composed as I waved good-bye. I replayed every exciting minute of the evening as I drove home. It was late, but I wanted to call and tell someone all about it. I had to fight with myself not to call Wendy and wake her up to tell her what a great find he was, how wonderful the evening had been, and how this really terrific guy wanted to see me again. I turned into my driveway, and as I did, I saw Collin sitting outside reading on his front porch.

Collin was my new neighbor. We'd talked a couple of times, and he was a really nice guy. He was in marketing but had a secret dream to be a farmer, something I had a little experience with, so he liked to talk with me and ask me questions. I did not want the evening to end, so I decided to walk over to say hello and find out why he was out so late.

As I approached he looked up at me, I could see from the look on his face that he was interested in hearing why I was out so late as well. I was in a pretty great mood, and I'm sure it was written all over my face.

"Hey, lady! It's kind of late for you to be out on a school night, isn't it?" he asked. "You been out on a date?"

"Well, not really," I replied.

"Yeah, well your face would say otherwise. You seem pretty happy tonight."

"Really?" I feigned ignorance and then said, "I do feel pretty great. Hump day, you know." Then changing the subject, I asked, "How come you're up so late? How was your day?"

"Well, I have some pretty exciting reading here, and I just could not put it down," he said holding up the book he was reading. "This here book is all about raising chickens," he said with a fake twang.

"You know, you really are a farm boy at heart.?"

"Yeah, I guess I am," he replied, grinning at me from ear to ear.

I sat down on the step and we chatted for several minutes before I finally stood up and said good night. As I slowly walked back over to my garage, I decided I was too tired to bother getting my brief case, purse, and phone out of my car. And besides, I was too distracted to concentrate on anything work-related. I was still too focused on the evening—and Dean. I really could not wait to see him again. I was wondering how long it would be before he called me. Yep, my report would just have wait until tomorrow, and I would have to get to the office early to get it done. I had more important things on my mind than reviewing that report.

I put my keys on the table next to the front door, walked into the living room, and sank down onto my couch to take my shoes off. I'd not been sitting there long before the doorbell rang. I looked at the clock—it was nearly eleven o'clock. No one could be stopping by at this time of the night—unless it was Wendy. Maybe Wendy had come over to see how things went with Dean. I looked through the peephole and there he stood! My heart leaped in my chest. Had I left something in his car? Or, wishfully, maybe he didn't want the evening to end either. With shaking hands, I opened the door and, with that winning smile on his face, he said, "Hi."

CHAPTER 4

Summer 2001

IT WAS STILL nighttime when I woke up feeling very groggy, and my head was just pounding. Wow, I thought, I must have had more to drink last night than I realized. My vision was very blurry, and as I looked around I could see just enough to know I wasn't in my bed. Where was I?

I patted the area around my body and I could feel carpet. It was then I realized I was lying on the floor. I held my hand up to my face and touched my eyes, which were wet and sticky. I pulled my hand back to see what it was and saw blood. I was so surprised and confused that I just lay there. I had to really strain to think. Why was I on the floor and what had happened? Then I noticed my arm was bare, and when I touched my chest and thighs I realized I didn't have any clothes on.

I struggled to make sense of my situation. I asked myself the same questions over and over hoping there was an answer somewhere. Why was I on the floor? Why was I bleeding? Why was I naked? Nothing made sense. My head was pounding and ached terribly, and my heart was beating so hard that it made the pain in my head hurt even more. I felt very disoriented and frightened. Nothing made any sense.

I finally decided that maybe standing up and turning on a light would help me figure out what had happened, give me a different perspective, and then perhaps answers would come. I was in a fog and had to think hard to do even the simplest tasks. First, I tried to roll onto my side. But that little bit of effort caused extreme pain in my chest and ribs. So I lay very still for several minutes before attempting any further movement that might be painful—which at this point seemed like moving anything at all.

It was clear there were several things wrong with me, and I needed to know exactly what they were. I tried putting my hand down to push myself up to a sitting position, but found myself nauseous with pain from the effort. So I slowly lay down again to wait for the nausea to subside.

My mouth was dry and my lips were stuck together. I was very thirsty. I ran my tongue over my lips and there was the metallic taste of blood. I could feel that the inside of my mouth was raw, and my teeth hurt when I pushed the tip of my tongue along the edge of my gum line. I reached up and touched my finger to my lips. I could feel that they were crusted with what must have been blood—and they were very swollen. I desperately wanted to look in a mirror. I wanted to see what my face looked like.

Slowly and carefully I rolled over on my stomach. There were stabbing pains around my ribs. So painful that it was hard to breathe. Every part of me was sore. With my cheek resting on the floor, I pulled my knees up under me with great difficulty. I lifted my head, and as I did, I felt something trickle down the inside of my thigh. It was then that the confusion and disorientation started to settle, and it dawned on me—I must have been raped. When that realization sunk in, my stomach started churning and, while feeling intense pain all over my body, I threw up and passed out again.

I'm not sure how much time passed, but when I awoke, I was lying face down in my vomit. And once the cloud started to lift, my brain began to put the pieces together—which made me panic and made my heart pound even faster and harder. As my brain worked to make sense of what had happened, I became two distinct people: the fearful me and the calmer me. The fearful me said in a very low whisper, "What if whoever did this to you is still in the house?" And then my calmer self said, "Keep calm, Lynne. You need to get control of your thoughts and body. You need a clear head."

I lay very still for several minutes, trying to hear over the pounding of my heart. Trying to listen for any small sounds that might reveal if there was someone in my house. But the pounding in my ears made it hard to hear anything. My calm voice kept telling me over and over, "Calm down. You are smart and capable. You can think your way through this. You need to get to your phone and call for help." But then fear would take over and remind me that in the excitement of the night, I'd left my phone and my purse in the car, which caused me to panic even more.

Tears ran down my face, and I was gasping for air. I knew I had to try to stay calm. I needed to focus on my next steps and how I could get help. So I began to evaluate my options. I could get to the garage, to my car, to my phone, or get to the front door and outside where I might be able to get to someone to help me. What would be the best way to escape or get help?

The fear started up again. What if someone was still in the house and they heard me? Would I make it? Would they kill me? Maybe they thought they'd already killed me. The more fear talked, the faster my heart pounded. But ultimately, my calm self was able to determine the front door was closer than the door to the garage. I'd go for the front door.

I looked to see if the door was locked, but it was too dark and too far away to tell. My blurred vision made it worse. Then the fear assaulted me with questions: "Could I get to the door, get it unlocked, and get outside before he saw me?" I was in no shape to outrun anyone. I didn't know whether or not my legs were hurt, or if I could even stand. There was so much pain coursing through my body that I didn't even know where the pain was coming from. It had overwhelmed my senses and was impeding my ability to make decisions. I had to try to calm down and determine what parts of my body were injured and whether I was capable of walking. Not feeling any significant pain in either leg, I decided they were probably okay, but worried whether I'd be strong enough to make it outside.

Shaking, my head pounding, and my vision blurry, I tried to get control of my body. In the state it was in, I would really need to focus. This was not going to be easy, and my life might depend on my next actions. There was no option for failure. I had to be successful. If he was still in the house, he would not want me to get out to get help, so I'd need to be ready for a fight.

I slowly pulled my feet under me and managed to stand up part way before I lost my balance and fell back to the floor. I was so dizzy that the room was swirling. I lay still on the floor and listened intently to hear if anyone was coming—or for any sounds indicating that someone was in the house with me. I didn't hear anything, and decided at that moment that regardless of whether someone was in the house or not, I needed to get out of there. I could not wait. The longer I waited, the more likely he was to return. If I was going to get help, I needed to get out and get out now.

I pulled my knees under me again, but this time I stayed on all fours. I crawled to the wall and, pressing my hands on it, used it for support until I was standing all the way up. Gasping at the pain in my ribs, I continued using the wall for balance, and as quietly as I could, I inched my way along it as I struggled to make my way to the door. It was only a few yards away, but it could have been miles with all the strength and focus I needed to get there. I was covered in sweat.

Finally, I reached the door, and fumbling, I tried the doorknob. It was unlocked! In a rush of relief I started crying. But I had to stop. When I cried, the tears obscured my vision. If I was going to get away, I needed to get control of myself. As quietly as I could, with a shaking hand, I opened the door. It squeaked. I felt my throat tighten and let out a gasp as I struggled to stay in control. I needed to hurry—to get out of the house and get help.

When I looked outside, it was pitch black. The only light I saw was the light on Collin's porch and somehow I would need to get there. I realized I would no longer have the wall for stability. I would have to get back down on my knees and crawl. If someone was still there and found me that way, I would be very vulnerable and not able to get away. But I didn't have a choice.

I inched my hands down the door frame to the porch floor, flinching in pain with each movement. As I extended my hands in front of me, the pain was so intense that I threw up again, which made the pain in my ribs worse. I'd never experienced pain like this before in my life. Inching along to the handrail, I gripped it and while trying to pull myself up, I became dizzy, lost my balance, fell down the steps and landed on the lawn. I think I blacked out.

Everything hurt. Everything. But the pain was still nothing compared to the fear. I rolled over and again pulled my knees up and got on all fours. I was crying now. I started crawling slowly across the lawn to Collin's house. I needed to get there, and the closer I got, the harder I cried.

I got to Collin's porch a knee and a hand at a time, inching up each step until I finally reached the door. By now I was sobbing out loud and screaming. Using every ounce of strength I could muster, I rang the doorbell over and over. When nobody came, I banged on the door with my fists as hard as I could until I couldn't stand the pain a minute longer. I slumped down in front of the door, and trying to make myself as small as possible, I hid in the shadows while continuing to bang my fist on the door. I decided that if Collin wasn't home, or if I couldn't get him to hear me, I would just have to stay there until morning.

I continued to pound for what seemed like forever. I said over and over, "Please dear God, let him hear me. Please let him hear me." I could taste the salt from my tears and blood from the injuries to my face as the mixture ran past my swollen lips into my mouth. I was crying aloud, and the sounds that were coming from inside me were like the sounds of a desperate and severely injured animal—horrible, pitiful, and scary.

The door flew open, and a furious Collin stood in the doorway. He looked around and in an angry voice screamed, "Who the fuck is it and what the hell is going on?"

I dropped my fist to my lap and, in a rush of relief, said softly to myself, *He heard me! I'm safe!*

Stepping out onto the porch, dressed only in sweatpants, he looked around until he spotted me. "My God, Lynne, is that you? What happened to you?"

"Would you help me?" I asked.

"Of course," he said as he reached down to help me stand up, but my legs wouldn't support me.

He tried to pick me up, and as he did, I screamed in pain as his arms squeezed around my ribs. He stopped then, not knowing what to do and said, "I don't know how to touch you without hurting you. Where are you hurt?"

I mumbled something in response, but was too overcome with emotion and pain to be coherent.

After several minutes of maneuvering, he was finally able to pick me up using my legs and bottom as leverage—with one arm under me and the other up around my shoulders. The jostling was very painful, but I tried not to make any sounds. All I wanted was for him to get me inside and to close the door, to lock me away from whatever or whoever was out there. I didn't even care that I was naked—the relief was overwhelming. My body began to shake uncontrollably and I was really crying now—loud uncontrollable, uncontainable sobbing.

CHAPTER 5

Summer 2001

WHEN COLLIN LEANED down to set me on his couch, I whispered, "Put me on the floor."

He looked at me in confusion and said in concern. "Why shouldn't I put you on the couch?"

"I'm such a mess—I'll ruin your couch."

"Oh, for God's sake," he said as he ignored me and set me down on the couch anyway. He tried to stand up, but I hung tightly to his neck, not letting him go.

"Lynne," he said calmly, "I need to take a look at you. You're covered in blood and we need to find out exactly where it's coming from. I think you must have some broken bones."

Through chattering teeth, I said hopefully, "I don't think I'm bleeding anymore. Most of the blood has dried. But I'm pretty sure I have some broken ribs." Like my diagnosis would end the investigation!

He smiled back at me with very sad eyes. He carefully pushed my hair back from my forehead, trying to get a better look at the state of my face. "Lynne, I need to get my phone so I can call an ambulance. You are safe now. I'll be right back."

I said, "Okay," but I didn't let go of him. I mumbled, "Call the police. Please call the police—but I don't need an ambulance." Looking at me in total

disbelief, he carefully unlocked my shaking hands from around his neck and rested them in my lap. He reassured me again that I was safe and he'd be right back.

I slumped back into the couch and closed my eyes. I felt like a rag doll. I couldn't even hold my head up. I'd quit sobbing, but the tears kept coming—flowing from the corners of my eyes, down the sides of my face, and into my ears. I could hear Collin talking to the police department as he quickly returned to the room. He placed his phone on the coffee table with the speaker on, and I could hear the dispatcher continuing to ask him questions, which he answered, while at the same time carefully wrapping me snugly in a blanket. I felt like I was swaddled in a protective cocoon.

Finally, he knelt down in front of me and said, "They're on their way, Lynne. Your face is still bleeding, and there's blood all over you, so I can't tell where you're hurt. I'm concerned that you may be badly injured and that I should be doing something else for you. May I look at you more carefully to see if there's something I can do to help you?"

My voice cracked as I struggled to talk and suppress my tears at the same time. "Will you just sit here with me? My heart is beating so hard I can hardly hear you—and I can't stop shaking."

Collin sat down next to me on the couch and put his arm around me. He didn't ask any more questions. He just sat there and allowed me to feel safe, all the while listening intently for the sirens. I put my head on his chest for what seemed like a very long time. My tears had started again, falling on him and the blanket. I could hear his heart beating inside his chest, and knew he was probably frightened too.

Softly I said, "I'm so sorry, Collin. I've gotten you up in the middle of the night and made a mess out of your house."

Carefully caressing my hair, he said, "There's nothing here I can't handle. I'm just grateful you survived, Lynne—that you're alive." And then he asked, "What happened?"

I wasn't sure what to say, *I* certainly didn't know what had happened. I felt stupid, like somehow it had been my fault and, after a minute, I said, "I don't know. I just woke up this way."

I could not see the look on his face, but I'm sure that answer must have surprised him. How could anyone look like I did and not know how it happened? But he didn't ask any more questions. He'd probably decided he would let someone else try to find that out. For now, he would just be there for me.

Soon, I could see flashing lights through the blinds in the living room, and then the doorbell rang. When Collin started to get up to answer the door—just as he started to move away from me—I began to panic again. I held tightly to his hand to try to keep him from leaving me. He said, "It's okay, Lynne. It's the police. You're going to be alright. I'm just going to walk over to the door to let them in."

I closed my eyes and wrapped the blanket more tightly around me. I could hear Collin's voice as he talked very quietly to the police. I could hear him say that he didn't know what happened, that he'd been awakened about twenty minutes ago when his doorbell started ringing and he heard someone banging on his door. He told them he found me on his front porch and that I appeared to be badly hurt, that I had no clothes on and was covered in blood. Then I heard him say again that he didn't know what had happened to me, and apparently, I didn't either.

Then I heard a woman's voice saying, "Lynne, my name is Officer Curtis. We have the paramedics here. May they take a look at you?"

Still clutching the blanket, I opened my eyes and said, "I'm okay."

"Lynne, you don't look okay. Please let them have a look at you," she said. I saw the two paramedics approaching me slowly as if I were a barking dog. "May I sit here next to you?" she asked.

"Yes," I said mechanically.

"They just need to look at you to see if you're alright. It will be okay." The two paramedics stood in front of me, looking very uncomfortable. "It will be alright, Lynne. They'll be very careful. They are trained professionals—trained to help people who've been hurt like you have."

I nodded my head, but didn't let go of the blanket.

Collin knelt down beside the couch. "It's okay, Lynne. Everything's going to be okay now," and then he took my hand in his and repeated, "It's going to be okay, Lynne," saying it over and over to me like he was soothing a small child. I needed to hear that, and he knew it.

"Yes," I said, nodding. "I *am* going to be okay." And I let go of the blanket.

The paramedics—a man and a woman—checked me over methodically, asking me where it hurt and sponging away the blood to see what was underneath. While they did, Officer Curtis asked me to tell her what happened. I told her I woke up on the floor of my living room, and that I had no idea how I got there or what had happened to me.

"What's the last thing you remember before you woke up on the floor?" she asked.

It was at that precise moment that I finally put things together. I gasped and started sobbing uncontrollably. I pushed the paramedics away and became irrational, screaming, "Get away! Get away from me!"

But Officer Curtis was undaunted and said calmly, "Lynne, we are here only to help you. But you have to help us. You're going to have to calm down so we can understand you."

Collin, in an attempt to calm me down, put his arm around my shoulders. But I screamed at him too, "Get your hands off me. Don't touch me!"

"It's me, Lynne—it's Collin. You are okay," he said gently.

Officer Curtis put her hand on her gun and said, "Get away from her, sir. Take your hands off of her and step away. Put your hands up where I can see them."

I don't know why I'd responded that way to Collin, who was totally stunned. I could see the confusion and pain on his face. He immediately put up his hands and moved away from me. As I looked at the faces of the police and the paramedics, I realized they thought it possible that he'd been the one who attacked me.

"Oh no, I'm sorry," I said. "I'm so sorry, Collin." Addressing the others, I added,

"Collin didn't hurt me. It was Dean." Officer Curtis' eyes were back on me, but everyone else continued looking at Collin, who didn't move. He continued to stand off to the side with his hands still in the air.

"Who is Dean?" Officer Curtis asked.

"It must have been him. It must have been Dean. Dean Simpson."

"Where's he now?" she asked.

"He came to my house—he did this to me."

When Collin offered to show them where my house was, Officer Curtis, without saying another word, motioned with her head and the other two officers were out the door, following just behind him.

"Now, who's Dean?" she asked again.

"I don't know," I sobbed. "I just met him tonight."

"How do you know him?" Officer Curtis asked.

I told her how we had met, and repeated what I could remember of what transpired earlier that evening. I told her how he'd driven me to my car, and that he must have followed me home. How I opened the door to him— and then there was nothing after that. I couldn't remember anything until I woke up on the floor of my living room.

Knowing what had just happened, I wondered to myself—how I could have been so stupid and so careless as to let my guard down. How wanting him to like me caused me to ignore any warning signs. How had I become so infatuated with his good looks and so desperate for attention that I didn't see that he was a predator and rapist waiting for me?

I put my face in my hands and began to cry. Officer Curtis put her hand on my shoulder and told me it would be okay—but she didn't know the real reason I was crying. I was crying because I believed that what had happened to me was my fault.

The paramedics brought in a stretcher, and in my panic on seeing it, I immediately blurted out, "I'm not going to ride in the ambulance. I'm fine. I don't need to go to the hospital."

Collin had returned by then, and he knelt down next to me. "Lynne, you are badly hurt. I don't think you know how badly hurt you are. You're going to need stitches and X-rays. Please let them take you to the hospital so they can check you over and give you what you need. This can't wait."

"I won't ride in the ambulance," I said.

"If you won't go in the ambulance, would you go by car?" Officer Curtis asked.

"Lynne, I could take you and then I could stay there with you," Collin volunteered, as he looked at me steadily, his face displaying deep concern.

"No, but thank you, Collin. I'll go with Officer Curtis." Then I added, "I'm so very grateful you let me in, and for everything you've done for me. You need to go to work in a couple of hours, and I've made enough of a mess for you for one night."

"Lynne, I worry about you going to the hospital by yourself. If you won't let me go with you, is there someone else I could call for you?"

To me, it was as if going to the hospital would make this whole nightmare true. But this was not a nightmare—it was real. It had actually happened, and now it had been reported; and more and more people were getting sucked into it. Seeing the concern on his face I lied. "I promise to call my sister once I get to the hospital."

Officer Curtis said, addressing Collin, "Don't worry, I'll keep an eye on her."

One of the officers who had gone to my house came back and told Officer Curtis that there was no one in the house, but there were clear signs of an attack. They had already sealed off the house and called forensics, who would search the house for prints and other evidence.

"Lynne, is there anything you'd like to bring to the hospital with you from your house?" Officer Curtis asked.

I wasn't sure what I would need. Something like this had never happened to me before. "I guess I will probably need my insurance card and my driver's license, right? My phone? My purse is in the front seat of my car," I told her.

I tried to stand up on my unstable legs, when Collin reached out tenderly to steady me. "Lynne, I worry about you going alone. I promise to stay out of your way and not bother you. I can just be there in case you need someone or something."

I smiled at him and, trying to make light of my situation and to make him feel needed, I said, "I'll be home in a couple of hours—and you should go back to bed and get some sleep so you can go to work in the morning. But first, would you help me out to Officer Curtis' car?"

He responded by first rewrapping me in the blanket, and then carefully picking me up and carrying me out to Officer Curtis' car. He was trying to be extra careful not to hurt my ribs, and at the same time watch his step so he didn't trip on anything. I tried my best to conceal the pain I felt as he very gently set me down in the backseat of the police car.

"You're going to be okay, Lynne," he said.

"Yes, I am," I said with tears running down my face. "It's going to take some time but you're right—I'm going to be just fine. Thank you again for your help, Collin. I'm so grateful you were home and let me in."

Collin leaned over to kiss me on the cheek, and pushed a piece of paper into my hand. "Here's my phone number. Please call me anytime, night or day. I want to do whatever I can to help." I could tell he meant it; and while he would have liked to do more to help me, it was the best he could do since I wouldn't accept his offer to accompany me to the hospital."

I leaned my head back on the seat, closed my eyes, and said again, "Thank you, Collin. Thank you for helping me," as someone closed the door.

CHAPTER 6

Summer 2001

I WAS SHAKING all over, as if I'd just been pulled from a frigid lake. I couldn't stop. The nurse explained that I was in shock. She quickly tucked warm blankets around me and carefully patted my leg. "You'll stop shaking soon. I'm here to stay with you, so you tell me if you need anything; or if you don't understand what's happening, I'll get answers for you. I'm your advocate." Then leaning over and whispering in my ear she said, "I'll do my best to stay up here next to your ear so you can hear me, or when I can, I will keep my hand on your shoulder. That way you'll know I'm close by."

And she did. She kept her hand on my shoulder so I'd know she was there as other nurses, doctors, and technicians walked in and out of my room poking and prodding and exploring my injuries. Throughout the entire time, she stayed with me with her hand on my shoulder. When I seemed confused, she would quietly explain what was happening or what to expect. The medical team were very thorough. I was a crime scene. Every statement, sample, or test was carefully completed and recorded. Eventually, I just closed my eyes and shut out anything or anyone except for her quiet, calm voice. I felt safe with her there. She was a huge comfort. Just knowing there was someone looking out for me—even someone I didn't know—who could explain what was happening to me, who wouldn't judge me or gossip about me. She took so much pressure off me at a time when I was stretched to my emotional limits.

I don't think there was even an inch of me that wasn't examined, sutured, and bandaged. Finally, after what seemed like days, my advocate patted my hand and said, "Lynne they are all done. I am going to see what room they have assigned you, and I will be right back."

As she stepped out into the hall, the doctor stepped in. "Lynne," he said, "I want to go over your condition." I opened my eyes as best I could, considering the swelling which had gotten even worse with all of my crying, and I tried to listen and maintain my composure. But I felt like I couldn't take one more thing. I didn't want to hear about my injuries. I wanted this night to be over so badly, and I could barely control myself any longer. I had to work hard to concentrate on what he was telling me while the tears began to flow down my cheeks again.

He spoke simply and clearly, without any emotion—he was very factual. He told me I had a concussion from a head injury. I didn't have a skull fracture, but my brain had been bruised. I would need to take it easy for at least a week and would need to see my doctor for a medical clearance before returning to work. Apparently, I had been hit on the front of my head with a hard object. The impact of the strike had split the skin on my forehead. Possibly this same object had been used to beat my chest and rib cage, thighs, and upper right arm. I had two fractured ribs. I was very bruised and would probably be sore for some time.

In addition, I had been raped and sodomized. My forehead, lower and upper lips, rectum, and vagina had required stitches. I closed my eyes and tried to take in what he was saying, but I was so tired. All I wanted was to be left alone.

He told me he would like me to stay in the hospital—for a day or possibly two—just for observation and, if I appeared to be doing well, they would let me go home. It all seemed so matter of fact. I appreciated the fact that he was very respectful yet unemotional. It was clear he'd been through this scenario many times before, but for me, even without the emotion, it was overwhelming.

When the doctor left, Officer Curtis came into my room. "Lynne, I know you are more than exhausted, but I want to let you know that no one was found in your house. As best as we can tell, there are no other signs of criminal activity beyond the attack. There is no evidence of forced entry." Then she paused and said, "It appears that whoever did this to you may have been let in."

It took a minute for that comment to settle in my mind. I had let the person in. I had let the man who did this to me into my house. That handsome, interesting man I had spent the evening with was the likely suspect. The man who I'd agreed to go to dinner with later in the week, who had kindly offered to drive me to my car and who had kissed my cheek so gently. The man who apparently followed me home, waited for me to enter my house before he rang my doorbell—and I'd opened the door to him. That man had hit me hard enough to knock me out. He had torn my clothes, raped, sodomized, and beaten me. That man who I'd been fantasizing about had done all of this to me. The tears began to flow again.

Officer Curtis stepped closer to my bed and said gently, "Lynne, you need to rest. We're going to leave you alone and let you get settled in your room. I'll be back to talk with you tomorrow. It's going to be okay. We'll get the person who did this to you and keep him from hurting you or anyone else."

Just then, my kind nurse advocate came back in to wheel me to my room for the night. As she raised the side rails on the bed, she asked, "Is there someone you'd like me to call for you? Someone who could come be here with you?"

"I'm fine, but thank you," I told her.

She patted me on my shoulder and said, "Honey, I am so sorry about what happened to you. You have been so strong through all of this, and I know it seems impossible now, but you are going to be okay."

And I could tell she truly was sorry for what had happened to me and that she truly did believe I would be okay. I prayed she would be right.

Minutes later, she left the room. I lay there in that unfamiliar place, relieved to be alone at last, totally exhausted, and I just let the tears flow.

CHAPTER 7

Summer 2001

I WAS SO mentally and physically exhausted that I finally slept. The nurses came in frequently to check on me, but while I was relieved that I could turn over the concerns about my health and safety to them, I just wanted to be left alone. I didn't even bother to open my eyes when they came in and, if they asked me a question, I gave a one syllable response. I just wanted to curl myself up into a tiny cocoon and be left alone.

Later the next day, as warned, Officer Curtis came by. She knocked on the door and, when she did not get a response, she came in. "How are you doing today?" she asked in a whisper.

I struggled to open my eyes and said, "I'm great, just great."

"Well, I don't think you are great, but I think you are doing a little better today than you were yesterday."

"Well, that's good," I responded sarcastically.

"I have a few more questions for you, and I know you are tired of all of this, but we really do need your help."

"I have told you everything I know," I said exasperated.

She smiled, acknowledging that she heard me, but continued with questions for which I still did not have good answers. Finally she said, "Your neighbor Collin called this morning to ask how you were doing and to find out when you would be coming home. I told him I was coming to see you and that I would let you know he was asking about you," she reported.

Blinking to be more present, I said, "Would you let him know I am doing well and will likely be released today or tomorrow? I would be most grateful. I . . . ," I stammered, "I just can't bear to see or talk to anyone."

"I understand, but Lynne, we are going to continue to have more questions for you until we can resolve the case. You are going to have to be patient with us and do your best to help us."

"I know, and I am grateful you are pursuing this. I'm just tired. More than tired," I said softly.

"Is there anything I can do for you?"

"No, thank you. I just want to be left alone," I said.

"Okay," she said. "I just want you to know I am here for you, Lynne, and we are working hard on your case. Rest and I will be in touch," and she put her hand on mine.

I did not thank her for coming or for asking about my welfare. I was irritated, not grateful. I was irritated to be in this situation. I closed my eyes and let her go. I wanted everyone to just leave me alone. What had happened had happened. I did not want to talk about it. I did not want people to ask me how I was. I had not come to terms with what had happened to me, and until I did, I just wanted to be by myself.

The next day, as soon as the doctor signed my release, I called a cab and asked to be delivered to the hotel down the street. I felt anxious about going home. I did not feel safe there, and I also wanted to be alone. I knew if I went home, Collin would come by. I felt guilty about keeping him away, but I could barely deal with being with myself and just couldn't handle anyone more than me right now. Disappearing seemed like a good solution and gave me time to figure out next steps on a timeline that I could control.

I looked a sight! The pain in my ribs made me hunch over, and because of the padding and swelling in my crotch, I could not put one foot in front of the other—I kind of had to rock from side to side in order to walk. My head was wrapped in a turban of bandages and, since I had arrived at the hospital only wearing a blanket, I only wore two hospital gowns. While they had tried to get the blood out of my hair in the emergency room, they ended up shaving some of it off to treat my head injury. The hair that was left was matted and crusty with blood.

The worst part though was my face. The swelling had gotten worse and the stitches seemed stretched to their limit. My lips looked like two purple bananas and my eyes like two fat plums. I definitely had a Bride of Frankenstein thing going on. I was frightening to behold!

The clerk at the hotel's front desk tried to keep his eyes on his computer screen as he registered me, but I was just too much—interesting and terrifying at the same time. He kept looking up from his computer to take in the scope of this apparition, and then quickly looked down, hoping I hadn't noticed. I can't imagine what he must have told his coworkers, and I was grateful there were no other people in the lobby when I checked in to see my macabre appearance.

While I was sure I could not go home and the hotel was a better option, I still felt very anxious and frightened. I had considered myself a strong woman and usually felt very sure of myself, but this experience had taken away any confidence and assurances I had. Sounds, movements, doors, hallways, drapes, you name it, everything around me caused distress. My heightened anxiety levels put me on sensory overload. I made my way toward the elevator to get to my room, but while I waited for the elevator to arrive, I stood as far away from the doors as I could while still being able to see inside, just in case. When I reached my floor, I held the elevator door open but hid inside, until I could be sure there was no one lurking in the hallway. The whole time, my heart was beating out of my chest, making my head throb and my eyes blur. I walked as quickly as I could, repeatedly looking over my shoulder, until I reached the door to my room and then, after getting the door opened, I propped it open with my foot and listened for any little sound—just in case someone was inside. Finally, I stepped in and slammed the door shut behind me, locking it as quickly as my shaking hands could manage. The whole experience was overwhelming, and I found myself leaning against the door, crying and gasping for air because of the panic and pain.

Finally, after getting myself under control, and moving slowly and carefully to keep the pain in check, I looked in the closet, shower, and around and under every piece of furniture and drapery. When I was satisfied that I was completely alone, I put the do not disturb sign on the door and locked it again. I hobbled over and pulled the drapes closed, and with my heart still pounding out of my chest, I pulled the covers back on the bed and crawled inside. I lay there with my eyes open, too afraid to shut them, and let the two parts of my brain battle it out for supremacy.

My illogical self kept my heart racing and my tears flowing. It constantly chanted, "You are not safe. He knows where you are. He is not done with you. He's going to come here and finish what he started." Then there was my logical self. It tried to suppress my illogical self by saying over and over, "No one will hurt you here. You don't need to panic. He has no idea where you are. You are safe here." But the illogical me was significantly stronger than logical me. My heart did not slow down, the shaking did not stop, and I did not feel safe.

I lay on my back so that both my eyes and ears were clear of any obstructions. Then I pulled the blanket up to my chin and let my tears flow once again. They streamed down my face, while the pressure in my chest released deep guttural gasps. No one was here to hear me, and I could just let it all out. I was mentally and physically exhausted. I ached from all my injuries. I felt embarrassed and angry. But, more than anything, I was relieved to be alive.

I don't know when I finally fell asleep, but I slept on and off for two days. On the third day, at around ten o'clock in the morning, my cell phone began to ring. I didn't want to speak to anyone, so I didn't answer it; and besides, it hurt just to turn my head, let alone reach for my phone. But whoever it was didn't give up. They just kept calling, so finally I reached for the phone, wincing at the pain in my ribs. It was Officer Curtis.

"Lynne? Are you okay?"

I stammered at first to get the lie out, "I'm fine."

"You don't sound fine. Are you sure you're okay?"

"Really, I'm fine," I said in an angry voice.

"I'm sorry if I woke you up. I just wanted to know how you're doing. Also, I wanted to tell you that your neighbor Collin called again. He's worried about you—especially since you did not come home. I told him I would check on you to make sure you were alright. I hope that is okay."

"I would appreciate it if you'd call him and let him know I'm doing fine," I said. I knew I should call him myself—I owed him that much—but I didn't have the strength to talk to him yet.

"I'll be happy to do that for you, Lynne. And I'm sorry to ask, but we need to ask you a few more questions.?"

"Could it wait until tomorrow?" I asked.

"I'm sorry, Lynne. But we need to keep this case moving along if we're going to catch the person who did this to you. Would you be able to talk with us around five o'clock today?"

Reluctantly, I agreed. I told her where I was, gave her my room number, and then, after she hung up, I turned the phone off. I lay there. All my muscles and bones ached. They'd gotten swollen and stiff while I'd been asleep. After several minutes, I tried to push myself up into a sitting position, and cried out from the searing pain in my ribs. Even simple movements were nearly impossible. I let my feet drop off the side of the bed and waited for my head to stop swimming. And then, hanging onto the furniture in the room like a handrail, I maneuvered my way into the bathroom.

When I looked into the mirror, I didn't recognize the image I saw. It didn't look like me. My face was disfigured from the swelling, and the turban of bandages didn't help either. My lips, still nearly twice their normal size, were dappled with small, dark stitches. It was hard to get my lips parted to get a look at my teeth. While they ached, and several were loose, it didn't appear any were chipped or missing. I started to feel queasy and slowly slid down the wall to the floor. I lay on the cool floor of the bathroom for several minutes, waiting for the queasiness to pass; and then holding my forearms up in front of my eyes, I studied the rows of bruises one at a time.

I wondered about the mind of a person who would beat someone, especially someone they didn't even know. What type of mental illness did Dean have? Would I forgive him if I knew? No. I didn't care whether he was mentally ill or not. He had done this to me, and I hoped the police caught him. I hoped he would go to prison for the rest of his life so he couldn't inflict this kind of physical and mental pain on someone else.

After a long time, I decided having a pity party was not getting me any closer to clean. I rolled over slowly and carefully until I was on all fours and used the wall to stand up—remembering how I had used this technique the night I was attacked. I slowly unwound the dressing on my head and was disappointed to see the jagged line of stitches from my eyebrow to my scalp. There would be a significant scar.

I tried to run my fingers through my hair, but it was so matted that it was no use and it really hurt. Even the roots of my hair hurt! I turned on the water and let the steam build —finally obscuring my image in the mirror. Hanging onto the grab bar, I carefully stepped into the warm shower and let the warm water run over me. I took a deep breath and closed my eyes as I felt the tension go from my sore muscles.

Delicately, I traced the row of stitches on my forehead using the tip of my index finger, moving down to my swollen eyes and bruised cheeks. I ran my tongue along the inside of my lips and teeth, felt the stitches inside and then outside my mouth, and wiggled my sore, loose teeth. I ran my hands softly over my breasts, so tender and sore, and then along my sides over my broken, aching ribs. Almost every part of me was either cut or bruised.

But it wasn't until I ran my fingers gently between my legs that I got sick. I could feel the stitches where he had torn me. Everything there was so swollen that it seemed like I'd been turned inside out. If the other injuries were not indication enough, this was clear evidence of the violence of my attack. But this was much more than physical violence. This violence was meant to emotionally scar me. It was in that moment that I realized—I would not just need physical therapy but lots of psychological therapy to get over this, and even then, I might never feel like my old self again.

Letting the water run over me, I wondered how anyone who was awake for an attack like this could ever be normal again. In that respect, I was lucky. I wasn't awake for his assault. What would it have been like to have the memory of his face, hands, body, or voice while he hurt me? It took me a long time to make the connection between the man I'd met only a few days before—his handsome face, beautiful smile, and nice hands—and the ugly monster with sharp teeth and claws who nearly killed me.

I wrapped my arms around myself and said, "It's a miracle you survived Lynne, and you will come back from this. You are strong."

After several minutes, I got out of the shower, dried off, and wrapped myself in the hotel robe. I called and asked for housekeeping to come and change my sheets and sat in the bathroom, door locked, while they cleaned and changed my bed, and then, after they were gone, I sat there listening intently just in case someone was still in the room. It took several minutes for me to get up the courage to unlock the bathroom door; and then, once again, I shuffled around and opened the closet, checked behind the drapes, and under the bed. Once I was sure I was alone, I was able to relax. I wondered if I would ever feel safe again.

By the time I had gone through my ritual, I was exhausted. I crawled back into bed and felt a huge sense of relief at having washed the stink of that man off me. I may still have the stiches, bruises, and broken bones, but I was alive—and I made a vow then and there he would no longer be a part of me. I started to weep again—but this time they were tears of joy. I was alive.

CHAPTER 8

Summer 2001

THE PHONE RANG, and without thinking I reached for it. The pounding in my head and the pain in my ribs immediately made me feel dizzy and nauseous. I had to lay back down. I tried to find the phone with one hand while holding my head with the other. Finally successful, I said, "Hello?"

"Hello, Lynne, it's Officer Curtis. May we come up?"

"Yes you can come up," I said. But really, I didn't want them to come up. I wanted to keep hiding and be left alone to try to recover. I didn't want to talk anymore about what had happened. It was over, and I was starting to heal. I wanted my pain and fear to fade away like it had never happened.

I heard the knock at the door and Officer Curtis said, without waiting for me to open it, "Lynne, it's me, with two other officers. Will you please let us in?"

I had never thought of myself as vain, but there it was. Before I opened the door, I stopped to look at myself in the mirror. I'm not sure what I was looking for, but it certainly wasn't what I saw. For some reason, I'd imagined I'd gotten better looking in the last few hours. No such luck; and now the image staring back at me from the mirror reconfirmed just how grotesque I looked.

Officer Curtis knocked on the door again, and this time I opened it.

"Lynne, these are my two investigators—Doughten and Frank. They're helping me with your case."

"My case? How lucky I am to have my own case," I said sarcastically. "Is it okay if I lay back down? I'm feeling a bit dizzy."

"Of course you can. Do you need any help?" she asked, trying to support me by taking my elbow.

"No, I think I can make it. Just make yourselves at home," I said with a smirk. Then I realized how that came across and added, "You know, I'm really sorry. If you haven't yet noticed, I'm being a bit of an ass right now, and I'm not sure why. I understand you're trying to help me, but you may need to remind me of that, especially if I go over the edge."

"You've been through a lot, Lynne, and you don't have to understand your feelings right now. Just try to remember we're on your side and only trying to help."

Then they started in with the same questions I'd been asked the day before. I did my best to answer, and tried not to be sarcastic or nasty, but it wasn't easy. And, when it all became too much, I just broke into tears.

"Lynne, we've not been able to find any address or record for a Dean Simpson, so we assume he was using an alias."

"Really? I'm surprised. I assumed that was his real name. How stupid of me. You know what, maybe there wasn't anyone—perhaps it was an immaculate rape," I said, hating myself as I did so. Then, after regaining my composure, I said, "Sorry. I told you—I really am an ass."

"Lynne, I think we're done, and I'm sorry to have made you go through this all over again. It's just that we need to be sure we have as much information as we can possibly get so we can find this guy. We're not challenging your story. We just want to be sure we have everything you can remember."

"I understand. I'm just exhausted. I want this behind me."

"Is there anything I can do for you?" she asked.

"Actually, there is. But after the way I've behaved, I wouldn't blame you if you said no."

"I'd be happy to do whatever I can. What is it?" Officer Curtis replied.

"I can't bring myself to go to my house yet, and I could use some things. If I make you a list, would you be able to get them for me? I just can't face going back there yet."

"Absolutely. I'd be glad to do that for you," she said, patting my hand.

As soon as she smiled at me, I could feel the tears well up. I thought, *what's wrong with me? I'm usually not so nasty and so weak.* This slight kindness seemed to send me into another tailspin.

CHAPTER 9

Summer 2001

I STAYED IN the hotel for more than a week. I'd tried to eat, but couldn't keep anything down. I think it was because I was still very anxious. In fact, for the entire time I'd been at the hotel, I hadn't turned the lights off, although I felt somewhat safe there. At least I could control when and who came and went, and I could hide in the bathroom when housekeeping or room service came so no one could see me or talk with me face to face. I put time on hold and just disappeared into that room.

Officer Curtis called me every day at five o'clock to check on me. She'd told me that all I had to do was answer, I didn't have to have a conversation. She seemed to understand what I'd been through and didn't push me. She just wanted to know I was okay. Then about ten days after the attack, she paid me another visit.

"Lynne, I'm worried about you. I think you were supposed to visit your primary care doctor and get rechecked, but you haven't done that yet. I also don't think you've told anyone close to you about what's happened. Isn't there someone I could call for you?"

"No," I said firmly. "I'm not ready to deal with any questions, and I don't think I could take being poked and prodded again so soon."

"What about family? Do you have any family you could talk to? I think you need to talk to someone. You need someone to help you come to terms with what's happened and talk through your feelings. You need to be prepared so that when we do catch this guy, you have a support system in place."

I paused and said, "I've been thinking about my sister—and I want to call her but I'm afraid to tell her what's happened. I know it will be devastating for her. She lives a couple of hours away on a farm. I don't think I want to tell her what's happened, at least not until I see her face to face. It will be very hard for her to hear what happened to me and not be able to see me."

"You don't have to tell her in advance, but I do think you should tell her. May I take you to her? You really must have some type of support."

"I'll go to her. I can get there on my own. But I don't think I can go to my house alone. Would you be able to go with me so I can get my car?

"I would be glad to," Officer Curtis said, with a warm, encouraging smile.

I didn't go inside the house. I went directly to the garage and got into my car. I only brought the few things that Officer Curtis had picked up for me, and that would be enough. I just couldn't go inside.

It was more than a two-hour drive from my house to the farm. I had time to think about how I would tell Betsy what had happened, but I didn't have enough time to figure out how I would deal with her reaction. I knew she would be all about hunting this guy down and taking care of him herself. Also, I was worried about her seeing my face—it was such a mess—so I decided to wait until dusk when the light would be dimmer and conceal some of the damage.

Stalling for time, I pulled into the main city park and sat there for quite a while before I got out of my car. It felt good to be in the fresh air after being shut up in the hotel for the past ten days. It also felt good to take a short walk and just stand on my own. But I still looked a bit scary. The skin around my eyes was deep shades of purple and green, and the whites of my eyes were red with pooled blood. My arms were black and blue, and I still walked like I was wearing a wet diaper.

People who passed by me tried not to stare, but I could tell they were startled by the sight of me. I decided it was worth it though, because I was so happy just to be outside. I just wanted to be able to sit in the fresh air and just be the old me for a few minutes. I didn't have to explain to anyone why I looked like I did or even think about what had happened. Finally, I got back in my car and finished the drive to the farm.

As I turned into the long lane to the house, I could see Betsy's dog Jasper race off the porch toward the car, barking the whole way. He seems quite vicious until you discover he's all bark and no bite. And despite how I looked, he recognized me—wagging his tail so hard it looked likely to fly off. He danced around me until I petted him on his head and he licked my hand as we walked to the porch. But before we even reached the door, it swung open and Ron stepped out to see who was making Jasper go crazy.

"Lynne?" he said—and stopped cold. He turned to yell inside the house, "Betsy, I think it's Lynne." Then he turned back to me and said, "My God. Lynne, what happened to you? Were you in an accident?"

"Hey, Ron. Good to see you, too. While that's not the welcome I was hoping for, I'll take it"

"What did you do to your head?"

"It's a long story. I'll tell you and Betsy at the same time, if that's okay."

Ron, staring at me, took my bag from me, and carried it up the steps as Betsy came to the door.

"Oh, my God! Lynne—is that you? What happened to you? Are you okay? When did this happen? Why didn't you call me?"

"Down boy, down," I said to her as poor Jasper looked up at me confused.

I could feel my tension uncoil now that I was in the protective custody of Betsy. A calm came over me that I hadn't felt since before the assault.

"I'll tell you all about it, Betsy, if you'll feed me first," I said. "I'm starved!"

Betsy wrapped her arm around my shoulder and said, "Come with me," and walked me into the kitchen. I sat at the kitchen table, across from Ron, while she made me poached eggs on toast—the go-to dish our mother used to make for us when we were sick or something was wrong. It tasted delicious. It was like a huge Band-Aid that covered my body and soul. I felt relieved, protected, and full of food and love. And then I told them what had happened to me.

Every once in a while, Betsy would stand up and pace back and forth. I know she was trying to listen without asking a million questions, but sometimes she had so much anger that she had to do something. When she realized what she was doing she'd stop, apologize, and sit down again. Ron. Dear Ron. He just sat quietly with his hand holding mine, trying not to interrupt. Just being there for me. I talked until well after midnight.

Finally, Ron said, "It's late, and you look so tired, Lynnie. Let's get you to bed. We can finish talking about this tomorrow." He took my bag to the guest room, and Betsy helped me unpack. She sat on my bed and waited quietly while I brushed my teeth. Then, together, we sat on the edge of the bed in silence as she carefully untangled and combed out my hair, just like she used to do when we were little girls. When she was done, she wrapped her arms around me and said, "I'm so sorry about all of this, Lynnie." Tears were running down her cheeks, and it was my turn to comfort her. I wrapped my arms around her and held her for several minutes. I wiped the tears from her cheeks and said, "It's going to be fine, Betsy. I'm going to be just fine."

She patted my back and waited for me to lay down. Then she tucked me in like I was a small child, just like Mom used to do to make us feel like everything was alright. She kissed me on the head and said, "Good night, dear Lynnie. You are safe here with us. We love you."

I closed my eyes as Betsy turned off the light and left the room. This time, it was tears of relief that slid down my face to my pillow.

CHAPTER 10

Summer 2001

THE NEXT DAY Betsy drove me down to see my doctor to get checked over. She wanted to be with me to hear what kind of care I needed. I was glad to let her take charge. She wasn't going to let me go home—and I didn't want to go home either. She brought me back to the farm to stay with her and Ron, and I stayed with them for two weeks. We got to the point where we could joke about my face and the different shades my skin turned. Each day I healed more and felt physically and emotionally stronger.

I didn't want to leave, but I knew it would only get harder the longer I stayed. I certainly had to go back to work or risk losing my job. I'd told my boss, Margie, what had happened to me, and she'd been understanding and supportive. And while she told me I could take my time, I felt like I was taking advantage of her at this point. I had to go back to reality sometime, and now was as good a time as any.

Betsy wanted to go home with me, but I told her I needed to face it myself. As a concession, she made me promise to keep my cell phone in the car all the way home so I wouldn't feel alone. We talked about all kinds of nonsense just to pass the time. I could feel my anxiety rising the closer I got to my house. I didn't want to go inside. I pulled into the garage, feeling my heart racing in my chest. I didn't even realize I'd stopped talking until I heard Betsy yelling into the phone. "Are you okay? Lynnie? Are you okay?"

"What if he's been driving by my house waiting for me to come back? What if he's in here?" I asked myself out loud, not realizing that Betsy could hear what I was saying.

"I'll call the police and have them come over right now," she said.

"No!" I said. "Give me a minute. I'm just anxious right now, but I'll be fine."

I finally found the courage to open the door and walk inside. I was protected by the kitchen, which separated me from the rest of the house. It looked to be just as I had left it, and like nothing had happened to change how I should feel about coming home. The walls were the same cheery yellow, and I looked fondly at the island where I liked to sit and drink my coffee every morning.

I stepped into the hall with my eyes closed, afraid to see the blood splattered around the front hall. But after I opened them and looked around, I saw the floor and walls were clean—there was no blood. There too it looked like nothing out of the ordinary had happened. I headed into the living room and stood where my unconscious body had been only a few weeks before. Everything was neat and tidy, the only sign of anything amiss was the faint sign of a blood stain on the carpet. Someone had been here and done their best to clean up the mess, understanding how hard it would be for me to face it when I came home again. They were right—it would have been an unbearable sight for me to see. I was so grateful. As I explained what I was seeing to Betsy, I could hear her begin to cry on the other end. She was as relieved and grateful as I was.

It took several minutes for me to walk methodically through the house, turning on all the lights, opening all the closets, and checking under the beds. But even when I was done with my search, and I knew no one was in the house, I still felt uneasy. My house was no longer my safe place. It was no longer my home. I was in a terrifying place where something unimaginable had happened to me. The experience had changed me and my home. In that moment, I knew it would never feel right again.

I had to fight with myself not to get back in my car and flee to Betsy's. I had to be strong, and I needed to focus on reality—not what I was making up in my head. Finally, I screwed up my courage and told Betsy that everything was fine and I was going to go to bed.

"Are you sure you're okay? You don't sound okay. I should have come home with you," she insisted.

"I'm fine, and no, you should not have come home with me. I just had to go through the initial shocks and now that they're over—I am just fine."

"Call me first thing in the morning, Lynnie—before you even get out of bed. Don't forget, or I'll have the police there at your door."

"I won't forget. Thank you, Betsy. Thank you for everything. I love you."

"Good night, Lynnie. I love you too. If you need me just call," she said.

I stood in the kitchen feeling empty—emotionally and physically—and even though I hadn't had anything to eat since lunch, I had no appetite. Besides, I was afraid to sit out in the open in the kitchen. I went upstairs to my bedroom, shut the door and locked it behind me. I put my desk chair under the doorknob, just in case, and closed the drapes. I lay down on the bed with all my clothes on, including my shoes. The silence in the house was deafening, but I couldn't stand to have the TV or radio on because the noise might cover any tiny sound that would alert me to the presence of someone else in the house. I just lay on the bed, with my clothes on, listening to the quiet until I finally fell asleep.

At eight o'clock the next morning, my doorbell rang. I sprang to my feet in a state of total panic and looked for a place to hide. I stood in the bathroom with the door locked talking myself down before finally daring to approach the bedroom window to pull back a corner of the drape. It was light outside. There were no cars in my driveway or out in front of the house. I wouldn't be able to see who was on the porch unless I went downstairs and looked out the side window, and if I did, I might be seen. The only thing I could do was wait to see who left the porch. I stood behind the drape and waited for several minutes until at last I saw who it was. It was Collin. I watched as he strode across the lawn to his driveway, got into his truck, and drove away.

I leaned back against the draped window and took a deep breath as I screwed up my courage to go downstairs. There, taped to the side window, was a note. I opened the door and reached out with trembling hands to grab it, then hastily closed the front door and locked it. I walked back upstairs to my bedroom, where once again I locked the door behind me before sitting down on my bed to read the note.

Lynne,

I'm sorry, if I woke you up this morning when I rang your doorbell. I saw your lights on last night and I wanted to check in with you before I left for work. I'm leaving you my cell phone number so you can call me if you need anything. I've been picking up your mail and I have it at my house. Would you like to come over for dinner tonight? I can give you your mail and see how you are doing. Call me to let me know. Whatever time works for you is fine with me.

Collin
847-525-4476

I sat for several minutes thinking about what I should do. I didn't want to do anything. I didn't want to go to his house and I didn't want to stay home. I didn't even want to call him! What was wrong with me? Collin had saved my life. It would be rude if I didn't call him back, plus I owed him. He knew I was home, and he'd been so kind to me. At the very least, I should call and tell him thank you but no thank you. But if I didn't go, I would be stuck in this house all night. I didn't want to be here alone. It would be a good excuse to get out of the house. I called him.

"Collin, it's Lynne."

"I hope I didn't wake you up this morning or upset you. I don't have your cell phone number or I would have called you instead," he said.

"No, you didn't wake me up," I lied. "I must have been in the shower when you came by."

"Officer Curtis let me know how you were doing. I was glad to hear that you were okay, and that you were staying with your sister."

"Yes, I'm fine."

"I've been worried about you."

"No reason to worry," I said in my best fake happy voice.

"Well, I'm glad to hear that. And I also wanted to let you know that I have your mail."

"I'd completely forgotten about my mail. Thank you so much," I said. "This is my first time back at the house, and it's going to take some time for me to get used to it." The moment I said it, I knew I would never get used to it. "Do you know who cleaned up the mess?" I asked.

"I did," Collin said. "But I need to apologize. I came over when the police were looking for evidence and took your house key. I just didn't want you to come home to . . . well, there was a bit of a mess with the fingerprint dust, and I was worried about the carpet. I hope that was okay. I put the key back after I was done."

After a brief pause, he added, "Listen, Lynne, if you ever need someone to walk through the house with you, just call. I'm sure it was hard coming back yesterday. I'd be happy to walk through and make sure everything is okay—anytime."

I began to tear up and my voice choked as I said, "Thank you, Collin. I can't tell you how much I appreciate all that you've done for me."

"Would you like to come over for dinner tonight?" he said, clearly trying to change the subject.

Forcing myself, I said, "Yes, thank you for inviting me." Then, sounding more enthusiastic and meaning it, I added, "Thank you for asking me, Collin. It's hard to be here, and I'm really grateful for the invitation."

"My pleasure," he said. "See you at seven, then?"

"Perfect. Thank you." As soon as I heard the phone disconnect, I began to cry. Why was it that the slightest acts of kindness completely upended me?

I lay back on my bed with my phone on my chest and began to think about how I was going to have to face everyone in my office that day. I practiced telling the story that "I'd slipped on the wet floor getting out of the tub." Followed by, "I decided to stay with my sister and take some vacation time to recover. Yadda . . . yadda . . . yadda." I hoped I sounded believable.

I looked at my arms, which were still a bit greenish in color. Those bruises would not be as easy to explain, so I decided to wear a long-sleeved blouse. My head and face were still a mess, so the wounds weren't easily concealed, but at least the stitches were gone and most of the swelling was too. I hoped my story would fit with how I looked.

Everyone bought my story and things were going fine at the office until I ran into Wendy.

"I've been calling you and leaving you messages. Why haven't you been answering your phone?" she demanded.

"Wendy, I'm sorry. I haven't even checked my emails or voicemails," which wasn't true, but up to that point, I didn't want to speak to her or anyone else.

"I've been dying to know how things went with Dean," she said in a voice practically breathless with excitement.

Instantly, my stomach fell and I felt lightheaded—like I was on a rollercoaster ride that suddenly took an abrupt dive. I'm sure that my face must have gone completely white too. I had to work hard to look nonplussed and then say nonchalantly, "Oh, that didn't work out."

"Damn, I wish I'd known that. I'd have nudged my way in and maybe I'd have gotten lucky," she yelled after me as I hurried away from her, heading toward my office. Once inside, I immediately shut the door and slid down the door frame to the floor to keep from falling. I sat there for several minutes as I struggled to regain my composure and tamp down my blood pressure.

Suddenly, there was a knock at my door and Margie stuck her head in. "Lynne?" she said, looking around my office before she spotted me next to the door on the floor.

"I don't think I was ready to come back to work this soon," I said as I started to stand up.

"Are you okay? Do you need a glass of water?" she asked as she came inside, closing the door behind her, and helping me to a chair.

"I'll be okay in a few minutes."

Sitting down in the chair opposite me, Margie said, "Please tell me how can I help you, Lynne?"

"I think I just need time. I also need to focus on something other than myself. That's all I've been doing for the last couple of weeks and I know it's not healthy."

Placing her hand on my arm, she said, "It will take time, Lynne, and there'll be some days when you think you have your shit together, and then something will happen that reminds you and you'll struggle. These things do not heal without leaving a scar," she added, looking at me sadly. "I know this doesn't fix what happened to you, but I want you to know you're not alone." And then, with obvious difficulty, she told me her story.

She'd been raped in college, and while she hadn't been dealt the physical violence I had, she still struggled with the experience all these years later. She told me she hadn't told another soul until that minute—she hadn't even reported it. And in fact, while she was still in school, she often ran into the man who'd raped her. He'd smile and say hi to her as they passed, like nothing had happened. After each time she saw him, she'd have to find a quiet place where she could be alone, or go back to her apartment to try to pull herself together. She'd relive the experience in her head every time. She believed if she'd pressed charges or even just gotten him kicked out of school, it would have helped her heal.

"To this day," Margie said, "I feel like a victim because I didn't take charge. Every once in a while, I'll see someone who looks like him and my heart will race. I relive it even now. I even wonder what happened to him—if he's living a happy life with a family someplace . . . and whether he raped other women. I don't mean to burden you with my story. I just hoped it might help you to know you're not alone. I understand a little bit of what you've gone through, and I want you to know that I'm here for you. I will help in any way I can."

"Margie, I am so sorry. I'm grateful to you for sharing your experience—and it does help to know that someone else understands. I had such a hard time coming here this morning and you've made it easier. Thank you."

"I hope you'll let me help you if I can."

"Thank you. Just knowing you understand is a huge help. You've been a tremendous support to me over these past few weeks."

Margie was right. It would take a long time for me to get over what had happened. Every morning when I woke up there would be that brief moment when I felt normal, but then I would remember. I'd get a queasy sensation in the pit of my stomach that would remind me I was not the same. I'd try to talk myself into feeling better, but the queasiness would stay until I got busy at work and was forced to focus on something else. But as soon as I slowed down, or if I saw something or someone who reminded me of the attack, it would come right back.

Every morning and every evening when I walked past my foyer to go upstairs to bed, I would look around and imagine I could see him at my front door. I would see his handsome smiling face and relive the excitement I felt at seeing him standing there. Then he would suddenly be transformed into a monster—the transformation happening in an instant—and because I hadn't been conscious while it happened, I would imagine what happened instead.

I would see him raise his arm, which held a club. He would strike me again and again in the head. Then slowly and calmly he would step over me and drag my limp body into the living room, where he would leave me, before walking casually back to the front door and closing it. When he comes back to me—with that monster face—I watch him beat me, mangle my body, and then sodomize and rape me. This requires such strenuous effort that he has to stop and wipe the sweat from his brow. He even has to take a rest. He sits down on my couch, and while he's resting, he looks down at me on the floor, deciding what to do next, waiting for his strength to return.

When it does, he resumes hurting me and violating me; and when he is done, he stands up and tidies himself. He walks to the front hall and looks at himself in my mirror, runs a comb through his hair, tucks in his shirt, and makes sure he looks good before walking out my front door. And just as his foot touches my front porch, he turns around and looks at me—wearing his handsome face once again. He's no longer the monster. He is the handsome, charming man I had met the evening before. He smiles and calmly walks away.

This happened day after day until I decided I couldn't go through it anymore. I decided that in order to make it stop, I would need to get out of that house. I would have to move if I was to ever escape those images.

CHAPTER 11

Summer 2001

THERE WAS A knock at my door, and I opened it to see Collin standing there.

"Hi, Lynne. What's going on?" he asked.

"Come in. What do you mean?" I said, standing aside.

Before he even stepped inside the foyer he said, "I'm surprised to see there's a for sale sign in your front yard. Are you moving?"

"Yes," I said quietly before looking directly at him. "I've decided to move."

We had spent nearly every evening together since I'd gotten back from Betsy's, and I loved the fact that we were literally steps from each other. If I needed anything, I could walk out my back door and be at his back door within seconds. This decision had been a hard one, and I had been avoiding telling him because telling him meant that it was true. I was moving and the easy relationship we had developed would not be the same.

"Have you had dinner?" I asked.

"No, I just got home," he said in a tone that showed he was hurt.

"Let me take you to dinner so I can tell you all about my plans. I'll grab my purse and you can pick the place."

On the drive over, Collin didn't say much, he just sat and waited patiently for me to bring up the move. I talked about my job, my sister, and everything but the move. Finally, when we arrived at the restaurant and before we got out of the car, he leaned over put his hand on my shoulder, and asked, "Are you going far away, Lynne?"

I looked up at his kind, sweet face and said, "No, I'm not going far away. I just can't live in that house anymore. Every day I relive what happened to me. That place is no longer my home, and it's a constant reminder of something bad that happened to me."

"I understand, Lynne. I guess I was just disappointed you didn't mention it to me; and today, when I saw the sign on your lawn, well, I was surprised is all. I'm worried about losing you. Do you know where you're going?"

"I want to stay close to work, so I won't be moving very far away. I just can't live in that house anymore," I said again firmly.

"I'll miss having you next door, but close is good enough. I would hate to lose you," he said as he got out of the car. He walked around to open my door and, as he did, he stood above me, saying, 'I'm so sorry about what happened to you, Lynne. I can't even begin to grasp what you've gone through—and I understand you not wanting to be constantly reminded of that terrible night."

Stepping out of the car and trying to lighten the mood I said, "Well, enough of that. Let's go and have a good time and not talk about this anymore."

We did have a good time. Collin told me hilarious stories about how he and a friend had discussed going into business together, and the wide variety of enterprises they'd explored. Crazy, disconnected ideas like a brewery, a farm, and even a trampoline park. Neither of them had any experience with any of them. They just wanted to do something that might make them happy and challenge them. I laughed and laughed as he told me about one funny scheme after another. It was great to have a good time and feel normal again.

When we got back to my house and we were standing in the driveway, he stopped and blurted out, "Lynne, I like you, and I'd very much like to keep our friendship going after you move. I hope we can."

"Of course," I said. "I'm not falling off the face of the earth. I'm just moving to a different house, somewhere I can start fresh and get my feet back under me."

"I had a great time tonight. Thank you for dinner," he said as he started heading towards his house. But then he stopped and turned around, came back over to me. "I expect you to call me and ask me for help with the move. If you don't, I'll be very hurt. I have a truck and friends I can call. So let me help you get settled in your new house."

"I will," I said, squeezing his hand. "I promise."

CHAPTER 12

Summer 2001

COLLIN WAS A far better cook than I was, so I would find recipes I wanted him to make for us and pick up the necessary ingredients on my way home from work. He would cook and supply the wine, and I would lazily sit back and relax at his kitchen table sipping my wine and watching him work.

We talked about everything and nothing in particular—just the familiar ramblings of two people who were comfortable with each other. After dinner, I would clean up the dishes and, when everything was back in place, we'd go out back and sit on his porch steps, drinking and talking long past dark. When it was time for me to go, he'd walk me back to my house and he would come inside until I felt comfortable enough for him to leave. He was invariably sweet and kind to me. I knew I'd miss those delicious dinners—and especially the ease of being so close with someone as special as he was.

Within two weeks, my house was sold. I was still so unsettled emotionally that I'd decided to rent rather than buy my new place. I found an apartment close to work, and better yet, close enough to Collin's house that I could bike over for dinner. I was so spoiled! After dinner and our usual long conversations, he would load my bike into the back of his truck and drive me home. Although I didn't have the same degree of anxiety about my apartment as I'd had with my house, he'd still come in with me, look around the whole apartment, and stay until I felt safe enough to let him go.

A few weeks went by, and then one morning my office phone rang. When I answered, I heard a familiar female voice. "Lynne, it's Officer Curtis. I think we may have him."

"What?" I said, despite having heard her words clearly.

"I think we have him. Would you be able to come in and look at some photographs?"

I couldn't respond.

"Lynne—are you there?"

"I'm here," I said.

"Are you okay?" she asked.

"I don't know. I don't think I can do it," I said, panicking. "I don't think I can stand to see him."

"Lynne, the person we have in custody attacked another woman last night. He thought she was home alone. But her roommate was there, and when she heard a struggle, she came running to find him attacking her. He ran, but the roommate followed him and was able to get his license plate number. We caught up with him a few miles away. We need you to take a look and see if this is the same guy who attacked you. You don't want this to happen to anyone else."

"No, I don't want it to happen to anyone else, but I . . . I don't know," I said. "I don't want to dredge all this back up again. I just can't."

"Lynne, we need your help."

"And then I said, "Can't she do it?" The moment the words left my mouth I knew it was wrong. I felt terrible. Why should she have to do this for me? I needed to do this for me. Finally, I said, "Yes. I'll take a look. When do you want me to come?"

"Well, could you come now?"

"Now!" This was sooner than I'd expected. It wouldn't give me enough time to let it all settle in. "I'm not ready. This is too fast."

"Lynne, there's nothing you can do to prepare for this, and no amount of time will make it easier."

"You're right," I said, thinking there would never be a good time. But it was all so frightening and unexpected. Finally, I said, "I'll come—now."

I was surprised at how emotional I felt. Officer Curtis was right. I'd been hoping and waiting for them to catch him, but I hadn't thought about what it would mean for me when they actually did. I'd been mistaken thinking I was getting over the experience. I hadn't realized how vulnerable I still was and how hard this had hit me.

I hung up and immediately called Collin to see if he could go with me. I was barely able to explain what was happening before he said, "I'll be right there. Wait for me to come pick you up from your office."

I was sitting outside my office on a bench when he arrived. He'd hardly stopped the car before he jumped out and raced over to me. I tried to look as normal as possible, but I had a hard time focusing and controlling my hands, which were shaking very hard. I couldn't hold onto my purse, and my legs were weak and wobbly. Collin could see by the expression on my face that I was in trouble.

"Lynne, are you up to this?" he asked, sitting down next to me.

I smiled up at him and said, "I'm not sure I'll ever be up for this, but I'm going to do it anyway."

I took his hand as I stood up to walk over to his car. As soon as we were inside, he asked me again, "Lynne, are you sure you have the strength to do this?"

"I have to," I blurted out more for me to hear it than for him. "If I don't do this now and something happens to someone else, I couldn't live with myself. I just have to do it." Then, trying to pretend that everything was fine, I smiled and said more calmly, "Thanks for coming to get me and helping me through this. I couldn't do I it without you."

He put his finger up and wiped away a tear that had begun to trickle down from the corner of my eye. "Lynnie, I'm happy to do this for you and

I'm glad you asked me." He held my hand tightly as we drove to the police station.

Officer Curtis was waiting outside for us. She smiled at Collin and then turned to me. "Lynne, I appreciate your doing this—I know it's hard for you. But it will take only a few minutes. We just need you to look at some photos and tell us if you see the man who attacked you."

As we walked through the front door, I could feel my heart pounding in my chest. I just kept telling myself that this would soon be behind me. Collin sat next to me and I continued to grasp his hand tightly.

Officer Curtis set a computer down in front of me and told me to tell her when I was ready. When I did, she said, "Take your time looking at these men, Lynne. Take all the time you need. We want you to be sure. If you don't see him here, we'll keep looking for him."

All the men looked very much alike. They had dark hair and were slender. Most appeared to have blue eyes—like Dean. I looked slowly at each picture, at each man, and was beginning to feel like I wouldn't find him there—when I saw him. My stomach leapt and I gave an involuntary gasp.

Collin squeezed my hand tightly. "Do you see him, Lynne?"

"It's him," I whispered, looking away from the computer screen feeling afraid that his photo might hear me. "It's him," I said again. "That's Dean."

Officer Curtis asked, "Are you sure, Lynne?"

"Yes. That's him," I said again, this time loud enough for her and the other officers in the room to hear. She walked briskly over to another officer and whispered something to him; he immediately left the room while speaking into his radio.

I felt a tear run down the side of my cheek, and I gasped again.

Collin looked at me with concern and confusion, like he was trying to figure out what to do to help me. "Do you want a glass of water, Lynne?"

I shook my head from side to side trying to keep my tears and sounds inside. I also didn't want him to leave my side, even for a minute.

Officer Curtis stood by, watching us.

"So do you have him?" I asked.

"Yes. We have him and you're safe now. He can't hurt you anymore."

I began to fill up with rage, and in a loud voice I said, "That's interesting, because I really don't feel safe. How is it possible that a person who looked so kind and was so charming could hurt me and other women the way he did? I didn't deserve what he did to me. None of us did. Why did he do it?" I asked, looking at Officer Curtis.

"Often there are no logical answers to these questions, Lynne. There's obviously something wrong with him. It was nothing you did. You were just in the wrong place at the wrong time. We have him, and I will do everything in my power to make sure he gets put away for a long time."

"What's his real name?" I asked.

"His name is David Hoffman. He'll go to trial for both attacks—and potentially others."

Then it hit me: *He'll go to trial.* I hadn't even thought about what would happen after they found him. Stupidly, I just thought he would go straight to jail—no trial, no complications. He would confess and be put away for life. It would be over and everyone would be safe. But no, there would be a trial, and he might even get off. A trial would mean that everyone would find out what happened. David Hoffman's arrest would result in the story—my story—getting out. Everyone I knew would soon know too.

"Officer Curtis?" I asked. "If he goes to trial, will it be possible for me to remain anonymous? The only people I've told about this are my boss, my sister, and Collin. I don't want people to know what happened to me."

I could see the concern on her face as she said, "We'll do our best to keep you out of the papers. But court proceedings are in the public record. I can't guarantee that you won't be identified. I wish I could."

I thought for a moment about how she'd been so kind to me and how she really seemed to care. "I owe you an apology," I said. "I've been so self-absorbed that I haven't told you or your team how grateful I am for all you've done to help me. So, thank you."

With a look of surprise she said, "That's what we're here for, Lynne. We're glad we could help." Seeing that I was still struggling, she added, "Feel free to sit here as long as you need to. I'll be back in a few minutes to check on you."

Collin and I sat silently at the table after Officer Curtis left the room. She was right, I was overwhelmed and needed some time to collect myself and get control of my emotions—but it was not going to happen here. I turned to Collin. "Would you mind taking me back to my office so I can get my car? I think I'd like to be alone for a while."

"Of course, I don't mind. Let's get you out of here."

As we walked to his car, Collin said, "Lynne, I'm glad you called me and asked me to come with you today. I would hate to think of you going through this alone."

He knew how hard it had been for me and how just seeing David's face had rattled me to my core. I could tell he wanted to reach out and hold me, but wasn't sure how I would feel about it. I was sending mixed messages—help me and leave me alone—both at the same time. Even I didn't know how I felt or how I would react to reassurance in the form of physical contact. Instead, Collin knew to keep his distance and wait to see how I was handling things; and then he made sure I knew he was there for me to do whatever he could to help. He knew I was fragile, and I knew that he would be careful with me.

I, on the other hand, took advantage of his kindness. I'd stayed tightly wrapped in my emotions and kept him at arm's length while he continued patiently to be there for me.

When we pulled up to my car, Collin said, "Are you going to be okay, Lynne?"

"I'll be fine," I said and kissed him on the cheek. "Thank you, Collin. Thank you again for coming through for me. I think I just need some time to myself to sort through all this. I hope you understand."

He leaned over so he could look into my face as he spoke. "Remember, Lynne, you know where to find me if you need me."

CHAPTER 13

Summer 2001

THE NEXT DAY was my visit with Dr. Goldman, my physician. I'd seen him for my post-hospital follow-up visit and now, finally, this visit was my last visit to give me a clean bill of health. He was a very kind man, grandfatherly in his manner. He didn't just focus on my physical health, he was concerned with my emotional well-being as well. He always left ample time to talk with me after he completed his examination to make sure I was doing okay. Today would be the same routine. After the exam, as I sat in his office waiting for him to come in and give me his assessment, I studied the photos and memorabilia displayed around the room. There were pictures of his patients, new babies, small mementos, and letters of appreciation. He was well liked by his patients. Within a few minutes, the door opened and he came in. I selected a chair and sat down across from him.

Lynne," he said, "physically, you're healing nicely—but how are you feeling emotionally?"

I told him they'd caught the man who'd attacked me, and that I was very anxious about the case going to trial. I told him I had been seeing a therapist, and she was helping me develop coping strategies that I felt certain would help me build confidence by the time of the trial. Finally, I told him that I'd feel huge relief when it was over—when I could get all this behind me.

"Good, I'm very glad to hear you like your therapist, and I'm doubly glad you feel she's helping you."

"Yes. I like her a lot and I definitely think she's helping me."

"How do you feel physically?" he asked.

Smiling at him, I said, 'Well, I think I'm doing fine based on what you've told me this afternoon."

"Remind me, Lynne, didn't you tell me you were in a sexual relationship prior to the attack?"

"Sadly no," I said, shaking my head.

"How about since the attack? Have you had a physical relationship with anyone since the attack?"

"No. Not yet," I said as my face flushed pink. "I've met someone and I like him a lot. He's a really great guy and we have the potential for a physical relationship, but I wanted to be back to myself one hundred percent before launching into anything. My therapist has helped me get my emotional groove back, and I'm hopeful you'll give me the all-clear physically."

"Lynne," Dr. Goldman said as he got up from his chair and came around to the front of his desk. "I'm not sure how to tell you this other than to come right out and say it. I ran several tests today, and one of them indicates that you're pregnant."

I sat looking at him, blinking rapidly in disbelief. I'd heard him say something, but I wasn't sure what he'd said. My ears were ringing and my head was spinning. "What? What did you say?"

Dr. Goldman could see that the color had drained from my face, and he took me by the arm. "Lynne, I think you should lie down."

He walked me over to his couch and put my feet up. He called his nurse and asked her to bring ice packs.

I lay on his couch, blinking, trying to focus my eyes.

"Take slow breaths, Lynne," he said. "Just focus on your breathing."

His nurse came in and put an ice pack on the back of my neck and another on my forehead. Then he dismissed her, and he sat next to me for several minutes while he repeated, "Take slow breaths. Focus on your breathing."

I closed my eyes as I felt the tears running down the sides of my head. Finally, I asked, "I'm pregnant? How is this possible? I thought they gave me something at the hospital to ensure this wouldn't happen."

"Lynne, I'm not sure what went wrong. It shows in your file that you were given the medication. I checked it twice. There could have been a mistake—or it just might be that the drug didn't work for you. Regardless of what should have happened, you are pregnant. What is important to know now is that you have options. There are choices available to you."

Dr. Goldman went on to discuss my options, but the more he talked, the sicker I felt. Finally, I thanked him and said, "As you can imagine, this is a lot to process and I'll need some time to think. This is certainly not the news I'd expected today."

"I'm so sorry about all of this, Lynne. It's not the news I'd hoped to deliver. Please be sure to discuss the matter with your therapist. If you decide to move forward with an abortion, we can get you in right away. You have options. Think about what you want to do. I'll have my nurse set up an appointment so we can talk more about it—after you've had ample time to think. That said, you shouldn't delay making a decision." He patted my hand and left.

His nurse approached me to set up an appointment, but I just wanted to get out of there. I told her I needed to look at my calendar before I could set something up, and that I would call later that day. I felt numb as I went outside, found my car, and then fumbled around in my purse, trying to find my keys. While digging around in the bottom I dropped it, spilling the contents out into the parking lot. That was it! My eyes were so filled with tears that I struggled to see as I knelt down to collect everything. I went into a full-blown ugly cry as I thought over and over again, how could this have happened?

CHAPTER 14

Summer 2001

I DIDN'T GO home, I didn't call—I just drove straight to Betsy. I wanted to get to her when she was still alone, before Ron came in from the fields. As I got out of my car, I could see her working in her vegetable garden in the side yard. When she heard my car, she stood up, and with her hand shielding her eyes from the sun, she tried to see who had come.

"Lynne?" she yelled as she wiped her hands on her pants. "Are you okay? Why are you here?"

I couldn't get even one word out. I fell to my knees before I could reach her. Dropping my head into my lap, I covered my face with both hands and just started sobbing. Betsy raced over to me. She knelt down and put her arms around me, cradling my head on her shoulder.

"What's happened, Lynnie?"

"I'm pregnant, Betsy."

She sighed and said, "Oh, Lynne," in such a sorrowful voice that I felt her pain for me. Then, without asking any more questions, she just stayed there with me and let me cry. I don't know how long we stayed there together, but it seemed like an eternity. Finally, I wiped the tears from my face with the palms of my hands and said, "What do you think I should do?"

"I don't know, Lynnie. What do you want to do?"

"My doctor said I have options, but he told me I needed to make a decision soon. I've been thinking about those options all the way here. An abortion would be a quick resolution, and it's certainly justified under the circumstances. But I'm not sure I could do it. I also can't imagine going through a pregnancy with that man's child."

"Regardless of what you decide to do, Lynnie, I will help you every step of the way. You won't have to do it alone."

"I've been overwhelmed by my thoughts and feelings, so I've been flip-flopping since the moment Dr. Goldman told me the news. Betsy, my hospital records show that they gave me the medication to stop a pregnancy from occurring. Do you think they made a mistake and didn't really give it to me? How is this possible? I've always been very open-minded about other women's decisions, and know full well, especially in the case of rape, there certainly is justification. You'd think these circumstances would make the decision easier, but I actually think they make it harder. Under different circumstances I probably wouldn't even consider an abortion." I paused to catch my breath.

"I wasn't planning on having children anytime soon. I'm just getting my career started, Betsy, and I don't think I can handle my career and a baby. Goddamn it! I've been so careful not to let people know what happened to me. I don't want to have to look into their faces and see pity for what's happened to me. My life was beginning to look normal on the outside. But this! I won't be able to hide this! And then there's Collin." After that, I started sobbing again. "I think I love Collin, Betsy," I said between gasps. "What do I do about him? I can't tell him about this."

"Lynne, I think you're trying to tackle too many decisions at once."

"All of these issues are related and weigh on my decision, Betsy," I said angrily. "Then there's David. What if he finds out I'm pregnant? What if he thinks he has rights to the child? I couldn't stand for him to be involved in my life, even if he is in prison—and he certainly shouldn't be involved in the life of any child. What rights does he have? What rights do I have, or, for that matter, what rights does the child have?"

"Lynne, surely David wouldn't have any rights. He committed a crime."

"I don't know. I need to find out. It's tough enough being a kid these days, then add to it, you're the product of a rape and your father is in prison!" I could feel myself getting panicky again and repeated my therapist's mantra in my head, *Breathe slowly. Focus on your breathing.* I lay down on the grass trying to get some oxygen to my brain, and Betsy put my head in her lap.

"Lynne, you don't have to think about all of this now. Let's just take this one step at a time. One step at a time we can handle. And I do mean we. I'm here for you and will do all I can to help. Step one—let's look at your options. Then, let's find out what rights David has. Once we know the answers to some of these questions, you can walk through them one by one and that will help you make an informed decision."

I lay there on the grass, unmoving, for a very long time. Betsy stroked my forehead and I slowly started to relax and breathe normally. Finally, Betsy broke the silence and said, "Let's go to the house and have some tea. We can sit on the swing and talk this through."

We walked over to the house, and I sat on the swing while she went inside and made us tea. I ran my hand across my abdomen. It was a strange feeling, knowing there was a fetus in there. I'd imagined what it would be like to be pregnant since I was a little girl. I had dreamed about being all grown up, falling in love, and having a family of my own. I'd imagined that it would be a happy time and that I'd be able to share it with someone I loved very much. Now here I was pregnant—and not by someone I loved. There was no joy; there was only anger and sadness over what was happening. All my hopes and dreams were now dashed.

Betsy handed me my tea and sat down next to me. She held my hand and said, "It's going to be okay, Lynnie. Everything is going to be okay."

CHAPTER 15

Summer - Fall 2001

LUCKILY IT TURNED out that in Illinois rapists did not have rights to a child that resulted from a rape. It boggled my mind to think that in this day and age any state would give rights to a rapist, but sadly there were some that did. I was grateful to have one less issue to struggle with.

Two weeks had gone by and the clock was running out. Dr. Goldman had called to remind me I needed to make a decision, and I knew the longer I waited, the riskier an abortion would become. I was grateful I had options. Not everyone did, and while it took me a while, I finally realized that by delaying a decision I was in effect deciding. I would not have an abortion. I would lie about the baby's father; I would claim that I didn't know who the father was; or I would give up the baby for adoption. Regardless, it was no one's business who the father was, and unless there was a DNA test, no one would ever know.

Again, I had to go to Margie and tell her about my newest problem. She'd experienced more with me than any boss should ever have to, and she rose to the occasion every time. She told me I could take a position at the company that would allow me to work remotely. It might not be a role that would put me on a fast track to advancement, but it would give me flexibility; and when I was ready, I could come back and take up where I left off—if I wanted to. This arrangement gave me the opportunity to move further away and conceal the pregnancy. And I would have more time to decide what to do about the baby. I could go anywhere I wanted to—someplace where no one would know me or anything about me, and where I could make up my mind without any external pressure. I was very grateful to her.

I spent a couple of weekends flying to different parts of the country, checking out locations where I thought I'd like to live. I settled on eastern Tennessee, where the winter was moderate, the people were nice, and the scenery was beautiful. Plus, it wasn't too far from home if I needed Betsy, who was sad about my moving away, but understood completely why I needed to go. I was simply giving myself the necessary time and space to make the right decisions for me and the baby.

The whole time I was making my plans, I kept them from Collin. It was one of the hardest things I've ever had to do. I loved him, and I hated lying to him, and now I had to decide how best to push him away. I'm not very good at concealing my emotions, so I had to work hard to pretend that everything was fine—all the while planning my departure. We'd gotten very close and spent all our free time together. He knew me and understood me. I also knew he could feel a new undercurrent in our relationship, but instead of prying, he gave me space and waited patiently for me to tell him what it was. But I didn't—I couldn't. Because he loved me unconditionally and would do anything for me, he would take on any problem or challenge I might present him with—and that meant I had to let him go.

Over the three months since the rape, we'd become best friends and more. We both wanted a sexual relationship, and he was waiting for me to give him the right cues. His primary concern was that I be healed physically and psychologically before taking our relationship to the next level. When I was finally ready, the visit with Dr. Goldman happened; and the news I received finished it with Collin.

Soon I would be showing and wouldn't be able to conceal the pregnancy. Everything was in place, and I was ready for the move—except I wasn't ready to push Collin away. It would be very difficult to do it in such a way that he wouldn't attempt or even want any further contact. I wasn't sure how I would do it—or even if I could do it. What strengthened my resolve was the knowledge that he deserved more. He deserved a life not complicated by me and the ongoing baggage of my attack—including, and especially, a baby. Ultimately, the lie I settled on was that I'd earned a promotion that entailed a transfer. What was especially coldhearted about it was that I'd have to convince him I was excited about it and that he didn't even weigh in my decision—in other words, this opportunity was more important to me than he was.

I knew it would hurt him, and it hurt me to even think about it, but I had to focus on the fact that I loved him, and because I loved him, I had to leave him. I would have to be strong enough to make the decision for the both of us. There was simply no future for us.

I didn't want to share the news with him in a public place. I needed somewhere private, so we could talk and not worry about being overheard. I decided to make dinner for us and take it to his place. When I called him, I told him I had something exciting to tell him, and I worked hard to sound happy. He would anticipate something special just because I was bringing dinner to him, which was a rare occurrence.

When I hung up the phone, my mouth had gone completely dry, and I had that all too familiar ache in my chest. The ache you get when your heart is breaking. I was going to hurt him and hurt him badly; and after all of the wonderful things he'd done for me, and in spite of the fact that I loved him— or because I loved him—I was going to have to leave him. I needed to sever all ties, which meant I'd have to be brutal.

My skills as an actor were not good enough to overcome the pain in my heart. He could tell from the second he opened the door and saw my face that something was very wrong.

"What's wrong, Lynne? I thought you told me you had some exciting news." He paused for a moment before adding, "You have something to tell me, and I don't think I'm going to like it."

"Actually, it is great news," I lied, trying hard to sound upbeat. Forgoing all of my plans for a slow, careful delivery, I blurted out, "I've been given a promotion—a position I've been working toward for a very long time. The only downside is that I'll be transferred to another office."

Collin looked at me in surprise. "What? Where are you going?"

"I don't know yet," I lied. "They're going to give me more than one option to choose from."

"Then you could choose to stay here, or at least close by?" he asked hopefully.

"Sadly, no." Then going on the offensive, I said in an angry tone, "You don't seem happy for me. This is a great opportunity."

"But what about us? Don't you know how I feel about you?" he asked, looking bewildered.

"You are my dearest friend, Collin. Of course, I know."

"Friend? Lynne, I've fallen in love with you," he said, "and I thought you loved me." I could tell from his faltering voice that he was very angry and hurt.

"Collin, I love you very much, but I love you as a dear friend. I'm sorry if I've led you to believe I felt anything more than that." My voice started trembling as I struggled to regain my composure. I had to keep it together, since convincing him rested on keeping myself as calm and unemotional as possible.

"Collin, I thought you'd be glad to hear my news and be supportive of me," I said, feigning an angry tone. "I feel like this is my big chance. . . . Maybe having dinner together was a bad idea," I added, realizing I wouldn't be able to keep up my act as I felt the tears start welling up in my eyes.

Collin came closer and raised his hand to my face to brush away my tears. "I'm sorry, Lynne. I don't mean to be unsupportive," he said.

I held my hand up to keep him from touching me. I knew if he touched me, I would lose it. More forcefully than I needed to, I said, "Collin, I need to take this position. Clearly dinner was a bad idea. I should leave. I'm sorry you can't just be happy for me."

After I said that, I looked at him and saw he was deeply hurt. I quickly looked away so he couldn't look closely at me and see that my heart was breaking.

"I can't pretend I understand or that this isn't hard for me to hear," Collin said. "I thought you loved me—or at the least you knew how I felt about you. I guess I must have misread the signs. Maybe I shouldn't be considered a good friend because I didn't show more enthusiasm about your promotion. But because this news came as such a complete surprise to me, I'm not sure I can respond appropriately. I need more time to process what this means to me and for us"

I just stood there looking at him. I wanted desperately to tell him I loved him and that I was going away *because* I loved him, but all I could do was open the door and walk away. As soon as I closed behind me, I began to sob.

CHAPTER 16

Fall 2001 - Winter 2002

I CRIED MORE in the three months since the attack than all the tears I'd cried in my entire life before, and the majority of those tears had been about my pregnancy and break up with Collin. I was heartbroken about what I'd done to him, as well as heartbroken for myself. I loved him. He was without a doubt the most wonderful man I'd ever met; and now, because of this pregnancy, any possibility of us deepening our relationship would never be realized. I had to keep telling myself that there was no other way. I hoped someday I'd find out that he'd found someone special and was living a wonderful life unencumbered by all of my baggage—he deserved that.

I worked feverishly to finish packing, and the next morning at seven, the movers arrived. By noon I was gone. The whole time I panicked at the thought that Collin would call or show up, since I knew I wouldn't have the courage or strength to repeat what had happened the night before. It had taken everything out of me. On my way out of town, I stopped and changed my cell phone number and gave my new number to Betsy and Margie, asking them not to share it with anyone. All ties were cut.

Betsy wasn't sure I'd made the right decision. She'd wanted me to come to the farm and stay with her and Ron, but I couldn't do it. If I could keep this a secret now, I would be able to keep my options open, allowing me time to make a decision unencumbered by external forces. No one in Tennessee knew anything about the attack, so they wouldn't connect the baby to the rape; and if I decided to give up the baby for adoption, I could just come home afterward and no one would ever know.

I made a vacation of the drive to my new home in Tennessee. I stopped along the way and viewed the scenery, visited small tourist towns, and enjoyed my time alone. When I arrived in my new community, I spent another few days getting acclimated and settling in. There was a great little farmer's market there and a number of antique shops. I rode my bike along the trail system. I worked hard to keep busy, to make my new life as full as possible. I was afraid if I didn't, I'd become depressed. I talked with Betsy on the phone every morning and evening, and sometimes we would video chat when I needed to see her beautiful, smiling face.

I actually really enjoyed that time. As each day went by, I became increasingly certain I'd made the right decision about Collin. I was also sure I'd made the right decision about having the baby. But the further along I got, the less sure I became about what to do with the baby. What I did know was that I didn't want it to grow up knowing its father was a violent criminal and that it was the product of a rape.

I practiced my stories—I had a relationship that didn't last, the father of the baby had died, I had adopted the baby, on and on the stories went; but at the end of each and every one I worried about the chance that someone—or even the baby when it grew up—would find out about the attack and make the connection. If I gave up the baby, that connection wouldn't be made, and it would have a better chance at a life unencumbered by my past. And if I gave up the baby, it would mean a fresh start for both of us.

Every day, I would struggle back and forth, trying to make up my mind. I would make a decision and wait for a sense of calm—but none came. I would make another decision and wait again—nothing. It was exhausting.

At the end of my seventh month, Betsy called and told me Officer Curtis was trying to get in touch with me.

"Lynnie, the trial date has been set. Officer Curtis wants you to call her to get the details. She's been working with the prosecutor and says you'll need to come up to give a deposition. She hopes that means you won't have to go to court.

"That's good news. Did she mention whether I could give the deposition over the phone?"

"No, she said you'd have to be there in person."

My heart stopped. I was going to have to go back to Chicago now, when I was seven months' pregnant. The only saving grace was that Chicago was a big place, and the chances of seeing someone I knew were pretty slim. But that didn't mean I wouldn't worry about it. Since this whole thing began, I'd felt like I would just start to get my head above water when another wave would wash over me. This was the next wave.

"You'll get past this, Lynnie. Once he goes to jail, it will be all over," Betsy said.

"You forget that I'm carrying his child. I will never be over this," I said angrily.

There was a long pause. "I'm sorry, Lynnie—that was thoughtless of me. You're right. You know, you don't have to do this. You could tell them no."

"No, I have to do this or I'll be sorry for the rest of my life. I don't want him to get off and do what he did to me to someone else. I have to give this deposition."

"Do you want me to meet you in Chicago? I'd be happy to come. Lynne. Tell me how I can help."

"I love you for offering, but I can do this, and I can do it on my own. I'll go and give the deposition, then get out of town as quickly as possible afterward."

I contacted Officer Curtis and she repeated what Betsy had told me. She'd worked with the prosecuting attorney, and they were doing their best to accommodate me. She thought the deposition could be completed in one day; and if I could get there early, I might not even have to stay overnight. Regardless, I had to keep a constant mantra running in my head to build up my confidence: *You can handle this. Just one day, and then you are done. It will be over. You can do this.*

I was notified that the deposition would be in two weeks. I would arrive early that morning, give my testimony, and then leave the same afternoon.

When I arrived at the defense attorney's office, I was so nervous my hands were shaking. I sat in the upscale, busy waiting room until they called me. The receptionist walked me back to the room where I was to give my deposition, and as I walked in, the four attorneys and the court recorder looked up. I could read the shock on their faces and imagined the thoughts running through their heads. I was like an insect under glass—trapped, scrutinized, and vulnerable.

I'd talked on the phone with the prosecuting attorney, Graham Smith, several times over the previous two weeks. He'd helped me understand what was going to happen and had done his best to prepare me for the questioning—but I'd done nothing to prepare myself emotionally, and it showed. He tried to be reassuring. He put his hand on my arm to let me know I wasn't alone, that he was there to help me—but I still felt very much alone.

On the other hand, the defense attorney, Robert Calvin, was there to push and poke me with questions to see if he could shatter my story. He wanted me rattled and on edge. The fact that I was very pregnant gave the entire process a heightened level of intensity and made me feel even more self-conscious, insecure, and vulnerable. When it was his turn, he introduced himself and then asked, "Should I refer to you as Miss or Mrs.?"

I felt sickened and angry. I tried my best to remain composed, but he'd succeeded in rattling me on question number one! It was going to be a long day, and I would have to work hard to keep from getting emotional.

"Ms.," I said with a quiver in my voice.

"Ms. Parker," Mr. Calvin said, "when is your baby due?"

Before I could respond, Graham said, "That is irrelevant and beyond the bounds of questioning. She does not need to answer."

"Well, it may be relevant for two reasons," replied Mr. Calvin. "One, I want to establish Ms. Parker's sexual relationships, and two, because we may need Ms. Parker to testify at the trial. I understand you no longer live close by, Ms. Parker, and it may be difficult for you to participate if your delivery date is soon."

Again, Graham responded. "Ms. Parker's sexual relationships are not on trial here."

"Well, I would disagree. I think they're very relevant. Ms. Parker, how many sexual partners have you had in the last year?"

At that, I really stumbled. I could feel my face becoming red, and I was also feeling very angry again.

Graham stepped in and said to me, "You don't have to answer that."

I sat quietly with my face red and my heart racing as Mr. Calvin looked at me and waited for an answer. I didn't answer, but he'd been successful in putting me on edge, and he knew it. I hadn't expected to have to defend myself. I'd only planned to tell them about what happened to me and who had done it.

There was a palpable layer of ice in the air as Mr. Calvin asked me one question after another. He worked very hard to confuse and badger me; but when he asked an inappropriate or irrelevant question Graham was right on him.

Graham kept smiling at me and telling me I was doing fine. At first, I didn't feel fine, but as each question came and I described what had happened to me, I became stronger and surer of myself. I kept telling myself that David Hoffman was not going to get away with what he did to me.

Finally, it was Graham's turn. He asked some of the same questions, but did so in a non-threatening way, and I knew he was on my side. It was obvious he was trying to get to the truth. I recreated the entire attack for him.

The deposition took longer than expected, and by the end of the day, I was exhausted physically and emotionally. Finally, Graham leaned in and told me they were done questioning me, and whispered, "Good job, Lynne."

Once we were done, Mr. Calvin said nothing to me. He just gathered up everything he'd brought and left the room without a word. I felt angry and wanted an apology from him for treating me as he had; but even more, I wanted him to disappear through the doorway and to never see him again.

As I was leaving, Graham said, "Thank you for coming, Lynne. I know it wasn't easy for you. Your testimony is critical to the trial, and we're very grateful for it. The other woman who was attacked is also providing testimony. We're going to put him away for a long time. And I'll do my best to keep you from having to come to the trial."

"Thank you, I appreciate that. Even this wasn't easy for me, so I'm hoping this is the last time I'll have to talk about it."

"When I reached the waiting room, I was surprised to see Officer Curtis waiting for me. I could see she was surprised to see me too—or at least my protruding stomach.

"Lynne," she stammered, trying not to stare at my belly, "I thought I'd come by and see if you wanted to get a cup of coffee or a bite of dinner before you head back."

"Oh, Officer Curtis," I said as I gave her a big hug. "How kind of you, but I would really like to get home as soon as possible. I'm simply exhausted— and the sooner I get there the better."

"You know you can call me Susan, right? I hope you consider me a friend, and at the very least you should be able to call me by my first name. Let me walk you to your car."

As soon as we were outside, I stopped and took her by the arm saying, "Susan, I know you're surprised to see me like this, but I'm not telling anyone about the pregnancy. I hope you'll respect that."

"I understand, Lynne, and I do respect that. I admire your strength in dealing with everything you've gone through. You are an amazing woman!"

When we got to my car, I gave her another big hug. "Thank you for being there for me, then and now," I said.

"You are most welcome, Lynne. Call me from time to time to let me know how you're doing," she added before we parted.

I felt a huge sense of relief at putting the deposition behind me. Other than seeing the attorneys, I hadn't run into anyone I knew except Susan, and I trusted her to keep my condition confidential.

I was so happy to be on my way back home and, while I felt optimistic that I would not have to go to court, I was not sure. There was nothing "sure" about any of this. What if he was found guilty and appealed the verdict? When would my connections to him stop? It was clear to me now. My connection to David Hoffman would never stop. And, in the midst of that revelation I finally got my answer. I would give the baby up for adoption.

CHAPTER 17

Winter 2018

I SAT IN the shack and told the shack girls my story, and when I was finished, I sat and waited for the questions to start.

"How long was his prison term?" Jo asked.

"He was sentenced to twenty years."

"But it hasn't been twenty years—has it?" Jo exclaimed.

"And twenty years would not have been nearly long enough. That piece of shit should have been put away for life," Sam said, standing up to stretch her legs. "How is it possible that someone like that can serve so little time after what he did to you? Where is the justice here? This makes me so angry."

"So, you gave the baby up for adoption," Callie said with a bit of a question in her voice. "Oh Lynne, it boggles the mind to think about what you've been through!"

"Yes, I did give the baby up for adoption. I know I did the right thing for the baby and for me. And now that I've seen David Hoffman again, I'm even more certain I made the right decision."

"What are you going to do about him? Are you going to call the police?" Jo demanded.

"I know it seems crazy, but I want to find out what my rights are first. I want to see if I can get a restraining order or other restriction so he can't even get close to me.

"You don't think you should call the police? " Callie said surprised at Lynne's response. "He's a threat to you, and they need to know that he's here."

"You may be right. But I want to see my options before I bring more people into this."

"I agree you need to know your rights. Why would he come here unless he wanted to continue harassing you? You should get a restraining order. His visit represents a threat. He wants you to know he's out there, and he wants something from you," Jo said firmly.

"I don't think you are safe alone. You should have someone with you at all times until they can do something about him," Smitty said. "Who knows what he's up to?"

"Do you have a gun?" Sam asked.

"No—I don't have a gun!" I responded, horrified at the very idea.

"Well, we need to get you one and get you trained to use it. You need to be prepared with that son-of-a-bitch out there. Telling the police is not going to protect you. It will only alert them to keep an eye out for him. If you find yourself confronted by him, the police aren't going to be able to get there in time. You're going to have to be responsible for your own safety," Sam said, nodding vigorously.

The thought of getting a gun was something I had never considered, and it did not appeal to me now. Trying to push Sam's suggestion to the back of my mind, I continued, "I've wondered about this day for a long time. I knew he would get out of prison, but I didn't expect him to come find me. I mistakenly thought he'd go on with his life and I'd go on with mine."

"We'll put your things away for you. Why don't you go ahead? Jo can you go with her?" Smitty suggested.

"Of course I can go with her," Jo responded.

"Thank you. I appreciate that. I'd like to see Betsy before it gets much later," Lynne said, picking up her purse. "I'm sorry to burden you all with this long and distressing story. You guys are terrific. I hope you know that I love you all, but I also want to ask you to keep my story to yourselves. I don't want anyone to know what happened, and I need time to figure out how to handle this. I need you to trust that I am doing the right thing." Then I hugged each of the women one by one before leaving the shack.

As I watched Jo following me, in my rearview mirror, I thought about my decision to not go to the police. If I did, there would be hours of questions. Betsy and Ron's children would be frightened. I would have to explain to the entire town why the police were following me around. And, while I had told the shack girls most of my story, I had not told them all of it.

I was frightened of what David could or would do. I also thought about what Sam had said. I was going to need to be patient and careful until I could talk to my lawyer and see if he could do something to keep David from getting near me. I'd wait to bring the police into this.

As we pulled up in front of the little farm house, I walked over to Jo. "I'm going to go over to the big house and talk with Betsy. I am sure she is waiting for me. I will be home in a little while."

"Do you want me to go with you?" she asked.

"No, I'll be fine."

"Would you please let me know when you come in so I know you got home safely?" Jo asked.

"Yes, I will," I told her. "I won't be long."

As I walked nervously across the drive to the big house, I thought how, I had come back to my hometown to help Betsy and her family and now, here I was exposing them and the shack girls to David Hoffman and my past.

CHAPTER 18

Winter 2017

"WHAT'S WRONG, BETSY?"

"Lynnie, I'm going to come right out with it. I need your help. I have cancer."

I was stunned. I felt sure I had misunderstood, and I desperately waited for clarification, for Betsy to tell me I had misheard her.

She continued, "It's the same cancer Mom had. The doctors think they found it early enough, so they're optimistic that I won't have the same outcome as Mom did—plus, treatments have gotten better since then. But I'm going to need surgery, and then I'll need to undergo a rather intense chemo and radiation regimen. I'm going to be okay. I know I'm going to be okay," she repeated to reassure herself and me.

"They want to do the surgery as soon as possible. I know you're planning to come for Christmas, but do you think you could come early? If you could, it would be a huge help for Ron and the kids, and I'd feel better knowing you were here. But if not, I can ask the shack girls if they can help out, I know they'd be glad to. But I think the kids and Ron would rather have you here, and so would I."

Betsy was trying so hard to be matter-of-fact about her news, but I could detect the fear in her voice, and I'd never known Betsy to be afraid of anything.

"Lynnie, we told the kids I have cancer but we are trying to play it down so they are not afraid. I don't want to worry them, especially if the surgery and treatments seem to be working."

There was a huge lump in my throat, so I barely managed to squeak out, "Betsy, of course I'll come. I'll be there as soon as I can arrange it."

"Thank you, Lynnie. That's a huge relief to me. I love you."

Within a few days, I was on my way. Ron picked me up from the airport.

"Hey Lynnie, we are so glad you could come," he said as he hugged me and took my bag.

"How's she doing, Ron?"

"Prepare yourself, Lynne. You won't recognize Betsy when you see her. She's lost a lot of weight and she looks very tired. And she's not her usual hyperactive, bubbly, demanding self."

Despite his attempt at levity, I could see from his face that he was working very hard to keep it together because we were in a public place. When we got into the car, he looked closely at me and said again, "Thank you for coming, Lynnie." It was then that his face and entire body crumpled. I wrapped my arms around him and just let him cry. I think it's especially hard when someone who's usually so strong, becomes suddenly vulnerable. Betsy was always the fearless one, the one we relied on to keep the rest of us strong. Now she was the one at risk and there was even a chance we might lose her.

"What will I do, Lynnie? She's wasting away right in front of me."

"Have no fear, Lynnie is here," I said in a dramatic voice, trying to make him laugh.

"It means a lot to me, the kids, and Betsy that you're here, Lynnie. I'm so glad you could come. I know it will be good for all of us. Betsy doesn't like to talk about it, but I think she's more scared than she lets on, and I know she's trying to be strong for me and the kids. She needs someone she can lean on and talk to about her fears. You're her very best friend and dearest sister. I know she can talk to you."

"Well, that's good, since I think I'm her *only* sister—unless you know something I don't," I said, squeezing Ron's shoulder as he started the car.

I studied him and noticed how much older he seemed. He'd aged ten years in the last few months. I decided to change the subject and asked him about his baseball league, what the kids were up to, and how things were going at the farm. I would pat his shoulder every once in a while, and I even tried to make jokes to lighten the mood. But the strain and concern were still there, hanging over everything.

As we pulled into the road to the farm and drove up to the house, Josh, Betsy and Ron's nine-year-old, threw the door open and yelled to the entire countryside, "Aunt Lynnie is here!" Both he and the new dog, Jimmy, bounded down the steps and jumped on me before I could brace myself. We tumbled backwards onto the porch, Jimmy barking and Josh whooping.

Ron grabbed Josh by the back of his pants and pulled him up. "Hey man, what do you think you're doing? You could have hurt her!" he said, sounding annoyed.

Without a beat, and paying only slight attention to his dad, Josh said, "Hey Aunt Lynnie, you've got to come see the new Lego set I got. Dad, you won't believe this, but I'm almost done putting it together."

Ron interrupted him. "Josh, why don't you take Lynnie's suitcase upstairs to the guest room before you drag her off to see your Legos. She hasn't even said hello to Mom yet."

Josh's chin dropped to his chest in disappointment. "Okaaay," he responded.

Inside, the house seemed empty. There was no Christmas tree. There were no Christmas decorations. Nothing had been done for the holidays. But most noticeably, there was no Betsy.

"Where's your mom?" I asked.

"Mom's upstairs. Mom! Mom! Come on, Aunt Lynnie. Let's go see her," Josh yelled as he bumped my suitcase up the stairs, and at the top of the landing, he threw open the door to Betsy and Ron's bedroom and yelled, "Mom, Aunt Lynnie is here!"

"Hi!" Betsy said as she stood up to hug me. I stared at the woman standing there. Ron was right, I wouldn't have recognized her. She was very thin, and I could see from her face that she was in a lot of pain. I walked over to her and held tight to her frail little body as tears started rolling down my face. It was fortunate that my back was to Josh.

"Josh, would you take Aunt Lynnie's suitcase to her room?" Betsy asked.

Hastily wiping the tears from my cheeks, I turned the spotlight on Josh. "Betsy, that son of yours gets funnier every time I see him. Such a bundle of energy."

Gently taking my face in her hands, she said, "Yes, he is—on both counts. I hope he doesn't wear you out. Let Melanie help you with him. She needs to feel useful and she can be a great help."

"Speaking of whom, where is that beautiful daughter of yours?" I asked.

"She had an after-school event. Her friend's mom is bringing her home. You'll find that you'll spend your time between three and eight every day driving them around someplace or other. I've made a list of names and phone numbers of people who can help you with all the running around—including the shack girls."

"I can't wait, and I know I'll love doing it."

"Come sit down here next to me, I need to lay down," Betsy said, patting the side of the bed. "Tell me how you are."

"I'm doing fine, but I'm not the one who's the center of attention right now. You tell me about you," I said firmly.

Betsy lay back on the bed before she answered. "They're going to do the surgery tomorrow morning, since they wanted to do it as soon as possible. And I thought if I could get it out of the way, I might be able to be home for most of the preholiday festivities. I'm so glad you were able to come so quickly," she said reaching over and squeezing my hand.

"You're in pain, aren't you?" I said.

"A little, but not bad."

"When did you find out you were sick?"

Betsy said matter-of-factly, "Oh, I hadn't been feeling well, and was always so tired. I just thought it was a stomach bug or the flu. But when it didn't go away, I went in to see my doctor. He ran some tests, and after that it didn't take him long to figure out what was wrong. He said the sooner I could come in for the surgery, the sooner we could get started on the radiation and chemo. That was the day I called you. I know it's not going to be an easy process, but I'm strong and I know I can do it.

"I remember it all from when Mom was sick. She just gave up, Lynnie. I can't give up and won't give up," she said defiantly. "I need to make it for Ron, Melanie, Josh, and you. I need to be strong, but I can't do it alone. I need your help, Lynnie. I'm so glad you're here."

"This is where your obnoxious obstinacy will finally pay off," I said with a chuckle. "You will sail through this, and I'll be here to go through it with you—every single minute! I'm here for as long as you need me. See, there are benefits to having a sister who is single and alone."

Betsy smiled. "I feel better already—and I know Melanie, Josh, and Ron do too. The shack girls have been great, but I haven't told them everything. They went through so much with Mom, so I know it will be a real blow. They do know it's serious, and they've already been a great help."

Josh came bouncing back into the room and whined, "Can you come see my Legos now, Aunt Lynnie?"

I turned to Betsy and said, "Stay here and rest. I'll have dinner up here in an hour." Turning to Josh I said in a fake threatening voice, "Hey! I'm tired of waiting around for you, mister. When are you going to let me see your Legos?"

Immediately, his face broke into a big smile, and he grabbed my hand and dragged me down the hall to his room, where I oohed and aahed until he seemed quite satisfied that he'd gotten the desired reaction.

The next morning, soon after the kids were on the bus for school, Betsy and Ron left for the hospital. Before they did, I gave Betsy a big hug and said reassuringly, "Everything is going to be fine, here and at the hospital. Focus all of your energy on you, and know that I'm taking care of everything here."

Then I turned and gave Ron a hug, saying, "I'm here for both of you, of course, so let me do what I can to help you, too. Call me as soon as you know something—and don't worry about us." Ron gave me an affectionate squeeze back, mumbling, "I'm so glad you're here, Lynnie."

Betsy hugged me one more time and said, "I love you, Lynnie."

CHAPTER 19

Winter 2018

MORE THAN A year had passed since I'd arrived at the farm to take care of Betsy and her family. Betsy's surgery had gone better than expected, and she was managing her treatments fairly well, but she still didn't have much of an appetite and became tired easily. Her doctors seemed pleased with her progress, and her spirits were good. She was getting into the rhythm of what she could and couldn't do, learning how far to push herself. But David Hoffman's sudden, unexpected appearance was an additional pressure she simply didn't need, and I worried what it would do to her and Ron.

"Ron, I'm really sorry about this," I said.

"Sorry for what, Lynnie? This guy showing up is not your fault."

"He wouldn't have shown up if I weren't here," I replied.

"Betsy feels terrible," he said. "He came by here this afternoon and she told him where to find you. She just thought he was a friend from work or something."

"He had to have talked to someone who knew where I was, or he wouldn't have found the farm. I wonder who told him where I was?" I said and paused briefly. "He said he came to talk and that he had unfinished business."

"Do you think he blames you for going to jail?"

"Well, I was responsible for him going to jail. I testified against him. But I don't think that's it. I wonder if he found out about the pregnancy."

"How would he know? He never saw you, did he? No one knew about the pregnancy except for me, you, Betsy, and Officer Curtis, right?"

"Right, except for the attorneys at the deposition. I wonder if his attorney said something to him."

"Well, I still don't think he knows anything. I'm guessing he just wants to make sure you know he's out—he wants to intimidate you. Do you think we should call the police?" Ron asked.

"Well, my first inclination was yes, but as I have thought about it, I worry that once we call the police, the news will be all over town. I think I want to talk with my attorney first, or even Officer Curtis, to see if there is a better way to handle this. If there isn't, then there isn't, but I would like to try that first."

"Come inside. You're safe here with us," he said standing aside. "I think Betsy is still up. She was waiting to talk to you, but she was pretty tired when you called before. She said that if she's asleep, you should wake her up when you got here. Oh, and by the way, she also said to tell you that if you didn't wake her up, she will be very mad at you," Ron said with a smile on his face, lifting the mood.

Betsy wasn't sleeping when I walked into their bedroom. She patted the bed next to her and said softly, "Sit down, Lynnie." I sat down next to her and ran my hand over her bald head. "I think I feel some fuzz coming in," I said in surprise.

Betsy reached up and ran her own hand over her head and smiled; and then looking at me intently she said, "Lynnie, I'm so sorry about what happened today at the shack. I should have called you before I told him where to find you. What's wrong with me that I don't have a brain in my head?"

"He'd have found me anyway. If he could find you, he could find me. I'm going to call my attorney in the morning to find out what I can do about him. I can't believe it's legal for a criminal to hunt down his victim—but who knows? Are you okay? I'm sorry I didn't get here in time to get the kids dinner and into bed."

"You've trained them well. Ron made a delicious dinner, and the kids were able to get themselves in bed. Melanie even made their lunches tonight so you wouldn't have to do it in the morning," Betsy said proudly.

"That makes me sad. I need them to need me," I said. Shaking off those feelings, I stood up and bent down to Betsy. "I'll come by in the morning and get them off to school. Good night, dear," and kissed her on her forehead.

Taking my hand so I couldn't go, Betsy said, "What do you think he wants? Why is he here?"

"I just think he wants to intimidate me and," I said pausing, "I'm guessing he may know about the pregnancy. Regardless, I'm going to see if my attorney can do something. He might be able to contact David's parole officer, or get some kind of court order to keep him away so we never see or hear of him again. You don't need to worry. You should go to sleep and we'll talk more tomorrow." But I could see the concern on her face. I gave her a gentle squeeze and said, "Everything is going to be alright, Betsy."

I said good night to Ron, and walked slowly from the farmhouse to the little house by the barn. When I first came to help Betsy and Ron get through her surgery and treatments, I'd lived in their house with them. But when it became clear that I'd be staying for a while, I decided to make more semi-permanent arrangements. I packed up my apartment, put my things in storage, and set up at the farm in the little house. I needed to be nearby to help, but I didn't want to be in their way. I wanted them to have as normal a life as possible, and that meant giving them some space and privacy to be a family. That's when I moved in with Jo.

Years ago, Jo, a budding young artist, had heard about the *shack* from a gallery owner and approached my mother to ask for space at the artists' studios, or "shack" as we called it. My mother, knowing Jo was fresh out of college with little money and needing a place to live, had offered her one at the farm. Back then, the little house by the barn was rather run down and needed some renovations. So Mom came to an agreement with Jo. She could live there rent-free if she did the necessary repairs. Jo worked on it a little bit at a time—with help from my dad—and eventually they turned it into an attractive and cozy little house. Jo now earned enough from her art to make a reasonable living, and could have gotten a place in town, but she loved living out at the farm in her little house. She asked to stay and paid a modest rent to Betsy and Ron.

When I asked Jo if I could share the space with her, she seemed genuinely pleased. There were two bedrooms upstairs separated by one bathroom. Downstairs there was a small living room with a fireplace, a small kitchen, and a mudroom. The house's best feature was the open porch that wrapped around the entire place. Plus, it was only a few steps away from Betsy and Ron, so I could be there in seconds if I was needed.

Before Ron left in the morning to work in the fields, he would hang a small flag from a post on their back porch. While a bit primitive, the system worked just fine. When I got up every morning, before I even got dressed, I would walk to the porch and look for the flag. It was a sign to me that everything inside was fine and that Ron had gone off to work. One of the best parts of our morning routine was that Ron got the coffee started. All I had to do was walk over to their house and pour a fresh cup to get myself going.

It was nearly impossible to get Josh out of bed in the morning. He was a very sound sleeper. I could tell it was painful for him to open his eyes and get out from under the warm covers. Melanie, on the other hand, was usually up and getting dressed before I arrived. I'd knock on her door to see if she needed any help and to let her know I was there, then I'd head back downstairs to make their lunches. But today Melanie had done that for me. This gave me a little extra time so, as a treat and to make up for not being there the night before, I made them pancakes for breakfast.

"Aunt Lynnie! I love pancakes!" Josh said, sitting down with fork in hand.

"Good," I said, "I made special shapes just for you." I placed what I had thought looked like a dog on his plate in front of him.

"Is it a horse?" he asked.

"Yes. It's a horse," I said, frowning in disappointment.

"Good morning Aunt Lynnie," Melanie said as she came in all ready for school.

"Good morning Melanie. Thank you so much for making the lunches for today. That was very thoughtful."

"Dad said you were busy, so I thought I'd help out."

"That was very nice of you. What's happening at school today?" I asked, addressing both of them.

"I have a math test," Josh said sadly.

"Did you prepare for it? I'm sorry I wasn't here last night to help you study."

"Dad helped me, but I still don't think I'll do very well."

"I bet you'll do just fine," I said hopefully.

"I have an English test today," Melanie said. "I think I'm ready for it. I've been studying all week."

"I know you have. I'm sure you'll do very well," I said as I started collecting the dishes from the table. "Grab your book bags and lunches, and let's head down to the bus stop."

Josh jabbered the whole way there. Melanie looked over at me, rolled her eyes, and said, "He never stops." Josh pretended to look hurt and we all burst out laughing. Before we even got to the end of the lane, the bus pulled up. I hugged the kids hurriedly and waved goodbye as they boarded the bus. I stood and watched as it disappeared down the road and thought about what great kids they were. I would miss them and our daily rituals after I left the farm.

By the time I got back to the house, Betsy was up and in the kitchen. She was even starting to load the dishwasher.

"What are you doing?" I asked.

"I'm loading the dishwasher," she said. "I feel pretty good today."

"Well don't overdo it and exhaust yourself."

"If I don't start doing some things for myself, I'll never get back to where I was," she said a bit sadly.

"Alright. Then while you're at it, pour me another cup of coffee, please."

Betsy poured me and herself a cup of coffee, and we sat and talked for a little while until she said she needed to lie down. I walked back upstairs with her and tucked her in. "Is there anything I can get for you? I was planning to go back to the little house to give my attorney a call this morning."

"No, I'm good. After I have a short rest I'm going to sort through that closet," she said, indicating the linen closet in the hall. Then, when she saw the look of concern cloud my face, she said, "I'll take lots of breaks and it'll be good for me. I promise not to overdo it."

"Keep your phone close. If you need anything call me—and don't push yourself," I admonished her, before giving her blanket another tuck.

As I walked back to the little house, I looked around at the beautiful farm. I had not thought of it as beautiful as a child, but now I did. Every surface was covered with ice crystals, and it felt so peaceful. The gently rolling hills, clear blue sky, chirping birds, and usually a feeling that all was right with the world. But today, that feeling was not there. I reached the porch of the little house, sat down on the steps, and pulled out my phone. When I called my attorney, his secretary answered and put me right through to him.

"Jim, it's Lynne Parker calling. How are you?"

"Good, Lynne, how about you?"

"Jim, I'm calling because I need your help with something. David Hoffman has been released from prison and he came to see me yesterday."

There was a long silence on the other end. Finally, he said, "Lynne, I didn't know. He's out early, very early. Did he say why he came to see you?"

"He said he wants to talk, and that we have unfinished business."

"What do you think he was referring to?"

"I can't be sure, and I don't care what he wants. I want to know whether anything can be done to keep him from contacting or approaching me."

"I will request an emergency order of protection as soon as we hang up."

"If he's here to find out about the child, what are my rights?"

"As far as his rights to knowledge about a pregnancy and the resulting infant, he has no rights."

I was somewhat relieved at his answer, but still felt the weight and ambiguity of his response. "How would he even know?" I asked. "I have done everything in my power to keep this information secret. Would he be able to find out about the adoption?"

"No, the records for the adoption were sealed. He has no standing and no ability to take the case to court. You shouldn't worry about that, Lynne. Your bigger concern should be your safety. Do you want me to contact the police?"

"I was hoping to go beyond that. Would you see if you can get an order of protection, to keep him from coming anywhere near me or even contacting me again?"

"Let me see what I can do. I'll call you as soon as I know something. Do not, under any circumstances, allow yourself to be alone with Mr. Hoffman—and do not go anywhere alone until we can get this matter resolved. And, if you feel the least bit threatened, please contact the local police immediately."

"I will. Thanks for your help, Jim." I hung up the phone and lay back on the porch, my feet on the step, and clutched my phone to my chest. I told myself I didn't know why David Hoffman had shown up and shouldn't make any assumptions. Everything would be okay. But until I heard back from Jim, I wasn't sure I'd be able to convince myself.

CHAPTER 20

Winter 2018

"OH MY GOD, Lynne, are you okay?" Callie yelled. Before I knew it Callie, Sam, and Smitty were down on their knees next to me on the porch.

"I'm fine," I said. "I had a pinch in my back and was trying to stretch it out," I lied.

"It's cold out here, aren't you freezing?" Smitty asked. "I was scared to death, Lynne. I worried that man came back and did something to hurt you."

"No. Just a pinch in my back."

"Well, that's good," Sam said, stepping over me to head toward the kitchen. "I need a cup of coffee."

"You'll have to make it, Sam. I just made one cup," said Jo, coming outside. "Why are you all kneeling on the porch floor?"

These four women couldn't be more different from each other, and yet emotionally they were very close. They had a common bond—their art. That, and working together in the shack every day, was the foundation of their love and respect for each other—including me. The heart of the group was Smitty. She'd been a huge support to Mom when she was sick, and a huge support to Betsy and me after Mom died.

My mother had been a very talented artist. Yet she'd put her ambitions aside to marry my dad and raise Betsy and me. After the two of us were in school, Mom bought an old building just outside of town lovingly known as "the shack," which she immediately began to renovate. Her very first project was converting a space into a studio for herself so she could paint while we were in school.

To help with the cost of the shack and to finance the renovations, Mom rented out studio space. She promoted the beauty of the countryside, the quiet rural town, and idyllic conditions for serious artists to find focus and commit to their craft. She worked with each artist she brought in, helping them to renovate their individual space, customized to accommodate their particular talent and expertise. She sought to find a variety of artists with different specialties, so it was often a surprisingly eclectic group. In its heyday, Mom had been successful in achieving something of a cult status for the shack, so there was often a waiting list of artists for the next available space. Not only was she very selective about who she picked, but each of the artists already there could vote on which newcomers would join the group of shack girls—as they were called. I don't think Mom was prejudiced against men, but to my knowledge there were never any shack guys.

Smitty was the first artist to rent studio space from Mom. She came from a rural area in upstate New York, and every once in a while you could hear her New York accent come through. She had a graduate degree from the Rhode Island School of Design and had taught in the program there before gaining enough attention to launch a career as a full-time artist, thanks to some consequential exhibits of her artwork in Boston and New York. Those put her on the radar of dealers from across the country. She lived in Brooklyn for more than ten years, building her client base, before she and Mom met through a common friend. My mother convinced her to come and see what the shack had to offer, and once she did, she decided to stay. That's what launched it as an official artists' enclave with studio space for up to ten artists.

Smitty had taught me to throw pottery when I was a little girl. I would sometimes accompany Mom to the shack, especially when Betsy was a teenager and didn't have time for me. Smitty would take me into her studio, show me what she was working on, and let me play with the clay—always complimenting me on my work. Now that I was living at the farm and helping Betsy,

Smitty was always encouraging me to come over to the shack, so as not to let my talent go to waste—as she put it. I'm not sure about how talented I was, but I did find going to the shack, working on a project, and being around the other women to be very fulfilling. And Smitty couldn't have been more supportive.

Although she never talked about it, it was my understanding that Smitty had been married and divorced when she was younger and didn't have any children. She'd never remarried either. I decided years ago that it was none of my business, so I never asked, although I would have liked to know. She often said, "One of the best parts of being 'out in the sticks' is being able to disappear into the landscape," which made me wonder about her past and what that statement said about her previous life.

She was conservative and practical in her dress. Her beautiful silver hair was always tied back with a thin leather strap. She wore practical black flats, thin-legged black slacks, and a white cotton button-down shirt every day. It was her uniform. Her clothes, like her nature, were simple, refined, and composed. She never varied from this combination—clothes or personality—regardless of the situation. She was very observant of other people and their joys or sorrows. She would be the first person to congratulate someone, or recognize a milestone, or see a need; and, without being asked, she would literally roll up her sleeves and help in any way possible. She'd been a huge help to Mom when she got sick, and when it was clear that she wouldn't get well, she'd known how hard her death would be on me and Betsy. So she stepped in and took over where Mom left off—not trying to replace her, but being there to support us even though we were adults. She was there for us, and we felt loved and cared for. I often wondered if Mom had asked her to look after us, or if it was simply her nature.

The only time I remember seeing Smitty visibly upset was when she found out Betsy had the same type of cancer as Mom. I remember that day so well. She'd come to me when Betsy was resting, and asked me if she had cancer. When I told her, her face immediately crumbled into an expression of pain and despair. Her eyes filled with tears, and as she looked up at me and saw the concern on my face, she quickly blinked away her tears and said,

"Well, treatments are better now, and together we'll help her get through this. She will be just fine." I could see that even in the midst of her own pain, she thought of me and Betsy and would not allow us to see her concerns. She would gather her strength and faith and share it with us.

The shack girls were very close, and Smitty, in part because she'd been there the longest, was the matriarch of the group. But she was closest to Sam—even though side by side, they were complete opposites, physically and otherwise.

Sam was always very direct and didn't have an ounce of diplomacy in her body. If you wanted an honest opinion, you could rely on her to give it to you—but you needed to be prepared to hear it with no sugar coating. She didn't care much for people and certainly didn't exhibit any patience for them. If she was being helped by a clerk in a store who stopped to talk to someone else, they could expect to be told to "put that on hold until we are done here."

Sam could also be hilarious. She could see the funny side of anything. She did great impressions of famous people and often acted them out in unique situations. We would be rolling on the floor in laughter by the time she was finished. She also had a pretty colorful vocabulary—and when she was angry, she didn't care who heard what she said. But if she liked you, there was no greater ally. She would back you one hundred and ten percent. Mom would often tell us not to take what Sam said to us personally, that Sam didn't mean to hurt our feelings. It's just that she didn't try not to; and as soon as she said what she needed to say, she would move on and we should too.

Sam, unlike Smitty, was very haphazard in her dress. She shopped for clothes at the local thrift shop, and if it fit, it was a sale. She always looked as if she'd selected the first article of clothing she spotted in her closet, and if it happened to go well with the next one she chose, that was a happy accident. She had reddish-brown curly hair that she kept short so she could just wash it and be done.

Sam had been raised in Kentucky in a very large family—sixteen kids! She'd also never married and stated categorically that, with the exception of her father, she had no use for men. Growing up, she'd been close to her father, and perhaps because there were so many children, she took advantage of every opportunity to spend time with him. He operated a small glass furnace, and she'd learned the art of glassblowing from him. She often mentioned that her father possessed exceptional talent, but because of the size of the family, he couldn't dedicate enough time to his craft. Sam and her sister co-owned a shop in Knoxville. Her sister ran the shop and Sam's connections helped to fill it with wonderful unique pieces, including Sam's pieces and those made by some of the other shack girls.

Sam had been the second artist to come to the shack. Mom met her at a show in Chicago, and when she told Sam about the shack, Sam was intrigued by the idea of becoming part of an elite artists' collective. She came almost immediately. Because of the modifications needed to accommodate Sam's glass furnace, Dad had to get involved. He usually tried to stay out of the goings-on at the shack, because it was Mom's pet project. But Sam and my dad soon discovered they were kindred spirits with very similar personalities, and they'd formed a strong bond when they worked together on the special requirements for Sam's studio. Mom didn't seem to mind, because the renovations that Sam needed were more than the two of them could do alone; plus, my dad was excited about the challenge.

Based on Sam's specifications, Dad had a new gas line installed, put in a new concrete pad for the furnace, and improved the lighting. Together they made it exactly what she'd wanted. Sam purchased a cremator from a funeral home in Chicago, and the two of them picked it up and drove it back to the shack, where they spent several weeks customizing and retrofitting it to function as a glass furnace. I'd have loved to have been a passenger with them for that trip!

Callie, another one of the shack girls, was a fiber artist and had attended high school with Betsy. She and her husband owned a little butcher shop in town; and while she hadn't garnered the national attention some of the other artists had, she was very talented. I think Mom felt an especially strong connection to her because she, like my mother, had set her artistic aspirations aside to marry, manage a family business, and raise a family.

Callie enjoyed a strong regional following, and people came from far and wide to purchase her unique hand-dyed textiles, fibers, and yarns. Callie was always very generous with her time, helping perfect strangers with their various projects. Eventually, Callie took over two studios so she had ample room to run classes and display all her materials, as well as have her own private space to work in.

Callie's appearance was deceiving. She looked delicate—like a ballet dancer—with long slender arms and legs, fair skin, and striking auburn hair that made her big brown eyes stand out. She put in more time working than any of the other shack girls and would often fill in at the family's butcher shop before coming over to the shack to host a class for several hours in the evening.

I didn't know her husband very well, but they seemed to have a good marriage and worked well together. They had two sons who were now in college, making it possible for Callie to spend more time teaching and selling fiber goods in her studio. She made enough money at the shack so that she and her husband could afford to hire help at the butcher shop, freeing up even more time for her work at the studio. Callie and Betsy were still good friends, and even though she lived on the opposite side of town, she would drop in daily to check up on Betsy.

There were many artists who'd occupied the shack over the past twenty-five years, and during the summers when Betsy and I were growing up, it was not uncommon for it to be full, with ten artists working all summer long. Some stayed for a few months and others for a few years. Smitty and Sam were the only two original occupants besides Mom. While Mom had remained the sole owner of the shack, she'd thought of it as a collaborative enterprise. and requested input and collective thinking about its operation as well as its new tenants. When Betsy graduated from college with a degree in fine art, she'd planned to teach school, but instead Mom talked her into coming to the shack to paint, cementing the dynasty of "Parker Painters."

Betsy had dated Ron all through high school and college. When they both graduated, they got married and came home so Ron could help Dad run the farm. Originally, she and Ron lived in town, and Betsy would drive

Ron out to the farm every morning so the two men could take off for the fields while Mom and Betsy would head to the shack. I have to admit I was very jealous of the time Betsy got to spend with Mom. I missed out on those years because I didn't possess Betsy's talent. Instead, I moved to Chicago and got started in advertising. Like most young people, I thought I was going to live forever and that Mom would too. When she got sick, the concept of mortality hit me hard and became my reality.

Ron and Betsy moved into the big house, so Betsy could be there to help Mom. Dad and Ron had to deal with the farm, and they would put in long days during the growing season. Jo would stop by on her way home from the shack every day to see how Mom and Betsy were doing. They would get Mom into bed and settled, and then go out on the porch to have a glass of wine together. Betsy could talk to Jo and Jo was a great listener. They became close friends during this time.

After Mom passed away, Betsy couldn't bring herself to return to the shack, so Smitty and Sam stepped up to take responsibility for finding new talent and keeping the place fully rented. It wasn't until both her kids were in school that Betsy went back to work at her studio there. Jo was the fourth artist at the shack; and if you didn't count the studios that Betsy or I used, there were three open studios right now, so Smitty and Sam had been scouting for new talent.

Jo was what you'd call a mixed-media artist. Her work was sculptural in nature, although most of the time the pieces were designed to hang on a wall. She was always collecting odds and ends for them, since she had a unique eye for transforming ordinary objects into something extraordinary. She had a large collection of bits and pieces, including pelts, feathers, sticks, and rocks. The tools required to fashion these bits into art were also interesting. She used power saws, drills, driers, torches . . . you name it. Her only limitation was her imagination, which amounted to practically no limitation at all since she was so creative.

Jo was fine boned with beautiful features. She had long dark hair which was always pulled up in a knot with two thin paint brushes holding it in place.

When she had her work smock on, and her hair pulled up, she almost looked like a Geisha from behind.

When Betsy was undergoing treatment, the shack girls would bring lunch out to the farm so they could spend more time with her and also give me a break. The entire mood would lift and we would laugh and share stories and experiences. It was therapeutic for all of us. After every visit, Betsy would be exhausted but so happy. They were the best medicine she could possibly get. Every day she was getting stronger; and now that her treatments were finally over, she could just focus on getting her strength back. I knew she was looking forward to getting back to the shack and her work there.

"How's Betsy today?" Smitty asked me one day when we were all having our morning coffee together at the shack.

"She's doing pretty well. I think she'll be back at the shack in a week or two," I said.

"That's great news," said Smitty. "I think spending some time painting will help get her back on the road to normal. It'll change her focus and give her something productive and creative to think about. Oh, and before I forget, I think we have another artist interested in leasing a space. I brought over her resume and background information so you can pass them along to Betsy. She's from New York, and she's a painter. She's looking to get out of the city and into the countryside for a while. I think she's closer to your and Jo's age. If Betsy likes her, I'll offer her a space, and she can room with Sam and me while she looks for a place to live."

"That sounds like a good plan," I said as I sipped my coffee.

"Did you call your attorney this morning?" Smitty asked.

"Yes, I did. He's going to request a temporary order of protection until we can get a hearing." I decided not to tell her the rest of the conversation because it would only raise lots of questions that I didn't have answers to— and besides, I was too upset to talk about it.

"What do you think that son of a bitch wants?" Sam asked.

"I'm not sure," I replied, "and I don't want to find out."

"If he shows up at the shack again, he'll be sorry," she said. "I know I wouldn't be sorry if something happened to him. I'm not sure anyone would be."

"What do you have in mind?" Jo asked.

"Don't tell us," Callie cried out. "I don't want to have that image in my head all day."

"What's the name of the new artist?" I asked, hoping to change the subject.

"Kellan," Sam said. "Here's her resume. She'd like to come as soon as possible."

"I think as long as you all think she'd be a good fit, Betsy won't have a problem with her. I'll take her the application later this morning," I said as I perused the resume. "She seems like a good fit to me too."

"Good. I hope Betsy thinks so too. She doesn't drive, so if she stays, she'll need to find a place close to the shack," Smitty said.

"Not for long. I'll teach her. She needs to be independent if she's going to live here. And with no cabs or mass transportation around here, she'll need to learn," Sam said decisively.

"Lord help her," Jo responded.

"Amen," Callie said as we all laughed.

CHAPTER 21

Winter 2018

WE WERE ABLE to get a temporary order of protection against David Hoffman and a hearing date was set for the permanent one. He was forbidden to contact me in any way, or come within two hundred yards of me. I was relieved but still uncomfortable, wondering whether someone like him even cared about what was legal or not.

His comment about "unfinished business" kept playing over and over in my head. I felt sure that, even with this measure in place, I'd have to deal with him again. This worry stayed with me all day, every day. If I saw a man about the same height and coloring, my heart would jump into my throat. If anyone came around a corner unexpectedly, I'd panic. All day, every day. Eventually, I had to backtrack and practice the skills my therapist taught me after the attack. I would meditate and practice my rhythmic breathing to help reduce the panic and anxiety I felt. It helped that I was busy with work, Betsy, Ron, and the kids; but occasionally, when I had a moment to myself, or a second to pause, I'd think about him and wonder when I'd see him again. I was certain it wasn't whether, but when.

Betsy immediately agreed that Kellan would be a good addition to the shack girls, and within a few weeks, she'd settled in at Smitty's and Sam's house. She had taken over one of the upstairs studios at the shack and was already working on some paintings. Betsy had not had a chance to meet Kellan yet, so she asked me to take her to the shack to meet her. It was also an opportunity to test her stamina. This would be her first time away from the farm since she'd been home from the hospital, other than to go for a treatment or a doctor's visit. By now, she was going absolutely stir-crazy, and I couldn't have kept her from going even if I'd wanted to.

We pulled up in front of the shack, and before I could even come to a complete stop, Betsy had opened the door.

"Wait just a minute," I yelled. "You may feel okay now, but you'll need to pace yourself. You don't have as much strength as you think you have. Let's take this slowly so we don't have any setbacks," I admonished her.

"Okay, Mom," Betsy mimicked. "I promise to behave."

"That's a good girl," I mimicked back. "If you don't, I won't bring you again."

We walked arm in arm up the steps to the front door. Inside the place was humming with activity. We could hear the blast of the glass furnace, accompanied by conversations and laughter emanating from the other end of the hallway and reaching all the way to the entrance.

Betsy went into Callie's studio and said, "How are you doing?"

"Betsy! What a lovely surprise," Callie said, running over and giving Betsy a big hug, all the while pushing away piles of wool with her spare hand. "Let me clear a space for you to sit down."

"I'm good, but save that space for me. I'll come back after I walk through and say hello to everyone."

"Are you sure you're up to that? Don't you want me to bring them to you?" Callie asked.

"No, I want to walk around a bit, but clear me a space. I promise to come back," Betsy said with a big smile.

We walked slowly to the next studio, which was Betsy's. It looked so empty.

"I think it's time for me to come back to work. I've had a long time to think about the restorative power of painting, and I need to get to it," Betsy said, running her thumb over the bristles of a paint brush before moving on to look at a stack of canvases. "I have several works in progress that are nearly done, and it'll be good to finish them and move on to something new."

"Well, we'll all be glad to see you back at work and to have you with us again," Smitty said as she came in and put her arm around Betsy's shoulders. "How are you?"

"I'm quite well and feeling better every minute I'm here."

"I'm so glad to hear that, Betsy," Smitty said, kissing her on the cheek.

"For hell sakes. Look who's here!" Sam yelled. "How'd you get out?"

"I was halfway to town when Lynne pulled over and made me get in the car," Betsy deadpanned.

"Really?" Jo said as she joined the group.

"No, but it felt like I was making a break for it when I shut the door to the house. You know how long I've been cooped up in that place? It's been forever."

"We're very glad you escaped," Jo replied.

"Did Kellan get settled yet?" Betsy asked.

"Yes, let me tell her you're here so you can meet her. She's just great," Smitty said enthusiastically.

"She's a valuable addition to the shack girls," Callie said. "She's only been here a couple of weeks, but we're all so comfortable together it feels like she's been here since the beginning. She seems quite happy with us too."

"How's it working out at your house?" Betsy asked Sam.

"Fine. Just fine. You don't even know she's there, except that she cleans up my dirty dishes—which is like living with a fucking elf. She comes in after I'm in bed and cleans the place," Sam said grinning.

"Hi, you must be Betsy," Kellan said as she approached her. "What a pleasure to finally meet you. Thanks for accepting me into your ranks."

"We're glad to have you," Betsy said with a warm smile.

Kellan backed up towards the door and leaned on the frame. "Everyone here is just great," she said, waving her arm around the room to indicate all of us. "Just great," she repeated.

"Have you started your driving lessons?" Betsy asked.

"Oh, my God," Sam said. "She's just terrible."

"Really?" Kellan asked Sam sadly.

"Really!" Sam replied. "I'm not sure it'll be possible to teach her."

"Well, maybe if I started with an automatic transmission it would be easier," Kellan said defiantly.

"What vehicle are you using to teach her how to drive?" I asked.

"The old truck. You think I want her wrecking Smitty's car?" Sam exclaimed.

"The truck? That *is* tough," I said, looking at Kellan sympathetically.

"We've driven to the grocery store, the coffee shop, and next we're heading out to the farm," Kellan said with a smile.

"Maybe we should call the police first and have them clear the road," Callie said laughing.

"Not nice," Kellan said. "I think I'm getting better every time I practice. Don't you think so, Sam?"

"That's not hard," Sam said.

"Do you need anything, Kellan?" Betsy asked, changing the subject.

"No. Everything is great, and everyone has been terrific to me."

"Feel free to help yourself to anything you need in my studio," Betsy said.

"When do you think you'll be able to be back here with us and painting?" Smitty asked.

"If today goes well, maybe tomorrow. But I won't be able to stay very long at first."

"That's great news, Betsy," Jo said, and everyone echoed her sentiments.

We'd been sitting and chatting for about thirty minutes when I looked over to Betsy and could see from her eyes that she was getting tired. "Maybe we should be heading back," I suggested.

"Oh, do we have to?" Betsy whined.

"We have to," I said firmly.

Everyone gave Betsy a big hug, and then followed us out to the porch and watched as we got into the car and drove away. Betsy turned to watch them wave good-bye.

"I need them," she said. "I think being at the shack, working with the girls, will be good for me. I may look tired, but right now I feel better than I've felt in months."

"I agree. There's something therapeutic about being around those strong, talented women. Maybe we could set up a cot in your studio so you could rest at intervals when you're feeling tired. At least then you'd have an option to stay longer. What do you think?"

"I wish I could say 'I won't need it, I'll be fine,' but I think you're probably right. I could drive out with you, and if I got tired before you were ready to come home, I could rest. I think that's a great idea."

CHAPTER 22

Winter 2018

BY THE TIME we arrived at the farm, Betsy was feeling very tired. I helped her upstairs to her bed so she could take a nap before the kids got home. As I was leaving the room, she said, "We need to do this every day, so I can get my strength back."

"That's fine by me. Maybe tomorrow we could take lunch to everyone. I can make a salad," I said.

"That would be so nice," Betsy said as she closed her eyes.

I shut her bedroom door and went back to the little house to work for a while. As I started going through my emails, my eyes rested on a message from my attorney.

Lynne,

David Hoffman has requested a hearing to discuss his rights as the father to the child that was placed for adoption. He's requesting that the records be opened to see who has possession of the child, and is also requesting DNA testing to verify that he is the father. His request will be denied but I thought you should know.

I will keep you updated as I get more information.

Jim

I sat looking in disbelief at my computer screen for several minutes. This man was delusional. Questions swirled in my head. It made absolutely no sense. He had no rights. Why would he even make this request? How did he even know about the pregnancy, and why would he assume that the baby was his? He was a criminal who had attacked and raped me. Still, sixteen years later, he continued to haunt me. The fact that he thought he had any right to challenge me or even talk to me about a pregnancy was beyond my comprehension. What I had worked so hard to avoid was coming true. That child was as much a victim as I was. I could feel tears running down my cheeks before I even realized I was crying. I had to do something to take my mind off this or I'd go crazy. I'd never been very patient, but I was going to have to accept that this was out of my control and, as I'd learned from my therapist, I needed to focus on things I could control.

After several minutes of just sitting and fussing, I decided to get busy with my work. But my thoughts kept coming back to David Hoffman. For sure, I was not going to tell anyone about this latest development—not until I knew positively that David would get a hearing. I didn't want anyone to worry—especially if nothing would come of his request—and I'd been assured that nothing would. It just couldn't—he had no rights! Then I reminded myself again to focus my attention on the things in my life I could control.

I worked distractedly until it was time to walk out and meet Josh and Melanie's bus. As it pulled up, I could feel the burden of the day's bad news lighten. Josh bounded off the bus.

"Aunt Lynnie! How was your day?" he asked, giving me a big hug. I wondered, how many more years before he was old enough to be too embarrassed to hug me?

"Hi, Josh. How was your day?" I said, hugging him back.

"Hi, Aunt Lynnie," Melanie said as she stepped off the bus and opened the mailbox to pull out the day's mail.

"Hi, Melanie," I said. "Your mom . . ."

But Josh interrupted me and blurted out, "Me first, Aunt Lynnie. I had the absolute worst day ever. I lost my math homework and had to stay in at recess to do it over. It was a horrible day. The worst day ever."

"I'm so sorry, Josh. How do you think you lost it?"

"I don't know, but it was the worst thing ever."

"So, Melanie, how was your day?"

"Wait! Please! I'm not done yet," Josh said. "I broke my shoelace and my shoe has been flopping around on my foot all day," he said, pointing to where he was holding up the foot with the gaping tennis shoe for me to see. "Then they ran out of pizza in the cafeteria and I had to have a hamburger instead. Their hamburgers are gross. I don't think they're made out of meat!"

I looked at him sympathetically and said. "I'm so sorry, Josh. You really did have a terrible day. Did anything else happen?"

"That's enough," he said as he continued towards the house, head down, kicking a rock along the way. I let Josh get about ten yards ahead of Melanie and me so she could finally tell me about her day.

"Now, Melanie, how was *your* day?"

"It was fine. He is such a whiner sometimes, isn't he?"

"He can be a bit dramatic," I said. "But I think he did have a pretty rough day."

"How's Mom?"

"She visited the shack today. How about that!"

"Wow. That's great. But is she tired?" Melanie asked, looking concerned.

"She is, but I think she feels like she's getting back to normal," I said. "She needed a little nap afterward, but she's up and ready to go again. I know her day couldn't possibly have been as tough as Josh's!" I said dramatically, ruffling Josh's hair, as we caught up to him.

As I entered the house, the kids ran past me and upstairs to say hello to their mom, so I fixed them a snack in the meantime. After a while, Betsy and the kids came downstairs together. She talked with them and helped them with their homework while I got dinner ready.

"What are we having, Aunt Lynnie?" Josh asked.

"Vegetables and more vegetables," I said, as Josh's smile turned into a grimace.

"No really, Aunt Lynnie, what are we having?"

"We're having broccoli, roasted chicken, and scalloped potatoes. Does that meet with your approval?"

"Yeah, that's better," he said, jumping down from his chair. "I'm going to play some video games."

"Are you done with your homework?" Betsy asked.

I added, "And did you put your homework where you can find it?"

"Oh yeah, I better put it in my backpack right now. I don't want another bad day tomorrow," Josh said.

Turning to Betsy I asked, "Would you like a glass of wine?"

"I would love one," she said.

I poured Betsy and me a glass of wine and Melanie a glass of juice while she continued to do her homework at the kitchen table. The three of us chatted and answered Melanie's questions while dinner cooked. Before long Ron came in and I poured him a glass of wine as well.

"Hey, I saw Jo on my way here," he said. "I hear you went into the shack today."

"Yes, I did," Betsy said proudly.

"How'd that go?" he asked.

"Very well," I added. "She's going to try it again tomorrow."

"That's great, honey. Pretty soon you'll be back to your old self," Ron said, working his way around the table, kissing Melanie and then me on our heads, and finally ending with a big hug and kiss for Betsy. "How was your day, Melanie?" he asked.

"It was fine, Daddy, but don't ask Josh how his day was because it'll take a long time."

"Come with me and I'll explain," Betsy said as she and Ron went into the living room to find a more comfortable place to sit and spend a few minutes alone with each other. I called Melanie and Josh in to set the table for dinner.

"You don't need to set a place for me," I said. "I'm going back over to my place tonight. I'll be back in a couple of hours to clean up and get you two into bed."

"Okay, Aunt Lynnie," Melanie said. Josh echoed her as he begrudgingly got out the silverware.

After I put dinner on the table, I decided to take a walk to clear my head. I was still flustered about the email from my attorney. I knew there was nothing I could do, other than wait, but I couldn't get it out of my head, and I hoped that fresh air would help. I loved to walk through the fields and inhale the farm smells. It had always been a place of peace and comfort for me, a place where the noise of the world could be shut out and I could simply live in the moment. I perched myself on the top rail of the fence and watched as the sun slowly set before I finally hopped down and walked back to the big house to clean up from dinner. When I entered the kitchen, Ron and the kids were happily chatting away as they washed the dishes and put everything away.

"Aunt Lynnie, Dad said *we* had to clean up tonight," Josh said, rolling his eyes.

"Yeah, and it was good for you too," Ron retorted. "We've got this—and we can get everyone in bed too. You go home and tuck yourself into bed."

"Wow! This is pretty impressive," I said. "Although it makes me sad that you don't need me anymore."

"We need you, Aunt Lynnie," Melanie said. "But we can do more to help ourselves too."

I kissed Melanie on the head, then Josh, and finally Ron, before I said, "You guys are the best! Call me if you need anything."

I walked out the back door and across the yard to the little house. I stopped on the porch and looked back at the big house. The lights were on in every room. The entire house glowed. It was a happy place where the people I loved most lived. I was grateful for them and the opportunity to be a part of their lives. I went up to my room and lay down on my bed. I lay there and mourned the fact that Melanie was right. They were getting older and could do more for themselves. Soon I'd move to an apartment in Chicago or some-place else, and then I'd be all alone. I'd miss the chaos and activity of these two great kids and having Betsy so close.

CHAPTER 23

Spring 2018

BEFORE I'D COME back to take care of Betsy, I'd gotten used to being alone; and when I left, I'd have to do it all over again. My desire for a family had pretty much evaporated when I gave up the baby for adoption. My life had been flipped upside down by David Hoffman. He'd not only damaged me physically and mentally, but he'd also completely erased my dreams for a future. I had accepted that and even gotten used to it, but now that I'd experienced more, during my time at the farm, I wanted more for my life.

I began to wonder about Collin and what had happened to him. I felt a strong pang of regret when I recalled how I'd left him; but now, especially after this recent email from the attorney, I was sure I had done the right thing. We never had a chance at a normal relationship, and it wouldn't have been fair to drag him into all my problems. It was better for him and me to just end it. It hurt to even think about it, but I couldn't help wondering, what was his life like, whether he'd gotten married, or if he'd had any children. He must have. Who would pass up a guy that great? He would be a wonderful husband and father.

In that moment, I just let all my memories of him wash over me. I'd fallen in love with him, but because of the circumstances of my life, I'd been forced to lie to him and hurt him. I'd left him and couldn't tell him why. Over the years, I'd dated a few guys on a relatively superficial basis, but there'd never been anyone who could even compare to Collin. I hadn't had an intimate relationship with anyone since the attack—now nearly sixteen years ago. I wasn't even sure I could have an intimate relationship. I hadn't been able to find anyone who could meet my expectations—which were perhaps unrealistic—but I always knew there was something better, because I'd experienced it with Collin. I knew that settling for something less would doom any relationship right from the start.

My thoughts were suddenly interrupted when my phone began to ring.

"Hello?" I said.

"Hello, Lynne? This is Officer Curtis, Susan. How are you?"

"Well, I'm fine. How about you?"

"Am I calling too late? I've been thinking about you and decided to check up on you."

"How great to hear from you Susan. I am doing very well."

"I just heard that David Hoffman is out of prison, and that he's filed a request for a hearing. I'm so sorry, Lynne. I'm sure this new development is very hard on you."

"Well, yes, it was a bit of a surprise," I said.

"I've been snooping around a bit. I hope that's okay," she said pausing. "I was glad to see that you filed a request for an order of protection. I am sure your attorney will tell you, but just in case, your request has been assigned to a judge, meaning you'll get a notice very soon with a date for the hearing. I know the judge assigned to your case. She is a strong advocate for victim's rights, and I would assume that your request will be approved rather quickly. I don't think that David Hoffman's request has been assigned a judge yet but, I would expect that no matter who the judge is, they would refuse to even hear his request."

Pausing briefly she continued, "I am sure this is a very anxious time for you, and I thought this information might help put your mind to rest. I also wanted to remind you that I'm here if there's anything I can do to help."

"Thank you, Susan. This is wonderful news. I'm so grateful you are keeping an eye on things. That means a lot."

Then I said, "So, did you know that he came here? He told me we had 'unfinished business'. I'm assuming it is about the baby, although I don't know how he would even know. How would he have found out I was pregnant? The only thing I can think of, is perhaps, his attorney told him."

"Lynne, this order of protection will put a stop to him bothering you. He could end up back in prison if he doesn't leave you alone, and I don't think he will want to risk it. I'll keep an eye on this case and I'm happy to help in any way possible so please let me know what I can do."

"Thank you, Susan. You've already been a great help to me, and I appreciate knowing you're still there for me."

"I'll keep you posted as I learn more. Be careful Lynne."

I hung up the phone and thought about all the strong women in my life and how they had helped me over these past sixteen years. First and foremost, there was Betsy, who was my rock. Throughout our lives, she'd been the one I'd leaned on, and now, even when she was so vulnerable, she still gave me strength. There were the shack girls, who were like sisters to me. Each of them was self-sufficient and capable, and I knew I could rely on them for anything I needed. And, if I was ever threatened in any way, they would circle 'round and protect me—they already had. I also had Susan in my life, who'd been there since the night of the attack and continued to look out for me. And now there was this judge who I hadn't even met. But she would fight for me too, for my rights, and the rights of the child.

I knew I'd done the right thing by giving up my child so it could have a normal life; and now I needed the courage to continue to fight to be sure that David Hoffman never found out where that child was. I understood adopted children may want to know who their birth parents are and the circumstances that resulted in their adoption. I also knew that it would be difficult to learn that your existence was the result of a rape and violence—especially at the delicate age of fifteen. No child deserved that.

I would have to fight to keep that from happening, and remember I had an army of women who would continue the fight with me. This was one more so-called growth opportunity, as so much of my life had been for the last sixteen years—but I was not in this alone. I had help.

Susan was right, within a few days, my case had been assigned a day and time. The day of my hearing arrived, and while both Jim and Susan had told me it was almost certain the court would rule in my favor, I was still a nervous wreck. Susan had offered to come to the hearing, and I gratefully accepted. Jim had another case earlier that morning and told me he would have to meet me in the hearing.

Susan suggested we meet at the coffee shop across the street from the courthouse. I arrived early and ordered a cup of coffee. I sat at a small table next to the window, sipping my coffee, and watching the people walk by. But, as the time got closer and Susan had not arrived, I began to worry. If she didn't make it, I would just have to muster my courage to go it alone. Then I saw her. As she approached my table, I jumped up and hugged her harder than I intended, then blurted out, "Sorry, Susan, I didn't mean to squeeze you so hard. I was getting worried you weren't going to get here in time."

"Me too," she said squeezing me back equally hard. "I'm sorry I am late. I had something come up this morning and had to shift some things around. Regardless, I wouldn't have missed being here with you."

"I'm most grateful," I said, beginning to feel emotional.

"We better get going or we'll be late," she said.

We crossed the street and were soon inside of the court house. It was an old building, with a huge lobby and a line of people waiting to get through security. As we stepped into line, I could see that it was moving slowly, and my anxiety returned. I looked at Susan. She could read my mind and patted my back saying, "We'll get there in time, don't worry."

As we waited our turn, I watched all of the people around me. Many were quiet, even solemn. People like me, anxious and worried, waiting for the court to make decisions that would affect their lives. Finally, we got through security and Susan quickly found the room assigned to us, and Jim was already there, waiting patiently.

"Lynne, I'm sorry I couldn't meet you ahead of time," he said shaking my hand, and seeing Susan he said, "I see you are in good hands."

"Yes, I'm in great hands," I said squeezing Susan's arm.

Just then David and his attorney walked in. I looked at him, and a big smile spread across his face. He was pleased with himself and the situation he had created. I began to worry whether others, especially the judge, would see him for who he was rather than what he appeared to be—if they could see beneath that charming handsome façade. He nodded at me as he took his place across the aisle.

Susan saw through that facade, but she had been with me through the whole horrible experience. She knew him for what he was. She bent her head to mine and said, "You are fine Lynne, don't let him rattle you. You are the one in control here."

She was right. Within a very few minutes the judge made clear that David had no right to have any contact with me. His actions were seen and understood to be hostile and potentially dangerous. He was to stay away from me. If he violated the order of protection, he would find himself back in prison. As he stood to leave, he was no longer the charming man who had come into the courtroom. There in his place stood the angry man I knew. He did not speak or acknowledge me. He just left.

CHAPTER 24

Spring 2018

I HAD BEEN driving Betsy to the shack three days a week, and she was getting stronger with each passing day. Every time we went, she would stay a bit longer. We put a cot in her studio so she could lie down if she needed to, but each day she needed it less and less; and there were many days she painted the entire time she was there, not needing to rest at all.

While taking care of Betsy, Margie had continued to send me projects so I could keep my foot in the door with my career and, since arriving at the farm, I'd set up a workspace on the back porch of the big house. This allowed me to be close to Betsy, Ron, and the kids if they needed me, while also having my own space to take conference calls and get my work done. Now, with Betsy going to the shack most days, I needed a workspace there. I settled into one of the empty upstairs studios where it was bright and sunny. Ron made me a makeshift desk out of a discarded picnic table, and I brought an old lamp from the little house for the days when I needed more light. Being at the shack reminded me of how much I needed other people and enjoyed being around them, which I'm sure was how Betsy felt too.

She continued to push herself. Most days we would arrive back at the farm just before the kids' bus pulled up. Betsy would lie on the couch and listen to all the stories about school, and together we would get the kids started on their homework. Most days now, Betsy would help prepare dinner, and I knew the day was coming soon when she wouldn't need me at all.

But not yet. Spring was here and Ron was already working long hours, getting the fields prepared and the seed in. His summer help started to arrive, which meant the farm would soon be in full throttle. There would be many evenings when Ron wouldn't get home until after the kids had gone to bed, and many mornings when he would already be out in the fields before they got up. That meant that Betsy would be the only parent around to take care of them, and with summer coming, that was a full-time job in itself. She would also have to do all the housework, manage a sizeable vegetable garden, take care of the chickens—and everything else that needed to be done while Ron was caught up in the height of the busy season.

I was very pleased to be there to help them both. Over the next few weeks, as activity on the farm ramped up, even with her strength increasing, it would be a lot for Betsy to handle on her own. But she would get there eventually, and that meant I needed to start thinking about returning to my old life.

But before I did anything, I would need to have a conversation with Betsy to find out what she thought. I needed to be careful how I handled it, or she would have me packed up and out the door to my new home before I knew what had hit me. She would tell me they were fine and could take care of everything by themselves. I know that asking me to come had weighed on her. When she'd first made the request, I don't think she'd envisioned that I'd still be here more than a year later. And I also think that when she asked me, she'd worried that she might not make it. I wanted to have this talk when I had the old Betsy back, the sister I knew to be a force of nature, the one who'd always taken care of me.

I wondered about how Kellan was liking her new life. She'd decided to stay on at the shack, but she and Jo had been on the road with their portfolios of work, trying to drum up clients. Kellan hadn't had the time to even begin looking for a place to live. For now, she still stayed with Smitty and Sam; and I wondered if she'd consider taking my place at the little house with Jo. I thought Jo would like the idea too.

One morning, when Betsy and I arrived at the shack, the girls were in Smitty's studio discussing their summer plans. Smitty and Sam planned to be at one event or another almost every weekend. And then in the fall, they were set to do a couple of shows out west. Callie and Kellan suggested the four of them meet in Wyoming so they could take a short vacation together.

"Why don't you come on vacation with us in Wyoming in the fall?" Smitty asked Betsy and me.

Turning to me, Betsy said, "I think that's a great idea, Lynnie. You need a vacation, and I think I'm ready to handle things on my own now. Why don't you go?"

"What about you? You could go and I could stay here with the kids. It might be your last hurrah for a while, if I leave for who knows where and refocus on my career," I suggested.

"No, I don't want to go anywhere right now. I feel like I'm seeing the light at the end of the tunnel on this sickness business, and I want to get back to normal. Taking a trip during Ron's busiest time is not my notion of normal."

"Well, in that case," I said, "since it will soon be time for me to leave, I'd like to spend what time I have left here."

"Oh Lynne, I hate to even think about that. I guess I'm pretty selfish, but I'd hoped you would stay here with us," Betsy said sadly.

"What about your art?" Smitty asked.

Laughing, I said, "You keep trying, Smitty, but I think we all know I'm not as talented as you shack girls. Pottery is therapy for me, nothing more."

"Well, I think you're wrong," Smitty said. "You're as talented as any one of us. You just need to invest more time in it."

"Ah, time—I'm not sure all the time in the world would be enough," I said with a sigh. "The time is coming soon to get my career moving again. It's been great to be here with you all, but I really do need to get back to my real life."

"But I'll be lonely in the little house all by myself," Jo said in a voice just above a whisper, looking glum.

"I bet you'll love to have your house back. And Betsy and Ron will be glad to have their little family back—just like it used to be. It'll be a new start for all of us," I said, trying to sound upbeat. I hoped no one could guess how hard it was going to be for me to leave. They'd become my support group, my family, and my very dear friends, but still I needed more. I had visions of getting my career back on track and maybe even having a family of my own.

"Well, we'll miss you terribly," Jo said. "You won't leave until we're all back together, will you?"

"I don't think so, but if I do, it's not like I can't come back here and visit—that is, *if* I'm invited."

"Of course, you're invited. You never need an invitation," Betsy said. "We would all be very disappointed if you didn't come back as often as you can."

"Enough of this sad talk—and you've not heard the last about that trip to Wyoming. But right now some of us are heading over to Nate's Place for a drink. Who's going?" Sam asked.

"I'm wiped out. I think I'll head for the farm," Betsy said. "Lynnie, why don't you go along? I'm fine by myself, and you can come back with Jo."

"I don't plan to stay longer than one drink, Lynne. So if you'd like to come with us, I won't stay too long," Jo said.

"Great. I'll come along then," I said, eager for the change of scene.

Smitty, Sam, Callie, Jo, Kellan, and I all walked down to Nate's Place. As we left the shack, Jo noticed a truck parked on the other side of the street. "Do any of you know whose truck that is?" she asked.

We all stopped and turned around to look back. As we did, I heard someone from inside the vehicle call my name.

The glare of the sun was in my eyes, so all I could see was the shape of a man emerging from the truck. My heart began to pound in my chest, and the first thought that came to my mind was, *"Oh God, he's back. It's David Hoffman"* Then the man approached, and I could see he was taller and his hair color was lighter than David Hoffman's. So I said hello and waited as he came closer.

"Lynne . . . it's me, Collin."

At that moment my heart leapt in my chest. I was momentarily speechless, waiting for my mind to clear so I could formulate a coherent thought.

"Who is it, Lynne?" Smitty asked in concern.

"Collin?" I called out.

"Yes, it's Collin," he repeated.

"Who the hell is Collin?" Sam asked suspiciously.

"He was her neighbor. The guy who helped her after she was attacked," Smitty said.

I stood there stock-still until Smitty leaned over and asked, "Are you okay? Do you want us to wait here with you—just to be sure you're alright?"

"No. I'll be fine, Smitty, but thank you."

"Girls, why don't we go on ahead and give Lynne some time with Collin? And Lynne, if you change your mind, please do join us at Nate's," Smitty added, as she herded the shack girls down the street.

I stood with my feet glued in place and watched as Collin approached me, hardly able to believe my eyes. I could feel my face go red and my heart speed up—thumping a mile a minute in my chest. My mind was flooded with thoughts. *Why is he here? What's happened with him since we last talked? Is this an impossible coincidence? He looks just as I remember him.*

His face bore a huge smile, and his pace quickened as he came closer to me. Before I could register what was happening, he'd lifted me off the ground as he caught me in a big hug and whispered, "How are you, Lynnie?"

I was overwhelmed by the emotions that washed over me in that instant—feelings of loss and joy almost at the same time. Choking back tears and working hard to camouflage all the feelings running through me, I said, "I'm fine, Collin. What about you?" I pulled back then to get a good look at his face, and I could see he was struggling like I was with a wide range of emotions.

"What are you doing here?" I asked.

"Well, I'm glad to see you too," he said in mock hurt.

"I didn't mean it like that. I'm just so surprised to see you. It's been a very long time. How did you even recognize me?" I asked.

"I'd recognize you anywhere, and I'm here because I came to see you," he said as he grinned from ear to ear. "Several weeks ago, a man came by asking about you, and I had to tell him I knew nothing about you, that we'd lost touch. After that, I couldn't get you out of my mind, so I decided to call Margie and ask about you myself. She told me Betsy had been very sick and you were here taking care of her. So I just decided . . . well . . . I decided I would come to see how you both were doing. Is that alright?"

"Yes, of course it's alright," I said, hugging him again. "I'm so glad you came. It's great to see you. It really is so great to see you," I repeated, because I was afraid if I said anything else I wouldn't be able to keep myself together.

"I remembered all our conversations about the farm, Lynne, which was why I was able to find your sister's address. First I went to the farm, but no one was there, so I came into town to get a hotel room. I stopped to get a cup of coffee, and I asked the man who runs the café if he knew you. He told me I would be able to find you here. I'm sorry to spring myself on you like this, but I didn't have a phone number or email address to use to alert you; and besides, I was pretty sure you'd tell me not to come. I'm not here to meddle in your life. I just wanted to see you for myself and find out what had happened to you. I also wanted to hear about Betsy."

I was both numb and overwhelmed at the same time. I didn't think I could put two words together and was afraid to even try. I pursed my lips in an attempt to keep control of my emotions and just stood there silently, hoping that the tiny tear that had leaked from my eye and rolled down my cheek was too small to be noticed. But Collin reached up with the tip of his thumb and caught it before it reached my chin.

"Is it okay that I came to see you, Lynne?" he asked tenderly.

I nodded my head while still tightly pursing my lips. "Yes," I finally managed.

"Is there someplace we can go to talk?"

"Yes, but please wait here for a few seconds first," I said as I headed to Nate's.

As soon as Smitty spotted me she stood up and came over. "Are you okay, Lynne?" The other shack girls followed in her wake.

"Yes, I'm fine," I said. "I just came to let you know that I have a ride out to the farm. My friend Collin is here to see how Betsy is doing."

"Yes, I'm sure that's the reason he's here—to see Betsy," Sam said sarcastically.

"From what I could see, he looks like a nice guy," Callie said.

"Do you need a key to the house?" Jo asked. "You can take mine."

"No, I have my key—but thank you. I'll see you in a little bit."

"No rush," Jo stated firmly.

"No rush," Sam called with a grin. "Take your time, and don't forget he's here to see Betsy."

Scowling at her, I said, "See you all later."

I turned to leave and, without looking back, I could feel the eyes of every one of the shack girls on me. I could only imagine the conversation that would now ensue. As I pushed the door open I could see Collin standing next to the curb waiting for me, and I'm sure they were able to see him too. I was surprised there were no catcalls coming from behind me.

I took a long look at him. I couldn't believe he was actually standing there in front of me after all these years. He looked just the same as I remembered him. I felt like I was looking at a mirage, and I was doing my best to maintain my composure, but I couldn't quit staring at him. He caught my gaze, and I could feel my face go deep red. He just smiled at me, full of confidence and warmth.

When I reached him, I said, "I'm not sure what your plans are, but I hoped you wouldn't mind taking me out to the farm. We can talk as we go, and you can meet Betsy."

"Sure. Sounds perfect," he said, staring at me.

I immediately thought about the last time we'd been together and how terribly I'd treated him. How could he be here and seem so genuinely glad to see me? I would just have to be patient and wait for those answers to come.

We walked along together without speaking, and oddly enough, it wasn't uncomfortable. He opened the door to the truck for me and helped me inside, and I watched him go around the front and get in beside me. I still couldn't believe this was happening. As the door closed I asked, "How have you been?"

"Well, it's been sixteen years since I last saw you, so a lot's happened since then," he said matter-of-factly.

"Yes. Yes, I know it's been sixteen years," I said apologetically. "But, has your life been good during that time?"

"Yes, it's been great—I've been great," he said.

"So, what have you been up to all that time?"

Collin turned and looked at me, with a big grin on his face. "Well, first, you have to promise not to laugh."

"Okay, I promise not to laugh," I said, not sure I could keep that promise.

"I bought a little farm about fifty miles from here, and my friend and I finally started that business there."

"Oh Collin, you always wanted to have a farm. I'm so happy for you."

"Well, it's not the traditional crop farm," he said, continuing to grin. "We make cheese."

"Cheese? You raise cows?" I asked incredulously, while trying to suppress a giggle.

"No, actually we raise goats."

"Really?" I said, struggling to control my impulse to laugh.

"Hey, you promised not to laugh," he said with a big, beautiful smile while trying not to take his eyes off the road. "It all started with goats and then moved on to cheese. It really is a long story and not a very interesting one, but it has been fun."

"Goats? Goats?" I said again, giggling openly now. "It sounds like a very great story and actually quite interesting. I think I would really enjoy hearing it."

"Well, maybe later. But first . . ." And then he paused before adding, "Hey, I'm just going to blurt it all out here. I don't want to rehash all the stuff that happened when you left so many years ago—although at some point I'd like to know why. But for today, is it okay to just let that sit? I want to start where we left off, unless of course you were unhappy with me—and in that case, I'd like to figure out how we can fix that," he said earnestly.

"Collin, sixteen years ago my life was very complicated. Some of the complications you knew about, others you didn't. I'd be so grateful not to have to rehash all of that, and I'd like to start fresh. There was never anything wrong with you. The problem was with me," I said, choking back tears. "I was in a very bad place back then, and by the time I got my life back together, I didn't contact you because I assumed you'd moved on. I thought it best not to stir things up."

"What do you mean, 'stir things up'?"

"I didn't want to . . . I don't think I could . . . well, by that time I was sure you'd gotten married and started a family. I didn't want to create any problems for you—or for me."

Collin pulled over to the side of the road. He turned and faced me. "I've dated a lot of women over the years, but things never worked out." I could feel my face flush, and I was grateful it was nearly dark. "I guess I just never found anyone I liked as much as I liked you." He paused then, resting one arm on the steering wheel. "I guess I can't make myself any more vulnerable than that, Lynne."

I looked down at my hands in my lap, unable to find the words to respond.

"How about you? Did you get on with your life?" Collin asked.

Slowly and softly I said, "No. No, I haven't. Even now, I've not gotten on with my life. For more than a year, I've been here helping Betsy and Ron." I paused, thinking carefully about what I wanted to say. "Betsy has been very sick, and I'm grateful I was in a position to come and help her. It means a lot to me that I could do that for her. But my life has never gone back to normal."

"Lynne, I'm glad you were able to help your sister and her family. I was so sorry to hear that she's been sick. How is she doing now?

Grateful to focus on something other than myself, I said, "She's doing pretty well. Her prognosis still has a bit of uncertainty to it, but for now, she's able to do most of the things she used to do prior to the surgery and treatments. I think she's almost back to being her old self, and she might even be able to resume her normal life a month or so from now."

"That's really good news. What do you think you'll do then?" he asked.

"Oh, I don't know. For a while there, I wasn't sure how things would turn out, and I didn't dare to even contemplate next steps. It's only been in the last few weeks that I've seen Betsy getting strong enough so that she may not need me anymore. I only just started thinking about what a future for me might look like. Career-wise, I'm hoping I can pick up where I left off—if Margie has room for me. I think I've deliberately put any decisions on the back burner because I know it will mean leaving Betsy, Ron, and the kids."

"Would you have to? Wouldn't Margie allow you to continue to work remotely?"

"I think she'd be willing to let me continue the work I'm doing now, but it's not a career I'd be happy with. The flexibility has meant that I've had to take on assignments that are less challenging and not very interesting to me. Margie hasn't said so, but it's true—I've moved from one personal problem to another, and my job has taken second place to these other issues in my life. It has happened time and time again over the past sixteen years. Don't misunderstand me—I think she and the powers-that-be at the office are happy with the work I do, and I think they would be fine with letting me continue as I am—but *I* still have ambition. A long time ago, I took on major projects and put in long hours. My career was taking off, but then life happened and my career—and other things important to me—had to take a back seat," I said reflectively.

Then I hastily added, "Don't get me wrong—my life hasn't stopped entirely. I've loved every minute with Betsy, Ron, and the kids, and I have an extended family with the shack girls, the women at the artists' studio. They are strong, talented women, and they've been such a huge source of support for both Betsy and me. When I leave, I'll miss them terribly. I guess right now, I'm struggling with what to do about almost every aspect of my life."

"Well, you don't have to decide right away, do you? You have time to think about next steps now that Betsy is doing better, right?"

"Yes, I have time, and nobody but me is rushing me to make any decisions. I'll take my time and try to consider all of my options." At that instant, it struck me that Collin and I *had* picked up where we left off. Those wonderful evenings after dinner at his house, sitting on the porch and just talking—they were here, in this moment. I felt this wave of warmth and comfort roll over me in a kind of déjà vu experience, like I'd been here before.

"Now that you know I didn't move on with my life, is there a chance you might consider adding me to the list of things you are considering? Would you be willing to call me once in a while—or even allow me to visit you?" he said carefully.

There was a long pause as I struggled to get control over my voice before I finally blurted out what I wanted to say. "Collin, I've thought about you every single day since I last saw you." I sat stunned and embarrassed at what I'd just said.

An awkward silence settled over us before Collin finally said, "Lynne, I wasn't sure what type of reception I'd get coming here to see you—especially since I came unannounced. I just knew that I wanted to see you and find out how you were doing. I didn't want to bother you, but I really wanted to see you."

There was a huge lump in my throat, as I struggled to speak. "I'm really very glad you took the time to find me and that you don't hate me. Or at least

I don't think you hate me," I said hopefully. "What I said just now, that I've thought of you every day, I mean that. I've thought about how I left you and the hurt on your face. I've wondered what you were doing and whether you were happy. Literally every day."

And then, feeling somewhat embarrassed about how open and needy I must have sounded, I went on to clarify my meaning. "I was in a very difficult place sixteen years ago. It took me a long time to get past what had happened, and I needed to focus on myself and getting well. The decisions I made were what I had to do to protect myself."

Which was true. Back then, I'd been hanging onto my sanity by my fingernails. Then I thought about how I was just getting my life back on track when I found out I was pregnant, and so then I needed to focus on what was best for me and for my child. I couldn't tell him the full story, but I could tell him how I felt.

As I paused momentarily, letting the silence settle between us, Collin said, "I think I understand, Lynne, and you don't have to explain anything else to me right now. After you left, I decided you had a reason for leaving like you did, and I had to accept that. I have only ever wanted what was best for you. Are you in a better place now?"

"I think so. I think I am. I feel like this time with Betsy, her family, and the shack girls has given me an opportunity to focus on what's important and think about something outside of myself. It's been a gift to me."

Collin said, "Again, Lynne, I don't want to dredge up the past, I just wanted to see you. I'm here for purely selfish reasons, although I would like to meet Betsy," he added with a twinkle in his eye as he steered his truck back on the road.

Soon we were at the farm. Collin came around and opened my door. Looking at me and taking hold of my hand, he asked, "Lynne, it may be too soon to ask this, but I guess one of the reasons I'm here is to ask you for another chance. A chance to get to know you again. Is that possible?"

Right then, I was afraid to respond with what my heart was telling me to say, so instead I jumped down to the gravel driveway and blurted out, "I'm very glad you came—and I know Betsy will be very glad to meet you. She's heard all about you."

Hanging onto my hand firmly, he said, "I'd very much like to meet Betsy, but maybe it's too late to do that tonight? If you think so, I could come back out tomorrow if that's okay. Are you planning on going someplace in the next twenty-four hours? Do I need to park at the end of the road to make sure you don't get away?"

"Hey!" I said in mock shame. "I'm not going anywhere. Why don't you come here for lunch tomorrow? How about noon? I promise not to run away overnight," I said.

"I'd like that," he said.

And then I looked up at him and managed to say, despite my warring emotions, "I'm so glad you came, Collin. It's wonderful to see you again." Then I turned and headed towards the little house. I didn't look back, but I knew he was standing there watching me right up until the second I went inside.

I closed the door and leaned against it trying to get a grip on what had just happened. My head was spinning. Collin had come back into my life. He hadn't gotten married and had a family. He'd found me. Me! After all these years and all that had happened. I just couldn't believe it. Did I dare even hope that this time it could work out for us? And then I remembered David. David was also back in my life. And feeling intense hatred as well as a sense of empowerment, I told myself I wasn't going to let him ruin my chances this time. I was a stronger person now, and I was going to take back my life. It was my turn to be happy.

CHAPTER 25

Spring 2018

THE NEXT MORNING, Ron hung the flag out as usual, and I walked over to help get the kids ready for school. As I opened the back door, I heard my sister's sing-songy voice say, "I heard that Collin was here last night. Is that right?"

"Yes," I said, blushing as I shut the door. "Who told you?"

"Never you mind," Betsy said defiantly.

"Well, apparently he ran into Margie, and he asked her if she knew anything about me. She told him I was here at the farm."

"Did you know he was coming?"

"No, he said he was afraid if he called I would have stopped him from coming."

"Would you have?" Betsy watched my face carefully.

"Probably." I was becoming increasingly uncomfortable with my sister's interrogation, but I tried not to show it.

"What's wrong with you?" she asked, sounding annoyed.

"I'm scared," I said.

"Scared of what?"

"I don't know. I've been convinced for so many years that he'd moved on or gotten married that I'd given up hope."

"Lynnie, he came all the way here because he wanted to find you. Are you at least going to give him—and yourself—a chance?"

"Yes. Yes, I think I will," I said, smiling, feeling relieved at last just to admit it.

Betsy ran up and threw her arms around me. "I'm so happy for you, Lynnie. I can't wait to meet him."

"Well, you'll get to meet him very soon. He'll be here at noon. He's coming for lunch."

"Lunch? I don't think I have anything to feed him," Betsy said, frowning.

"I have something in mind, so I'll take care of it. All you have to do is get dressed," I said looking at her ratty old robe.

When I headed back to the little house, I was surprised to see all the shack girls sitting outside on the porch holding cups of coffee. And from the looks on their faces, I wasn't sure I wanted to face them, since I wasn't in the mood for another interrogation.

"Well? What happened?" Sam asked before I could even put one foot on the porch.

"Collin's just an old friend," I said and then watched as she rolled her eyes.

"You looked pretty happy to see your so-called 'old friend,'" Jo said.

"When will you see him again?" Callie demanded.

"He stayed in town last night, and I invited him to come for lunch today."

"What are you going to make?" Sam asked as I walked past them and opened the door to the kitchen.

"I haven't decided yet, but I'll need to pick up some things from the store if I'm going to have lunch ready," I said, hoping that would end all the questions.

"Do we get to meet him?" Kellan asked.

"Well, I'd assume so, but right now I'm taking it one day at a time. And it won't be today."

"We don't want to be nosy. We just want to be sure you're safe and happy," Smitty said as she stood up to leave.

"Speak for yourself," Sam said. "I don't care if I am nosy or not. I want to know all the details."

"Of course I'll introduce you to him, but probably not today." Addressing them all, I added, "Don't you know you're like family to me? When I see him again, I'll make sure to bring him by to meet you. But for now, don't you have work to do?" I said as I nonchalantly let the screen door slam behind me, leaving my friends outside. Inside, I could still hear them talking on the porch and an occasional girlish giggle. They were happy for me, and that made me happy.

Promptly at noon, Collin pulled up in front of the little house. He had flowers with him and he looked nervous. As for me, I could hardly contain myself. I had to work hard to keep from shaking as I opened the front door.

"Good morning," he said, grinning from ear to ear.

"Good morning to you too." I smiled back.

"I picked up some flowers for you—and some for Betsy." He handed me a bunch of colorful spring blooms as he leaned in to give me a kiss on the cheek.

I felt a huge rush as he gently lifted his lips from my cheek. The fresh smell of him made my heart flutter. "They're lovely," I said as casually as I could, bending my head to smell them before looking up at him. "Make yourself at home while I put these in some water."

"This is a cute little house," he said as he headed back to the kitchen with me. "How long have you lived here?"

"Well, for a little more than a year. I wanted to give Betsy, Ron, and the kids as much privacy as I could, while still being close at hand."

"It's so hard to believe you've been this close, and I had no idea you were here," he said, looking at me sadly.

"It's been a difficult time," I said. "Betsy was very sick. I was afraid she wouldn't make it, that the disease wouldn't go into remission. Our mother had the same cancer and she didn't survive," I explained as I placed the vase of flowers on the table. "But now things are looking up, her prognosis is good, and I think she's nearly back to normal."

Collin stood, leaning against the door frame, watching me. "Lynne, I hope she continues to do well—and I'm so glad I found you again."

"Well, like it or not, you did," I joked, trying to lighten the mood.

"Lynne, are you here?" Jo called from upstairs.

"Yes, I'm in the kitchen," I called back.

"Hey, I was wondering," she said, stopping mid-sentence when she spotted Collin. "I'm sorry, I thought you were alone."

"Jo, this is Collin, an old friend of mine. Collin, this is my roommate, Jo. She's one of the shack girls, and she's been kind enough to let me live here with her during Betsy's recovery."

Collin had such a confident, easygoing manner that he put anyone he talked to at ease. He smiled and stepped over to Jo, extending his hand. "It's a pleasure to meet you, Jo."

"Nice to meet you too," she said, matching his smile with one of her own. "I'm sorry to interrupt. I just wanted to let you know that I was on my way to the shack if you wanted a ride—but it looks like you're busy," she said, knowing full well that Collin and I were having lunch. I was slow to catch on at first that she'd actually staged this whole thing because she wanted to meet him and size him up.

"I don't think I'll be going over to the shack today. Collin and I are planning to have lunch with Betsy and visit with her for a while." And then meeting her gaze directly, so she knew I knew what she was really up to, I said, "But thanks for asking, Jo."

"Well, I'll be off then. It's very nice to meet you, Collin," she said awkwardly before she left.

Once she was gone, I said, "Jo came here to live just before my mother died. She helped Betsy care for Mom, and they became very close. She's been like another sister through all of this. She just stepped in and helped with anything we needed. I'm also very grateful to her for letting me live here with her." I paused and then added, "Let's walk over to the big house now so you can meet Betsy."

"I'd like that very much," Collin said.

As we walked, I told him about my parents and the farm. Every time I looked up to see his face, he'd gaze at me with such an affectionate expression that I felt like my heart would explode. This all seemed so surreal, like I was having an out-of-body experience—watching something I'd only dreamed about happening in real life.

Finally, as we reached the back porch of the farmhouse, I said, "Get ready to be grilled. Betsy has heard about you for a long time, and she's very excited about meeting you in person. That said, she's also my big sister and is very protective of me. No pressure—just a warning," I said with a grin.

Betsy must have been watching us walk towards the house, because she was waiting for us in the kitchen. When I opened the door, she walked right up to Collin, wrapped her arms around his shoulders, and gave him a big hug. "I'm so happy to meet you at last," she said. "I've heard a lot about you."

"Thank you. It's great to meet you too," he exclaimed, pleasantly surprised by the warmth of her greeting.

"I hope you're here to talk her into going back to Chicago. She's been here too long taking care of all of us. It's time she did something for herself."

I looked at my sister in disbelief. It's not what I expected to hear her say so soon after meeting Collin.

"I'm just glad I found her again. I'd love to get her back in Chicago, but I think she has to be the one to decide," Collin said, looking pointedly at me.

Betsy was on her best behavior. She didn't interrogate Collin like I thought she would. She was very comfortable with him and seemed to genuinely like him. In fact, it was as if Collin and Betsy had known each other their entire lives. After lunch, Collin helped me do the dishes, while Betsy sat at the table and told Collin all about our childhood, what I'd been doing at her house for the last year, and then, repeatedly, how much she hoped I'd finally focus on my own life now.

The afternoon flew by, and before we knew it, it was time to meet Melanie and Josh at the bus stop. I offered to walk down to get them, but Betsy insisted she had plenty of energy and would walk down by herself. Before she left, she gave Collin a big hug, telling him that she hoped she'd get to see him again soon. Then she came over to me and gave me a hug too. Whispering in my ear, she said, "Don't let him get away this time, Lynnie," and then she was out the front door and on her way down the road to meet the kids.

"Do you want to walk with me back to the little house, or do you have other things you need to do this afternoon?" I asked.

"You're the only thing on my schedule today."

We closed the door behind us and walked at a leisurely pace, stopping along the way to look in the barn, since Collin was interested in seeing what kind of equipment and machinery Ron used. We spent the rest of the afternoon just talking about everything and nothing at all. We compressed sixteen years into a few hours. We sipped tea, then walked some more, out along the fence rows to look out at the fields. It was a beautiful day, with blue skies and fluffy white clouds.

When we were on our way back to the little house, Ron drove up, rolled down his window and said, "You must be Collin. I'm Ron, Betsy's husband. Nice to meet you."

Collin went over and shook Ron's hand through the open window. "It's good to meet you too, Ron. I met Betsy earlier today and had hoped to meet you as well. Lynne and I have been out exploring your beautiful farm this afternoon."

"Are you staying for dinner?" Ron asked.

"No, I need to get back to my own farm."

"Well, I hope we see you again soon," Ron said with a wink to me.

"Me, too," Collin replied.

Ron tipped the end of his cap to us and was soon on his way home.

"I hope it's okay to come see you again, Lynne."

"I would like that very much."

"Would you be willing to come out to my farm next weekend? I could tell you how to get there, and you could come and meet my goats."

"That sounds like great fun. I'd love it."

"Great. I'll email you the information." Then he took my hand and looked into my face as he said, "I'm so glad I found you, Lynne. It's been great to spend time with you again."

As he got into his truck, I struggled with letting him go. And then I just stood there in front of the little house and watched as he drove away. It seemed like a dream—like the last sixteen years had never happened, and we were back where we'd been before.

CHAPTER 26

Spring 2018

I DECIDED TO walk over to the big house, where I found Betsy waiting for me in the kitchen. She couldn't wait to tell me her feelings about Collin. "He's wonderful. I love him. He's perfect for you. Did you know you blush every time he looks at you?"

"Really?"

"When who looks at her?" Josh asked as he came in.

"Never you mind. You need to get to your homework, mister," Betsy said.

"I don't have any homework."

"Really?" I said again, only this time to Josh.

"Okay, maybe a little, but who makes you blush?" he asked.

"A friend of mine who I haven't seen in a very long time," I told him.

"Okay," he said nonchalantly, not needing any more information. He turned and went off to retrieve his book bag and homework.

Melanie was sitting at the dining room table doing her homework. When she saw me, she looked up and smiled without saying anything.

"What are you smiling about?" I asked.

"Nothing," she said with a giggle.

"You really shouldn't talk about this stuff with the kids," I said to Betsy.

"It's kind of fun seeing you squirm," she said.

"Not funny."

"When will you see him again?"

"Next weekend. I'm going to meet him at his farm. Is that okay? I'm sorry, Betsy. I forgot to ask you first. Will you be okay?"

"What do you mean asking me if it's okay? We can take care of ourselves. You have done your job, Lynnie. We're all back to normal, and you need to start thinking about yourself and what's best for you. No more babysitting us!"

"Oh, don't say that. That makes my heart hurt. My time with you guys has given me more than it's given you," I insisted. "It's been a very special time for me, and I've loved every minute of it."

Betsy came over and put her arms around me and gave me a big hug. "What will we do without you, Lynnie? You're part of our family and I don't like you leaving us, but you need to get on with your life. I'm so glad Collin has come back to you. That makes it just a tiny bit easier to let you go."

"Where is Aunt Lynnie going?" Josh asked.

"It is time for Aunt Lynnie to leave us and set up her own home," Betsy replied.

"She can't leave us," Josh said, sounding distressed at the idea.

"Who's leaving us?" Melanie asked, not having heard the whole conversation.

"Aunt Lynnie needs to leave us soon. We're doing quite well these days, and it's time for her to get back to her regular life."

"Aren't we her regular life?" Josh asked.

"You are my best life," I said, kissing him and ruffling his hair.

"Where will you live, Aunt Lynnie?" Melanie asked. "Didn't you move all your things out of your apartment?"

"I did, and I'll need to figure out where I'll move to. But I hate to even think about it. I'll miss you all terribly," I said, curling my bottom lip into a pout. "If you don't need me here right now, I'd like to go over to the little house for a while. Is that okay?"

Before I could get an answer, Ron walked in. I said, "How are you doing with your summer help? Have most of the hands arrived?"

"We're nearly up to full capacity. Why do you ask?"

"I'm just trying to determine the state of things so I can make some decisions. I need to talk to Margie to find out if she has a place for me so I could go back to work full-time. And depending on how that goes, and where that is, I'll need to start looking for a new place to live. I want to be sure everything is good here—just in case you guys need some extra help. Of course, I wouldn't plan anything until I discussed it with both of you first."

"You don't need to stay here, Lynnie —although we'd love it if you did. Betsy is almost back to full steam, and Melanie, Josh, and I can step up our game to help out around here. Can't we guys?" he asked.

"Speak for yourself," Josh said, shuffling along with his head down.

"School will be out soon, and we won't need lunches or help with our homework," Melanie pointed out.

"I like Aunt Lynnie's lunches. She always puts extra cookies in my lunch," Josh whined.

"You don't need extra cookies in your lunch," Betsy said.

I put my fingers up to my lips and said to Josh, "Shhh! Don't give away our secrets, mister."

"Sorry," Josh said sheepishly.

"See you all later," I said, shutting the door behind me. As I walked over to the little house, I thought about what a lovable family they were and thought about whether they still needed me here now. Everything seemed to be going well with Betsy's health. The doctor was pleased with her progress. Both Josh and Melanie had grown up a lot in the year. They'd become far more independent, and Ron was more confident in his ability to help manage the household."

"Hi," Jo said with a big smile as I entered the kitchen of the little house. "How was your afternoon?"

"It was great," I said.

"Collin seems like a very nice guy."

"He is a great guy," I said back.

"Hey, I only said he was a *nice* guy," she said, teasing me. "I'm so happy for you, Lynne. I'm on my way upstairs to read before I go to bed. Do you need to talk or anything before I go?"

"No, I'm good," I said, peeling a banana. "Actually, I'm great."

After Jo went upstairs, I stepped out onto the porch and looked over at the big house and the barn. I felt a sense of peace come over me—something I hadn't felt in a very long time. There had been a weight on me for many years. The weight of the attack, the pregnancy, moving, losing Collin, the adoption, Betsy's health, David's recent release, and the court ruling. I felt like things were about to take a turn for the better, and through it all I'd gotten stronger and was better able to handle difficult situations. I was a strong, capable woman, and I knew it—something I hadn't known before all this happened. I had tackled each challenge head-on and was better for it. I inhaled deeply and then let all the air out of my lungs—I could feel the pressure leaving me, a pound at a time.

The next morning, there was no flag on the back porch when I looked out, and Ron's truck was gone. I felt a twinge of sadness. He and Betsy must have talked last night and decided I needed a nudge to get off on my own. I walked over anyway, into a kitchen filled with happy sounds. Sounds that I would very much miss. Betsy was making the kids' lunches and both of them were eating breakfast.

"Hey, what about me?" I asked. "You guys went ahead without me. I'm hurt!"

"Aunt Lynnie, we love you, but we've got this!" Melanie said.

That really did hurt. I got a lump in my throat, and she could see I was upset.

"I'm sorry, Aunt Lynnie. I didn't mean to hurt your feelings."

I walked over to her and kissed the top of her head, and then I kissed Josh. "I will really miss you guys," I said as I went to pour myself a cup of coffee.

"You can still take care of me, Aunt Lynnie. I need you," Josh said.

"No, you don't," Betsy said. "Aunt Lynnie has been training you for this moment and now it's graduation time, my little man."

"I'll walk you both down to the bus if you aren't too grown up for me to do that," I said.

Both kids got their backpacks and kissed their mother good-bye, and we headed out the door to the bus stop. We walked slowly. Josh jumped on the bus as soon as it pulled up, but Melanie lingered for a moment.

"Aunt Lynnie, I know you are not leaving yet but, thank you for coming to take care of us. We love you." She kissed me on the cheek and stepped onto the bus, waving good-bye.

It was very hard to see them drive away. It would be a few months before I left, but that was the moment it really hit me. I would soon be leaving.

When I came back to the big house, I found Betsy sitting in the kitchen waiting for me.

"Lynnie, we'll miss you so very much. What would I have done without you?" Betsy said sadly. "I shouldn't have kept you here for so long."

"Don't be silly. There's nowhere I would rather have been these past months than right here with you, Ron, Melanie, and Josh. I'm very grateful you let me into your lives."

"What are you going to do today?" Betsy asked.

"I'm going to call Margie and talk with her about job opportunities, and hopefully she'll be able to take me back full-time. Then I'm going to start looking at apartments in Chicago. Ready or not, it's time."

Only a few hours after I called her, Margie got back to me saying she would have something for me full-time beginning in the fall, which would give me plenty of time to transition to a place of my own and get things wrapped up at the farm. Leaving the farm, I got in my car and headed for the shack. As I passed by all the familiar sights, I seemed to see things I hadn't noticed before, things I'd taken for granted and would miss. I had to keep telling myself that I wasn't leaving forever, I was just moving a little ways away. I could come back whenever I liked, but I knew it wouldn't be the same. I would be a guest when I returned next time, not one of the family—and thinking about that made me sad.

CHAPTER 27

Spring 2018

WHEN I ARRIVED at the shack, I found the place humming. In the back I could hear the glass furnace blazing away, with Sam's music competing to be heard. Up front, I could hear Callie's voice. She was teaching a class to a group of textile artists. Across the hall, Jo was in her smock laying out her tools, getting ready to work on a project. From Smitty's studio, I could hear Sam and Smitty laughing about something. Everything was in motion, and the place was alive with creativity and love.

"Good morning," I said as I entered Smitty's studio and hung up my purse on the hook.

"Well, good morning to you," Sam said with a wry smile. "How was your day yesterday? Or I should say, how was your day with your 'old friend'?"

"It was great. Collin is a really terrific guy, and I like him a lot," I said, rolling up my sleeves.

"Does he like you as much as you like him?" Sam asked, sounding more serious now. "If not, don't let yourself get too attached to him. You can use him to your advantage and not get your feelings hurt, you know."

"What a thing to say! Of course he likes her. He'd be crazy not to—and Lynnie is not the type of woman to lead a man on," Smitty said, sounding annoyed.

I smiled at the two of them. I knew Sam's comments were not meant literally, but were more than anything said to get a rise out of me. Also, she wanted me to be careful so I didn't get hurt. They both did.

"I'm ready," Kellan said as she walked in.

"Oh, God. Is it time for a driving lesson again?" Sam said, feigning terror. "Kiss me good-bye, everyone. We're taking the truck out on the open road today."

"Wow! You're really making progress," I said.

"Not really. I think that's why Sam wants to take me out on a long stretch of open road—fewer stops and starts."

"My neck needs a break," Sam elaborated. "I'm not going to allow her to take over until we are well out of town."

"Good luck to you both," Smitty said with a wink at Kellan as the two walked out.

Smitty and I settled into a peaceful rhythm as we worked around each other in her studio—until she stopped suddenly and blurted out, "Lynnie, you've spent such a long time getting over what happened to you years ago and then taking care of Betsy and the family—it should be your time now. Time for you to do something for yourself."

She knew what I knew, that it was time for me to leave.

"I guess it is," I said reluctantly. "I think I've been using Betsy's health as a crutch and an excuse not to have to go back to my old life. But I think it's time, and I was thinking of leaving in the fall."

"Well, I'll miss you. We'll all miss you. We've loved having you here in the shack, and I hope you'll visit here often so you can continue working on your art. You're becoming an excellent artist. It would be a shame to let your talent go to waste."

"Hope all you want Smitty, but there is no real talent here. I 'play' with this just because I like hanging out with all of you shack girls."

"Not even remotely true. I mean it, Lynne," she said sternly. "You need to keep on with your artwork. It's a sin to have a talent like yours and not use it."

Changing the subject, I asked Smitty about her new glazes, her new commissions, and other upcoming projects until we heard a loud screech and a bang outside, followed by an ominous silence. At first, Smitty and I just looked at each other, stunned, until she said, "Do you think someone hit the shack?"

We ran out into the hall in time to see Jo and Callie racing out to the front porch. There, parked in the driveway, were Kellan and Sam in Sam's truck. The entire driver's side of Jo's car was mangled from the collision. Jo walked solemnly down the steps and toward her car as Kellan got out slowly. "I am so sorry, Jo. I am so very sorry. I put my foot on the gas when I should have put it on the brake."

Then we all watched as Sam, who was still in the truck, tried to open the passenger side door without success. Then she calmly slid over to the driver's side, got out, and without a single word, walked right past us into the shack, shutting the door behind her.

"Well, that was interesting," Callie said. "I don't think I've ever seen Sam so calm and with nothing to say."

"What could she say?" Kellan said. "I think she may be in shock. This was my fault. She's been trying to be patient with me, but I think it's very hard for her. I think she just decided if she couldn't say anything nice, she wouldn't say anything at all."

"Well, then she must be in shock, because that's not like her!" Smitty declared.

At that remark, we all burst out laughing. A few minutes later Sam came out with a glass of whisky, the bottle still in hand. She sat down on the steps, drank a glass, and poured another. We stood staring at her until she finally said, "What? I didn't do it."

Jo and Kellan stood with their arms around each other, looking at the truck and the car. "It's going to be fine," Jo said as she gave Kellan a little squeeze.

CHAPTER 28

Spring 2018

IT WAS SATURDAY morning, and before I could even get out of bed, Betsy and Melanie came into my bedroom, sat on my bed, and began to pepper me with questions about what I was going to wear on my "date" with Collin.

"This really isn't a date," I said. "He's just going to show me around his farm."

"What do you mean, this isn't a date? If it's not a date, what is it?" Betsy asked. "This *is* a date! So you need to get dressed like it's a date."

"What do you mean? I look fine every day."

"This is not every day—and no, you don't always look fine. Today you need to look great," Betsy said firmly.

"Aunt Lynnie, you should wear the new jeans you got at Christmas and that baby blue t-shirt. It will make your eyes stand out," Melanie suggested.

"What are you going to do with your hair?" asked Betsy.

"You should curl it and leave it down. It looks pretty like that. I like your brown boots too. Those would look good with your jeans," Melanie called out since she was now inside my closet.

"Hey, you guys!" I said, pulling my pillows over my head.

"I'm sorry, Aunt Lynnie, but you haven't been out with a guy in a long time, and I think you're a bit rusty."

"Yeah, who made you Miss Porter?" I sneered.

"Who's Miss Porter?" she asked.

"She's right, those jeans you got for Christmas make your ass look great," Betsy said.

"Mom!"

"Sorry, Melanie! You're right. I shouldn't have said that, and you should never think about what your rear end looks like in a pair of jeans, young lady."

"She's right though—your ass does look really good in those jeans," Melanie added.

"Melanie! Just because your mother has a foul mouth doesn't give you license to talk like that," I said.

"So what exactly are you going to do at his place today?" Betsy asked.

"I would guess I will get to see some goats."

"Is he making lunch for you?" Melanie asked. "That would be *so* romantic."

"I think we're going to have lunch with his business partner, Grant."

"So much for the romance," Betsy remarked.

"Well, I think it's very romantic that he wants to spend the whole day with you," Melanie said. "I also think he's cute."

"He is cute, Lynnie, and he seems like a great guy. You shouldn't let him get away this time," Betsy suggested, and then looked as if she'd like to take back what she'd just said. I could tell she'd suddenly remembered why I'd let him get away the first time. "Sorry, Lynnie, I didn't mean that."

"Believe me, it's not lost on me that I'm lucky he found me. I decided long ago I had to just let him go. I assumed by now he was married and had a house full of kids. So I know how lucky I am. But who knows, we've both changed a lot in the last sixteen years. Maybe we won't be able to recapture that spark we had."

"Why *did* you break up, Aunt Lynnie?" Melanie asked.

Betsy glanced up at me with an apologetic look on her face.

"Well, it's hard to say. I'm not sure you could say we ever really dated—but we were close friends. I had to move away for business, and well, we just lost touch. Back then, we had other things going on in our lives and weren't ready for a relationship." In saying that, I felt I was being as honest as I could be. Then I got up to take a shower while the two of them chose the outfit they wanted me to wear.

As I was getting dressed, Betsy dropped my short suede boots on the floor in front of me.

"I like this look on you," she said. "I think you're just about ready for us to let you out of the house. We did a fine job, Melanie," she said, giving her a high five.

I smiled at them both. "What would I do without you two?" and then added with a pout, "What *will* I do without you two?"

What was supposed to be only a forty-five minute drive from Betsy's took me about twice that. The GPS couldn't identify the address, so I had to rely on a map and my best navigation skills, which were not nearly good enough—and a call to Collin for directions. By the time I finally found the "bright red barn," Collin was standing outside, watching for me.

When I emerged from my car, ignoring the fact that I was late, I said, "Hey, I like this," as I pointed up to the roof of the barn. It was painted with huge white letters that read "Pasture Prime."

"It looks like a very professional operation," I added with a grin.

"Yeah, it does, doesn't it?" he said, smiling warmly at me. "I is quite proud of this here operation," he said with a fake twang in his voice. "How was your ride out here—other than getting lost, I mean?"

"I could have been here sooner if I hadn't turned right instead of left twice. The GPS doesn't recognize your address, and your place is hard to see from the road," I said, turning to indicate the long road past the grove of trees. "You have great camouflage."

"Yeah, sorry about that. I've been coming here for so long that I forget we are a bit off the beaten path. Next time you'll get here in no time."

"Thank heavens I had your phone number, or I might still be out there."

"Us folks out here in the sticks do have some technology, you know," he said, again with the phony twang. "Come on, let me show you around before it gets dark," he teased, holding his hand out for mine. "First, let me introduce you to Grant and our team."

As we walked to the office, Collin reminded me that he and Grant had been friends since childhood, and they'd always wanted to own a business together. They decided if it was ever going to happen, they'd better get to it, since they weren't getting any younger. I watched his face as he talked, and it was lit up with excitement and pride.

"You know, we never thought seriously about raising animals and running a dairy," Collin said. "But for the past eight years, we attended organic farming conferences, visited other small farms, and spent a lot of time talking with farmers. What we learned is that it's a lot of work and you have to really want it in order to make it a success. We decided that with both of us wanting it as much as we did we could only succeed, so we had to give it a shot."

At that moment Grant came over to greet us. "Hey, you must be Lynne," he said. "I'm Grant. The 'Prime' part of Pasture Prime."

"Ha, ha," Collin said. "I would assume that means I'm the 'Pasture' part?"

"Yeah, that would be about right," Grant said agreeably.

"Moving right along . . . Lynne, this is my lifelong friend and now business partner."

"It's a pleasure to meet you," I said, extending my hand.

Grant leaned past my hand and wrapped his long arms around me, giving me a tight squeeze and kissing me on the cheek. "We're very friendly here," he said, "and besides, I feel like I've known you half my life. Collin has talked about you since the day he met you. I was amazed when I heard he was so fortunate as to run into your friend and ended up finding you after all these years."

Just then a tall, beautiful woman entered the office.

Collin said, "Lynne, this is Grace, Grant's fiancé."

"Hello, Lynne," Grace said in a sweet clear voice. "I'm the brains of this operation."

"That literally is the truth," Collin said. "Grace is our accountant and business manager. She keeps us on the right track."

Grant reached for Grace's hand and pulled her towards him. "I don't know what we'd do without her," he said, as they exchanged loving glances.

"Now that you've met the brains of the operation, how about we take a walk around the place?" Collin asked.

"That would be great," I said, my eyes still glued to Grant and Grace.

Collin walked to the door and held it open for me.

"Hey, when will you two be back?" Grant asked. "We'll have lunch ready whenever you tell us."

"Why don't you give us an hour or so. I'll give you a call when we're headed back this way," Collin replied.

As we walked, Collin told me how they'd taken the leap to get Pasture Prime up and running. Individually, neither of them had the financial freedom to quit their jobs or the ability to tackle this project on their own. They'd been driving back from a farm conference when they saw a roadside sign that said, "Farm for Sale." They looked at each other and without a word turned down the long drive toward the grove of trees.

"We didn't realize it was a dairy farm until we got to the barn and saw all the cows—and then we saw the little goats. After that, we were hooked. At first, we thought we'd just sell goat's milk to companies that made the cheese. But then one thing led to another, and before we knew it. we were up to our ears—literally—in cheese."

"How did you learn how to do it?"

157

"We hired a consultant. He helped us evaluate our stock, equipment, number of acres, types of feed, etc., and then the rest we learned—or rather are still learning—through trial and error."

At that moment, a small group of little goats left the barn and headed out to the pasture.

"Oh, Collin, they are darling!" I said.

"I told you. The minute I saw them, I was smitten. They're not really that hard to care for, and they're tremendous milk producers. They literally give more than they receive."

"Do you think you're over the learning hump?"

"Well, I think there's always more to learn, and that's one great reason why our project is so interesting and fun. We are invested in learning. Early on we agreed that one of us would work our regular job while the other worked the farm. For the most part, Grant has been the one to work the farm. We didn't invest a lot of money into the venture to begin with. We focused on educating ourselves about goats. We wanted to keep them as healthy as possible so they'd produce high-quality milk for other cheese producers. In year four, I mortgaged my home and went to Europe to study artisanal cheese-making. That experience turned out to be a real eye-opener.

"For instance, I learned about the significance of what the goats eat and how that flavors the milk. I learned about how different bacteria can really make the difference in our cheeses. I made lifelong friends and developed a strong network of cheesemakers who were willing to experiment with us.

"I also learned that if the goats are happy, their milk tastes better. We consulted with an animal behaviorist who helped us add stimulation for the goats: They like to climb, and they like to interact with each other, and even with us humans. That stimulation impacts the quality of the cheese. Who would have thought? It may seem obvious to most people, but Grant and I were clueless!"

"It seems like what makes them happy makes you happy," I said with a chuckle.

"Laugh all you want, smarty-pants. But happy goats make for a happy wallet."

"Sorry, I will try to be more respectful."

"In any case, all our experimenting paid off. We've gotten some national recognition for the quality of our cheese—and it's in high demand. We've had to invest more in the farm to up our production in order to keep up with demand, and we've been careful to keep demand high without saturating the market with our cheeses."

"Keep them asking for more," I added.

"Yeah, keep them asking for more," Collin said, nodding.

"I love the name of your business. That is pretty clever."

"Pasture Prime—yeah, I thought that was pretty clever too," he said proudly. "Come on into the pasture and meet some of our little herd."

We spent the next hour just petting the goats and letting them eat grass out of our hands. They were very cute, the weather was perfect, and I felt content. I became so absorbed in the animals that I didn't even notice Collin looking at me. As soon as our eyes met, I looked away quickly because I felt so self-conscious.

Collin said, "Hey, Bo-Peep, it's time to head back and meet Grant and Grace for lunch. We can come back later if you've haven't had enough." Taking my hand, he walked me out of the pasture and towards the house. My heart was pounding.

There was a delicious lunch waiting, all ready for us. We sat outside under a beautiful old oak tree at a very rustic picnic table. I enjoyed hearing the three of them talk about the experiences they'd had—some funny, some not—getting Pasture Prime to this high level of success. The time just glided by. Finally, Grant stood up and said, "Why don't the two of you continue with your tour. Grace and I can clean up," and he leaned down and kissed Grace gently on the lips.

"Hey, guy, you can do this. I have work to do," she said with a disarming smile.

"I can't do what you do, so that's fine by me," he said agreeably.

"I could help you," I offered.

"Don't be silly. It will only take me a minute," he said. "You need to go with Collin so he can coerce you into coming back to see us again."

Collin stood up and extended his hand to me, "Come on—he's got this. Anyway, you're our guest."

We spent the next few hours walking leisurely through the fields, petting the goats, and enjoying being together. It was amazing we were so comfortable with each other after all the time that had passed. We'd picked up right where we left off—before I so painfully left him.

Finally I said, "I should probably head back. Who knows how long it will take me to find my way home?" I added with a smirk.

Collin looked genuinely sad. "Lynne, would you consider coming back again soon for another visit?"

"Yes, I think I could be persuaded to return. I like these little guys," I said, petting one of the goats.

"When you come back, will it be to see them or to see me?"

"Well, that's a hard question. They are pretty cute. But, yes, I think I could be persuaded to see you again too."

"On a somewhat related note, what are you doing next Friday night? Do you think you'd have time to go out to dinner with me if I stopped by?"

"Stop by? That's quite a journey for just stopping by."

"I would be coming from home on my way to the farm, and it's not that much further to you. I thought we could have dinner, and then afterward, I'd drive back here for the rest of the weekend."

"That sounds great. I'd like that," I said, feeling confident that I was headed in the right direction.

CHAPTER 29

Spring 2018

I WAS SITTING in the kitchen, sipping on a fresh hot cup of coffee, and watching Josh follow Betsy from place to place complaining, "I have nothing to do. I'm *sooo* bored." Betsy sat down across from me with a grimace on her face and reported that this had been going on every day since school had gotten out. He was driving her crazy.

"Where's Melanie? Maybe she'll do something with you,." I suggested to Josh.

"She's reading, and I don't want to read."

"Why don't you ride your bike to Tom's house? He probably has nothing to do either," Betsy said.

"He's helping his uncle this summer. I am *sooo* bored!" Josh repeated with new emphasis this time.

Ron had just come in for lunch and overheard Josh complaining. "I have a cure for that. Get your work clothes on. You're coming with me today."

Josh must indeed have been terribly bored, because without another word, he ran to change his clothes.

With a stunned look on his face, Ron said to Betsy, "Well, that was a first. I'd expected a long, protracted argument about how working with me was no fun."

"I guess it just goes to show how desperate he is," Betsy replied.

"I could take Melanie out with me too. Where is she?"

"She's upstairs reading," I said.

"Melanie," Ron called upstairs. "Do you want to work out in the fields with me this afternoon?"

We could hear her door open, soon followed by her footsteps on the stairs. When she appeared, she said in a serious tone of voice to all of us, "I've been meaning to talk to you about something."

"Is there something wrong?" Betsy asked, looking concerned.

"No, it's something good," Melanie said with a huge smile. "I asked Mr. Saunders if I could have a job at the café, and he said I could waitress there a few hours a week. I was planning to tell you about it this afternoon. What do you think? I'd really like to. Please? Please?"

"What?" Betsy said. "What do you mean? You got a job?"

"Well, I don't have a job yet. I have to get permission from you and Dad first. Please, Mom. Let me do it. Mr. Saunders said I would get an hourly wage and share in the tips. It's only a few hours a day. You could drop me off when you go to the shack, and I can walk over to you when my shift is done so we can drive home together."

"What? Melanie has a job at the café?" Josh called as he raced in from the hall. "Cool. Can I come and get some free food?"

"No, you can't get free food," Melanie stated emphatically. "In fact, you're not allowed to come into the café without Mom, Lynnie, or Dad. Do you hear me?"

"Well, it sounds like you've thought a lot about this, missy," Betsy said, frowning.

"It will be good for me. It'll teach me to be responsible, and I'll have my own money so I won't have to ask you and Dad for it anymore. What do you think, Aunt Lynnie?"

"Well, I think it's better if I keep my opinions to myself so I don't get into trouble."

"Yeah, what *do* you think?" Betsy chimed in.

I thought carefully about whether I should weigh in with my opinion and decided I would. "Well, Betsy, as I recall, both you and I started to work at that very same café at the very same age that Melanie is now. That's all I'm going to say on the matter."

"It just doesn't seem possible my little girl is old enough for a job," Betsy said. "Ron, what do you think?"

"I think she's old enough. If she wants to work a few hours a week, I think it's a good idea."

Melanie's face began to beam. "Please, Mom?"

"Well, I guess it's okay as long as it's part-time, because you're too young to work full-time. A few hours, a few days a week would probably be okay."

Melanie wrapped her arms around Betsy's neck and said, "Thank you, Mom." She skipped out of the kitchen and back up the stairs to her room where we could hear her shut her door and let out a little whoop.

"It hardly seems possible she's old enough to get a job," I murmured. "She's turned out to be a great kid, and she's very mature. You guys have done a terrific job."

"Hey, what about me?" Josh asked in a hurt voice.

"Well, that remains to be seen," Ron said, plopping a baseball cap on top of his son's head.

Ignoring Josh, Betsy said sadly, "And just think, it won't be long before she's off to college, has a real job, and has moved into a place of her own."

"Don't get carried away," Ron said to his wife with an affectionate kiss. "She's still our little girl." Then turning to Josh, he said, "Come along with me, mister."

As we left the house, Betsy picked up where she left off. "Melanie's all grown up! It seems like only a few months ago she was a baby—and now look at her. She has a job!"

"I know. It doesn't seem possible. Has she started talking to you about colleges yet?" I asked.

"Yes, she's interested in a few schools, but I don't think she's decided yet what she wants to do with her life."

"She mentioned possibly going to law school," I said. "Melanie would be good at that. She's very calm and presents a good case. Look how she just handled all of us! Can't you see her as a lawyer?"

"Yes, I can," Betsy said, smiling at the thought. "She'd be a good lawyer. What do you think about this job at the café?"

"I think she'll do fine. She's always careful about not taking on more than she can do well, and her grades are excellent. Do you think she'll want to keep working in the fall when school starts up again?" I asked.

"I don't think Ron will let her work and go to school. But we'll see. Who am I kidding, he'll let her do whatever she wants to do! She has him wrapped around her little finger."

"Only because she's a great kid and he knows she has a good head on her shoulders."

Before we got in the car, we heard Melanie call out to us excitedly. When she reached us, she said, "I called Mr. Saunders, and he said I can start tomorrow. I can't wait to call my friends. They'll be so jealous!"

CHAPTER 30

Spring 2018

ON MORNINGS WHEN Melanie was scheduled to work, she was up and dressed, sitting on the steps, ready to go almost before I even got out of bed. And now Betsy was doing well enough to tackle her household tasks without any help. They literally went through their days without needing me! It was a bit scary to be responsible just for me with nothing to divert my attention—nothing and nobody to focus on but myself.

It began to dawn on me that for the past sixteen years, I'd been focusing on things that would divert my attention away from forming a happy and successful independent life—one just for me. And while I was a bit anxious and unsettled at the idea of facing this task, I was ready. It was a good time for me to leave, not just because Betsy and her family were able to take care of themselves, but also because I was finally able to take care of me.

Today, as soon as Melanie and Betsy drove off, I thought about my plans for the day. I was going to drive up to Chicago to meet with Margie to discuss some projects I'd be starting in the fall when I returned to work full-time. While I was there, I would check out some apartments I'd found online. I had my fingers crossed that one of them would work out, and I'd be able to move in the early fall. That would give the kids ample time to resume their school routine and Betsy and Ron ample time to settle into theirs. Melanie would also have her driver's license by then and could help Betsy get Josh where he needed to go.

As I pulled up in front of my old office and parked my car, a flood of memories washed over me. I remembered all the happy times when my bike club gathered in this lot. We would meet on Saturday mornings and ride our bikes for miles, then stop and get breakfast before we returned to load up our bikes and head back home. I remembered coming down from my office to the front entrance at lunchtime to meet up with colleagues for "a walk and talk." Of course, I also remembered sitting out front and waiting for Collin to pick me up and take me to the police station to identify David Hoffman; or David driving me back to my car after our time together at Byron's Bar. A lot had happened since then—good and bad—and today it felt like the good memories outweighed the bad.

Margie was waiting for me in her office, and we spent the morning going over the projects she'd assigned me. They were more involved and challenging than any I'd had in a long while, so I was looking forward to tackling them.

"Have you found a place to live yet?" she asked when we were done.

"I'm planning to look for an apartment this afternoon. There are several good prospects. I've decided to rent for now, so I can take my time looking for a place I want to buy."

"That sounds like a wise decision. There's no need to rush into anything, and you don't want to have to deal with too many new things at once." After a brief pause, she asked, "And how's your sister doing?"

"She's doing really well. She's in remission now, so she can focus on rebuilding her strength. She gets stronger every day. I think she is nearly back to herself physically, so it's the right time for me to leave."

"I'm sure they'll all miss you—and I know you'll miss them," Margie said sympathetically.

"Margie, I want to thank you for all you've done for me these past sixteen years. I couldn't have gotten through everything without your support, patience, and understanding."

"Well, it's been my pleasure to have you on our team, Lynne. And I fully understand how difficult and frustrating it's been for you to have to set your career goals aside—not once but twice—to deal with the challenges in your life. I want you to know how much I admire you for that."

"Thank you for saying that, Margie. I'm very excited at the prospect of this new chapter of my life—actually, excited and scared at the same time!"

"You're very talented and dedicated, Lynne. You'll do just fine."

After I left her office, I stopped to chat with a few of my old friends. I felt lucky to work for such a great company. It was amazing that I had friends here after all of these years. I felt especially grateful that Margie was still there. I also felt lucky to have such a good support system in place: Betsy and her family, the shack girls, Collin, Susan, and now my old friends from work. I knew I'd be okay—and I was looking forward eagerly to my next adventure.

CHAPTER 31

Spring 2018

ON SUNDAY MORNING, Josh came along with me when I drove Melanie to work. We decided to stay and have breakfast so she could show us how grown up she was. She walked us to our table and handed us our menus, just like she'd done it a million times already. Originally, Mr. Saunders had told Melanie she'd only be able to bus tables. But she proved so mature and responsible that he'd allowed her to waitress just a few days after she started.

Today was her big chance to show us her newly-acquired skills. Mr. Saunders watched her quite closely, but she handled everything beautifully, especially since Josh was trying to make it as difficult as possible for her. First, he complained that his fork wasn't clean even though it was, he asked for items not on the menu—and even snapped his fingers to summon her once. Thank heavens Mr. Saunders had known both Melanie and Josh since they were babies, so he knew what Josh was up to.

After Melanie brought us our food, Mr. Saunders approached us and asked how our service was. Even Josh was complimentary. "She did fine," he admitted.

"That's high praise coming from you, Josh, because I noticed how thoroughly you tested her," Mr. Saunders said with a chuckle.

"He did, didn't he?" I said with a laugh. "Josh can be a real pill."

We finished our breakfast, said good-bye to Melanie, and drove back to the farm. I dropped Josh off at the house, and then went over to the little house. Smitty, Callie, and Jo were there.

"Where have you been? We haven't seen you in over a week!" Callie demanded. "We've been waiting to hear how your date went."

"It wasn't really a date, just a visit with a friend," I said, trying to sound casual.

"Really?" Jo asked.

"Yeah, really," I replied, knowing I wasn't fooling anyone. "Those little goats are just darling. And the cheese is absolutely delicious."

"Well, if you don't have more to report next time you see him, maybe I'll go after him," Jo said. "He's very handsome and seems like a great guy."

"Are you coming to the shack today?" Smitty asked.

"No, I don't think so. I'm going to start sorting through my things and pack up what I won't be using for the rest of the summer."

"I'm so sad to think you're leaving," Jo said. "Who will I talk to late at night or share my breakfast with in the morning?"

"I thought you were going to talk Kellan into moving in. Once she gets the driving thing down, she should be able to get to and from the shack."

"If we're relying on her driving, it might be a while," Callie stated matter-of-factly.

"She could ride in with me until she gets her license, but regardless, it still won't be the same without you," Jo said in response.

We spent the better part of an hour chatting and reminiscing about some of our funnier moments over the past year or so. I looked around at these women and thought about how much I'd come to love and respect them. I would really miss them.

When I started going through my things at the little house, I realized I didn't have that much to sort after all. I'd left most of my belongings in storage, so what I had was mainly clothing. It was then I realized that while

I had a great life before coming back to the farm, I had not really felt settled.

When I finally finished, I was relieved to have everything organized— and one box I could check off on my to-do list. I sat down to work on the next item—an apartment. On Monday, I planned to drive back down to Chicago and continue my quest for the perfect place to live. None of the places I had looked at so far were what I wanted. Many of the photos online were deceiving, making the spaces look larger than they really were when you read the actual dimensions. Even at the little house, I was used to having some space, and most of the apartments I looked at were relatively small. But I knew if I kept looking, something good would pop up. I would just have to be patient, but I hoped it would pop up soon.

On Monday, I dropped Melanie off at the café and then drove to Chicago. In the morning, my realtor took me to look at two apartments, and one of them was actually quite nice. One of its best features was being located not too far from Collin's house. The realtor asked me if I wanted to get lunch, since I had time before our next appointment, but I begged off, saying I had to be on a conference call. I told the realtor I would meet up with her at the next apartment in the afternoon. I'd been consumed with curiosity, wondering what Collin's house looked like now, and I wanted to take a look.

As I drove down the street, I recalled many happy events and experiences I'd had while living there. And then, as I rounded the bend in the road, I could see my old house. My heart started pounding in my chest and my head got all fuzzy. I stopped my car right smack in the middle of the road— not pulling over to the side. The car behind me nearly collided with me because I stopped so abruptly. He honked, waited for me to get out of the way, and when I didn't, he glared at me as he drove around me.

I was simply paralyzed. Eventually, I was able to inch the car over to the side, and just sat and looked at the house. I'd been so stupid—not even considering the impact that seeing my old house might have on me. Feelings and memories I'd suppressed in anticipation of seeing Collin's house now overwhelmed me. I remembered starkly now why I'd left that house in the first place. I spotted Collin's house next to mine. But it was like there was an invisible barrier that kept me from getting there. It was so close, yet I knew I wasn't capable of getting any closer.

It wasn't like me to run away from a challenge—I'd proved that time and again. I'd taken on the rape and the pregnancy at great cost to myself and my happiness. But I'd left this house in order to get past those memories—and now here it was again, sixteen years later, and the memories still haunted me.

So I decided now was as good a time as any to face up to this unexpected challenge. I inched along the road until I was in front of my old house. I couldn't see Collin's truck in the driveway, so I figured he must be at work. There was no reason to stop other than to face my fears. I got out of my car and slowly walked up to my old front door. I stood there on the porch and remembered the night of the attack. I turned and looked at the handrail and ran my hand over it. I looked down the steps and remembered how I'd struggled to get down them to get to the lawn. I took each step slowly, and when I got to the last one, I stepped down and looked across the lawn to Collin's house. I remembered crawling along in terrible pain and blind with fear before reaching his door and banging on it for help. I had done that. I had, despite my horrendous state, managed to go for help. I had nothing to be ashamed of, or afraid of, anymore.

I walked over and sat down on Collin's back porch steps and thought about all those wonderful evenings at his house, sipping wine together and talking until well after dark. I hadn't walked away from Collin out of fear, but rather because I loved him. I knew it wasn't fair to drag him into the struggles I had to face then. Now he was giving me a second chance, and I resolved not to allow anything to mess that up.

CHAPTER 32

Spring 2018

FRIDAY NIGHT ROLLED around—time to get ready for my date with Collin. And again my personal fashionistas showed up to pick out what they thought I should wear. Betsy and Melanie had gone through my closet several times during the week, and Betsy had even pulled some items out of her closet for me to consider. Looking at them both, I said sarcastically, "No pressure, right?"

"What do you mean?" Melanie asked.

"Well, you guys put so much work and thought into this that it makes me feel a bit self-conscious about my looks."

"Don't be silly, Aunt Lynnie. You're one of the prettiest people I know."

"She's right," Betsy said. "You'd look good in anything, but we just want to be sure you accentuate your best features."

I tried on at least ten different outfits and modeled each one of them. Each time they would size me up and provide a critique. Finally, we found the right combination of dress, shoes, jewelry, and hairstyle.

When I was all dressed, I said, "Well, do I pass muster?"

"What is muster?" asked Melanie.

"Something old people say," I said.

"Well, actually, you look absolutely beautiful!" Melanie exclaimed.

"Wow, that is really saying something! Talk about a confidence bump! Thank you."

"It's nearly time," Betsy said, and then looking at Melanie added, "We need to take off before he gets here."

"Oh," Melanie sighed forlornly. "I was hoping we could stay and see his face when he sees her."

"Not tonight," Betsy replied. "Let's let them have that moment without us."

Melanie gave me a kiss on the cheek. "Have a good time, Aunt Lynnie."

And with that, they gathered up the clothes and jewelry they'd brought over to the little house and left.

I was dressed and ready to go. Nothing to focus on now but how much I was looking forward to seeing Collin. I paced, sat down, and then paced some more. Even though it was only a few minutes, it seemed like an eternity until he arrived. I heard his truck pull up and then the knock at the door. My heart was pounding as I opened it. He smiled broadly and simply said, "Hi." I could feel my face flush, and I was sure it flushed some more when I realized I was behaving like a teenager on her first date.

"Hi back," I said.

"You look very pretty."

"Why, thank you."

"Did you have your stylists helping you again?"

"Yes, as a matter of fact, I did."

"Well, they're a good team."

Then, as I regained my composure and remembered that I was over thirty, I said, "Yeah, I feel pretty good tonight."

"It shows," he said with the same smile still on his face.

We drove into town to a small restaurant that was humming with activity. The place was packed and very noisy. We were able to get a small table in the back where it was not quite so loud, but we still had to sit close together to hear each other. I could feel his breath on my neck as he leaned in so I could hear him. Every time he laughed and spoke to me, I felt a warm buzz. I even shivered once, and he asked me if I was cold. "No," I said, feeling embarrassed, "I'm good." What I wanted to say was—I'm actually rather hot!

We ordered several small dishes to share as we talked, laughed, and ate for several hours. It was just like when we used to talk over dinner in Collin's kitchen and then afterward on his back porch with a glass of good wine. It was like no time had passed since those days so long ago.

"Do you remember those evenings on your porch?" I asked.

"Yes, I remember them very well," he said, smiling fondly at the memory.

I started to laugh before I said, "Do you remember talking about the different types of businesses you were interested in investing in? I would never have guessed you would end up with a goat farm. Would you?"

"Well, actually, I'm not sure it was that much farther afield than any of the other opportunities I was considering back then."

We continued on for another hour or so until Collin said, "I'm so sorry to end our beautiful evening together, but I need to get on the road before it gets much later. Will you do this with me again soon?" he asked, leaning in close.

"Yes, I would like that," I replied softly.

And then leaning in even closer he said, "Lynne, I would like very much to kiss you. Would that be okay?"

I looked up at him, and without answering, I kissed him. It was a long, slow, soft kiss and as I pulled away I could feel his hand come up to the small of my back as he brought me towards him to kiss me again. Then he said, "I've wanted to kiss you for nearly sixteen years, and I must say, it was well worth the wait."

I smiled at him, and when I looked into his eyes, I could feel my throat tighten and my eyes fill with tears. I looked down quickly since my reaction took me by surprise, and I felt embarrassed. He was sensitive enough not to say anything, but I know he saw how much he'd moved me. He stood up and retrieved my coat. I gathered up my purse and when I got up, he pulled me toward him for a gentle hug. "Do you want to come with me?" he whispered.

I looked up to see if he was kidding, and I could see by the expression on his face that he wasn't. "Oh, Collin, I . . ."

"I know, I know. But I just couldn't help myself. I guess I'll just have to wait until I see you again."

"Does that mean I'll see you soon?"

"I hope so. Would you be willing to repeat this evening again next Friday? My routine has been to drive to Pasture Prime every Friday after work, and now I have this nice stop along the way to look forward to."

"Yes—and I'm glad I can be a stop for you," I said with a laugh.

The week whizzed by, and suddenly the weekend arrived. As promised, Collin came back, but he had to delay our date until Saturday afternoon, because something had come up at Pasture Prime that he needed to attend to. I'd been so looking forward to Friday night, but my disappointment was tempered by the idea of seeing him Saturday instead. I had suggested—if he had the time—that we plan for a picnic, and include Betsy, Ron, and the kids. He agreed, and that Saturday afternoon, he arrived.

It was only a short drive down to the river where we set up our picnic and built a fire to cook on. The day was perfect—not a cloud in the sky and only a few mosquitos. We had more than enough food even though everyone was hungry. There is something about a picnic and eating outdoors that makes the food taste better, so we ate more than our fill. Melanie, being Melanie, had brought along a book, so as soon as she finished her dinner, she found a quiet place by the river to sit and read. Josh, being Josh, found sticks to poke into the fire that resulted in several warnings from his parents about getting too close to the fire.

Ron and Collin got along great. They talked about their farms and the challenges of trying to bring a crop—or in Collin's case, a product—to market. Collin asked Ron lots of questions, and Ron enjoyed the role of mentor, graciously giving advice. Betsy watched me watch Collin, and every once in a while I would catch her at it—and she would break into a great big smile. She was clearly very happy for me.

After a while, Betsy and Ron took the kids down to the river to try to catch some fish. Collin and I watched them all in amusement. They were so funny together. Josh kept flipping his rod around with the hook attached, and Ron had to work hard not to lose his temper. The fourth time Josh did it, he got his hook caught in Ron's pant leg and even Betsy couldn't keep from laughing. Melanie looked back at us to be sure we could see what was going on and rolled her eyes.

"They're great, aren't they?" I said to Collin.

"Yes, they are pretty great," he replied, wrapping his arms around me. We'd gotten comfortable on the blanket with Collin sitting behind me so I could lean my back against his chest. We sat there together silently for several minutes, absorbed in the moment.

Betsy came back and sat down next to us, watching Ron and the kids fishing. She said, "I'm so grateful for my little family. I couldn't have picked a better man than Ron, and we love those kids so much. You know, I think that was the hardest part about being sick. I worried about missing these precious moments. I think I cherish them more now because of it."

I reached over and squeezed her hand. "Well, you are pretty great, too. I couldn't imagine a world without you, Betsy."

Just then Josh came running up the hill yelling "Mom? Mom? Can I roast a marshmallow? Fishing is *sooo* boring!"

"Yes, but you'll have to find a stick to roast it on first," she told him. So Josh went off to find a stick. A few minutes later he was back, stick in hand, and Betsy helped him push the marshmallows onto it. Betsy, Collin, and I continued chatting and watched as Josh proceeded to let the marshmallows catch fire and blow out the flames, until he gave up and just kept poking the stick around in the fire instead.

Before too long, Ron and Melanie joined us, having been unsuccessful in catching any fish, and we all sat by the fire until the sun went down, laughing, telling stories, and of course, roasting marshmallows. But it wasn't long before the mosquitos got to be too much. So we gathered up our picnic things, loaded ourselves into our respective vehicles, and headed back to the farm.

"What a great family," Collin said. "It's nice that you and Betsy are so close and that you have such a great relationship with the kids."

"I know, I *am* very lucky. And while I'm very sorry that it was Betsy's illness that brought me here, the time I've spent with them has been a gift to me. They count me now as a member of their family, and I will forever be grateful for that."

"Well, it's easy to see you are one of them," Collin said matter-of-factly as he pulled up to the little house. He got out and walked around to help me out of the truck. Then he wrapped his arms around my shoulders, pulled me in, and kissed me. "I hope that was okay," he said. "I've wanted to do that all day and decided now was my chance."

"Actually, you didn't give me much of a choice," I replied, feigning dismay.

"Did you mind, Lynne?" he asked, looking concerned.

"As a matter of fact, no, I did not," I said as I stood up on tiptoe and kissed him back. "I didn't mind it at all," I said afterward, savoring the kiss.

Collin retrieved the picnic baskets from the back of his truck and brought them into the house, placing them on the kitchen table. I'd just started unpacking them when Jo came in.

"Oooh, that looks tasty," Jo said, eyeing the pie I was still holding.

"It is very tasty," Collin replied. "In fact, I'd like another piece. Would that be okay?"

"Of course, that's okay. Would you like a slice too, Jo?"

"Well, now that you're twisting my arm, I guess so."

The three of us sat around the kitchen table talking and eating pie. Collin and Jo got along well. They had a similar sense of humor, and one could outdo the other with funny stories about how they each grew up, their love of pie—they both loved peach pie in particular—and the long, languorous summers they'd enjoyed as kids.

After a while, Collin pushed his chair back and said, "Well, it's getting late, and I'd better go. I didn't check into the hotel before I came over. I hope they still have a room for me."

"If you need to, you could stay here," I said. And then hastily added, "I could make up a bed for you on the couch."

"If they don't have a room for me, then I may be back," he said with a wink. "It's been a long day, and I could really use a hot shower and a nice soft bed."

As I walked him out to his truck I said, "Are you headed home in the morning or would you have time to meet for breakfast? I could meet you at the café. Melanie works there, and I usually take her into town. We could let her wait on us, if you're up to it."

"That sounds great. What time should I plan to meet you there?"

"How about six?" I said, cringing at the early hour.

"Six is fine," he said without hesitation.

AT FIVE-THIRTY, MELANIE and I were in the car, ready for our drive into town.

Out of the blue, Melanie said, "I like him, Aunt Lynne."

I almost asked her who she was referring to, when it dawned on me she could only be talking about Collin.

"He's cute too."

"He is pretty cute, isn't he," I said.

"He likes you a lot. He looks at you all the time. Even when you're not talking, he watches you. Even if you're just listening to someone talk, he is focused on you."

"Well, that's very observant of you," I said, feeling embarrassed.

"It's not hard to see. And I think Mom and Dad like him, if that matters."

"Yes, it does matter. Have they said they like him?"

"They like that he seems to make you happy. Mom said it's been a very long time since she's seen you this happy."

"Well, it has been a very long time since I've had a guy in my life," I said. "It *is* nice."

We pulled up to the café and Melanie hopped out. "Thank you for driving me," she said. "Are you coming in?"

"Yes, Collin is going to join me here, and we expect you to wait on us."

"Great!" she said with excitement. "I'll go get clocked in and then get ready for you. See you inside."

After I parked, I entered the café and sat in Melanie's area. She came over quickly and offered me coffee, which I gratefully accepted while I waited for Collin.

The door jingled and in he came. He was all smiles. He sauntered over and stood across from me, waving to Melanie as he sat down. She came right over.

"Good morning, ladies," he said.

"Would you like a cup of coffee?" Melanie asked.

"I would love one," he replied.

"How did you sleep?" I asked.

"Like a brick. I took a long hot shower, brushed my teeth, and before I could get the covers pulled over me, I was out cold."

"I didn't realize you were so tired. You should have told me, and I wouldn't have suggested that we go on a picnic."

"Are you crazy? I worked extra hard so I could get done most of what I needed to do so I could go with you on the picnic. It was the reward for my efforts," he said enthusiastically.

"You didn't get all of the work done that you needed to at the dairy?"

"Not quite. I'm going back there before I head home."

"I'm sorry about that," I said.

Melanie came back to take our order. We ordered our breakfasts, and Collin also ordered a lunch to take with him, to tide him over during his trip to Pasture Prime and then home. The food was delicious. Melanie did an excellent job of waiting on us, as well as getting Collin's lunch packed and ready for the road.

"Excellent service," Collin said smiling at Melanie. "You are perhaps the best waitress I've ever had."

Melanie blushed and said, "Thank you."

We stepped outside the café and stood there for a minute in the brisk spring air and bright sunlight, reluctant to part so soon.

"Would you have time for a short walk to the shack?" I asked.

"Sure, that sounds like a nice idea. Let me put my lunch in the truck first," he replied.

There were no sidewalks, but the shoulder of the road was wide enough so we could walk against the traffic—at least what traffic there was that early on a Sunday morning. Several pickups and a tractor passed us. Everyone waved, even if they didn't know who we were. Collin reached over and took my hand in his and squeezed it as we talked and walked to the edge of town to the shack.

"Remind me again how you got connected to the shack and the shack girls," he said.

"Well, my mother was a frustrated artist, and while she dearly loved my dad, Betsy, and me, she needed something of her own. The shack came up for sale, and she asked for a loan from Dad to buy it. He told her she didn't need a loan because his money was her money, but she insisted on a loan anyway. She even had the bank draw up the papers."

"She sounds a bit like you."

"What do you mean?"

"I could see you doing that. You are a bit stubborn, you know."

"Well, I think she wanted something that was truly hers. Something she could say she had done by herself. She bought the shack and spent several years fixing it up, all the while pursuing her painting. She was a very talented artist. so she would sell her paintings at craft fairs and art exhibits to pay the mortgage on the shack as well as for improvements. In that way, she was able to renovate it, studio by studio. As each one was finished, she would take on a new tenant. It took several years, but by the time Betsy and I were both in school, she had leased most of the space and was spending most of her days there."

When we arrived, I walked him around inside and showed him where my mother had worked—the space where Betsy worked now. "Betsy took over for Mom after she passed away. We agreed years ago that any money that came in from the shack would be reinvested as a memorial to her. So far, we've been able to make some improvements to the building and property. Right now, we have six artists, including Betsy."

"What's your special talent?"

"Oh, I don't really have one in particular, but sometimes I like to play with clay. Smitty taught me, and she often tells me she's frustrated with me for not being more serious about my work. But I don't see myself as having any talent. It's more like therapy for me, plus it gives me an opportunity to spend time with the girls."

Collin walked from studio to studio as I told him about each of our current artists, their specialties, and more stories about the shack. He seemed genuinely interested. I picked up the materials I'd come for and bagged them up to take with me. Collin carried them back to town. By the time we got back on the road, there was more traffic, so we had to walk single file back to the café—and I regretted that since it robbed us of more time to talk.

After Collin put the bags in my car for me, he asked, "When will I get to see you again?"

"You're welcome to come anytime," I said.

"How about you come to Chicago to visit me next time?"

I thought for a minute about coming to his house, and how I would have to fight through my feelings to go there. He studied my face as I remained silent, and apparently my apprehension showed.

"Lynne, is that a problem?"

"No, actually it's not a problem. I was just thinking about it."

"I'm so sorry. That was very insensitive of me. I stupidly forgot about that aspect of your meeting up with me there."

"No, it's good. I'd like to come visit you at your house. Maybe one day next week when I'm apartment hunting," I said cheerfully.

"Are you sure? What happened to you in that house was horrific. You have every right to feel the way you do." He paused thoughtfully, and then added, "Maybe you could come to Pasture Prime? Would you consider spending the weekend there?"

"Assuming everything is okay with Betsy, I would love that," I said with a sense of relief.

Collin leaned down and kissed me tenderly. I could tell he was remembering how damaged I'd been after the attack. I was mad at myself for not hiding my feelings better and unwittingly evoking his pity. I leaned in and kissed him back so he knew I wasn't frail, weak, or afraid. I was a strong woman. I hit the mark. He pulled back and looked down at me in surprise. "Wow," was all he said before he got into his truck.

I waved at him as he drove away and thought about how happy I was now. Happy to have him in my life—but more importantly, to have found myself again.

CHAPTER 33

Summer 2018

ON SUNDAY MORNING, Sam noticed that there was a water spot on the ceiling next to where the chimney for the glass furnace exited the shack. She started down the hall to the ceramics studio and called out to Smitty.

"Hey, I think we have a leak in the roof. Do you have a minute to check it out with me?"

"Sure, let me clean off my hands, and I'll meet you outside," Smitty said, dipping her hands in a bowl of water.

Sam was standing outside, shielding her eyes from the sun to get a better view of the roof as Smitty approached.

"Do you see anything?" Smitty asked.

"Not yet," she replied, walking toward the front of the shack to change her angle of vision. It was then that a car pulled up and a man got out. When she recognized him, Sam turned around and asked Smitty if she had her phone with her.

Fumbling around in her apron pocket, Smitty found her phone. "Yes."

Pointing at the man, Sam said, "Be prepared to call the police." Addressing him, she said sharply, "What do you want?"

"Ladies, how are you?" David said, ignoring Sam's tone.

"You're not allowed here. You better get back in your car and leave, or we'll call the police," Smitty said.

"I'm not breaking any laws. I'm standing here on the sidewalk, which is public property, speaking politely to two rather rude women. Nothing illegal about that."

"You have no business being here —and you are not allowed to be anywhere near Lynne."

"Actually, I'm here to see Betsy. Would you tell her I'm here and that I need to speak to her?" he said firmly.

"No, I don't think I will," Sam said.

"I think you will because what I have to say is important to her," he said, this time with a bit of frost in his voice.

Just at that moment, Betsy came out onto the porch. "What do you want?" she asked.

"Everyone here is so pleasant," David said sarcastically. "I've come to talk, and I'm not sure you'd want these ladies here for the discussion."

"You have nothing to say to me, and I'm not going to tell you anything about Lynne, so you should leave immediately," Betsy said.

"I don't want to talk about Lynne."

"Well, we have nothing to talk about," Betsy said as she turned to go back inside, when David said, "I'm here to talk to you about Melanie."

Betsy's stomach lurched. "What do you mean?"

"You know what I mean," he said.

"No, I don't know."

"Do you really want these women to hear what I have to say to you?" he asked.

Both Smitty and Sam looked at Betsy in alarm, and then at David. They could see the fear in Betsy's face, and Smitty started dialing her phone saying, "I'm calling the police."

"You may want to wait until after I talk with Betsy. She may like to exercise some control over how Melanie finds out about her real parents. You know, she's getting old enough so that a judge may bypass you entirely and let Melanie make that decision herself."

Betsy gripped the handrail of the porch and said, "What exactly do you want?"

"I want my daughter," he said emphatically, "and I think she'd like to know the truth about who her parents are."

"You are not allowed to get near her," Betsy said.

"Well, that's not true. I'm not allowed to go near her mother. The court did not rule on whether or not I can approach Melanie."

"The court has ruled that you have no rights, and I will get another order to keep you from getting near her," Betsy said, the terror in her voice apparent.

Ignoring her words and stepping even closer, he demanded, "You'll tell her, or I will. She doesn't need to know all the details, but I think she has the right to know who her father is."

Smitty looked closely at Betsy. She could see from her face that he was speaking the truth. Standing between the two of them, and trying to deescalate the situation, she said quietly to David, "We will call the police if you don't leave."

Addressing Betsy he said, "I'll be back tomorrow at noon—and you better have told Melanie who I am, or I will." Then with a slight softening in his tone, he said, "I think it would be better coming from you rather than from someone else. Don't you?" After a pause, he repeated, "I'll be back tomorrow at noon. And you should tell Lynne to stay away. If she's here, I won't give you another chance." Then he turned around and headed to his car.

Once his car was out of sight, Betsy slumped down onto the bench. Sam sat down next to her, and Smitty joined them.

"Are you okay, Betsy?" Smitty said.

Betsy didn't talk, she just nodded her head.

"Is it true, what he said?" Sam asked.

Betsy nodded her head again, and Smitty put her arms around her as Betsy started to cry.

AS RON'S TRUCK pulled up in the driveway, Betsy could feel her heart start to race. Smitty and Sam had taken Melanie and Josh out for pizza so Betsy would be able to talk with Ron about what had happened with David that afternoon. Betsy could see he was happy but tired. She didn't want to tell him what had happened, but she knew she had to. Before she could even speak, Betsy wrapped her arms around him and her eyes filled with tears. Ron whispered in her ear, holding her tight. "What's wrong, Betsy?"

Betsy told him all about the confrontation with David, and when she was done, Ron sat down on the kitchen stool and didn't utter a word for a very long time. "Does Lynne know he was here?"

"No."

"Don't you think we should tell her?"

"I don't know. I just don't know what to do. I did contact Lynne's attorney this afternoon, and he's working on an order of protection to keep David from having anything to do with Melanie. But I'm afraid that even with a court order, he'll either ignore it and get to Melanie himself, or he'll get someone else to tell her. I don't know how we can stop him. I think we need to be the ones to tell her before she hears it from anyone else." Betsy paused to take a breath.

"David told me this afternoon that I didn't need to tell Melanie all the details, so I don't think he intends to tell her about the attack and being in prison—why would he tell that part? But he was quite clear he wanted her to know that he was her father and that he would tell her if we didn't."

"Well, isn't he a gentleman," Ron blurted out. "Of course the son-of-a-bitch doesn't want her to know what he did. Betsy, if I see him I, I'll kill him!" Ron said through clenched teeth. "Getting orders of protection are going to do nothing. This man has no sense of what's right or wrong and doesn't care who he hurts to get what he wants. He's a psychopath. He's going to continue to be a threat to us as long as we're all alive. We're going to have to tell Lynne."

"Tell me what?" I said happily, as I entered the kitchen. But then, after looking more closely at their faces, I knew something was terribly wrong. "What happened?" I asked. "Tell me what happened."

Betsy sat down in one of the kitchen chairs. Patting the one next to her she said, "Why don't you sit down? We need to talk, and this is going to take some time."

As Betsy talked, I could feel myself sinking lower and lower in my chair. I'd been so unbelievably happy only a few minutes ago, and now here I was, back down in the depths of despair, having to deal with David Hoffman yet again. Betsy kept talking but I wasn't listening anymore. I was completely lost in the thoughts inside my head. It had finally dawned on me that there was no getting around this problem.

I'd been horribly mistaken to think I could pretend the rape ended when I woke up the morning after, that by giving up the baby for adoption I had concealed her beginnings, that his going to prison meant I was done with him. He was never going to go away. He was going to be with me for the rest of my life, and I'd been a fool to think otherwise. I'd been blinded by my desire to get past this horrific event by concealing what had happened. I'd been so greedy that I thought Betsy and Ron would be the perfect solution—I would see this little girl grow up and at the same time make Betsy and Ron happy too. But in the process I had risked the chance at happiness for that little girl. She would hate me and herself now. I'd also dealt a devastating blow to Betsy and Ron—and even Josh. I'd been so stupid.

Betsy's voice broke into my thoughts. "Lynne, Ron and I haven't had a chance to talk about this yet, but I don't see that there's any way to avoid telling Melanie. First, we need to talk to a child psychologist and get some professional advice. We can hold David off for a few days while we work out the best way to handle this. But ultimately, if we are careful about how we explain it, I think Melanie will be able to understand. She is a bright, strong, and kind young woman. She has known her entire life that she was adopted and that we are so are grateful she came into our lives. She knows she is loved. I think she'll understand why we didn't tell her about her origins, and she'll also understand that you made a tremendous sacrifice for her."

"Oh Betsy, I'm so sorry about all of this. I should have known that David Hoffman would somehow find out I was pregnant. I shouldn't have dragged you two into this. Since I saw him a few weeks ago, when he implied that he knew about a child, I've thought long and hard about the impact this situation could have on Melanie. I've also thought about a wide range of potential scenarios, and I feel like I'm out of my depth. I agree that it's critical we consult a psychologist.

"And while Melanie is a bright, strong, and kind person, she's also very young and vulnerable. She's still trying to figure out who she is and, even with professional advice, this news might devastate her. The world as she knows it will be gone—who she knows herself to be, what she's always known about where she comes from, and even who we are. We need to find someone who can help us determine how best to tell her—and be sure we have a support system in place. She's going to need someone she can go to who has no part in any of this other than to serve as her advocate. Someone she can trust and who can be objective."

Betsy reached over and squeezed my hand. "You're right, Lynnie. You're absolutely right. But David told me he's coming back to the shack tomorrow, and he wants an answer. Either we tell her or he will."

"Stop right there, Betsy. We're going to do this on our terms—not his," Ron said. "We can keep her close to home until we can get everything arranged. I can keep Melanie with me. She can help me in the fields. I'll keep an eye on her every minute until we have something figured out."

"What about Josh? If you take Melanie, our Josh will be upset that he's not included," Betsy said.

"Well, he can come with me too. I can keep them both busy until we get this worked out." Ron said.

"We can tell Mr. Saunders that we need her for a week or two to fill in at the farm. And I could fill in for her at the café for the next couple of weeks if he needs the help," I said. "It's been quite a while, but I'm sure I'll quickly get the hang of it again, and I bet Mr. Saunders would understand."

"We need to take as much control over the situation as we possibly can," Betsy said. "The challenge will be how we make these changes without setting off any alarms."

"Maybe we could include the kids in the problem-solving process so they feel they're helping us come up with the solutions," I suggested. "If you tell Betsy in front of Melanie that you need extra help out in the fields for a few days, she'll offer to help. Then Josh will say, 'No fair,' and you can tell him to come along too."

"I think that could work," Betsy said.

Just then, we heard Smitty's car pull up, and Josh came bursting in through the back door.

"Hey, how was your evening out?" Ron asked.

"Great," Josh said. "Smitty and Sam took us to the bar, and there was live music. They danced, and I got to play the pinball machine!"

"What?" Betsy asked.

"Hey, it was all good," Sam said.

"Even Sam danced," Melanie said.

"That must have been something," Betsy said, hugging each of her children in turn.

Ron said, "Why don't the two of you go get ready for bed?" And to Smitty and Sam, "And how about a beer for you two party animals?"

Betsy wrapped her arm around Melanie's shoulders, looked over at me, and then smiled. "Let's head up to bed, you two."

A few minutes later, after the kids were settled in their rooms, Betsy came back downstairs. "Melanie's reading, and Josh hadn't even put his head down on his pillow before he was out cold."

"Why don't we go and sit on the porch," Ron suggested.

When everyone was outside, Betsy closed the door to the house behind her, and sat down next to Ron on the swing. Smitty, Sam, and I leaned on the railing.

Sam was the first to break the silence. "We're making some assumptions that we know what this is about."

"Well, I would guess you're probably right," I said. "You already know I became pregnant from the rape. You know I gave the baby up for adoption, and now you know who adopted her."

Ron put his arm around Betsy and held her close. "We'd been trying to have a baby for years, and we'd just about given up. Then Lynne called and said she'd decided what to do about her baby. We'd never even dared to think she would consider us, until she said, "'I've found a wonderful family for my baby. I want you and Betsy to take her.'"

"Lynne gave us a gift beyond what we could ever have imagined," Betsy said. "She'd gone through the most terrible ordeal imaginable; and then when she discovered she was pregnant, she moved far away to conceal the pregnancy so she could give the child the best possible start in life. She did all this alone. She worked through a very difficult decision, one that would impact her for the rest of her life. Her only goal was to do the right thing for that little girl. I am, to this day, in awe of my sister and her tremendous strength." Betsy looked at Lynne with an expression of pure love.

"Her decision to choose us to be Melanie's parents has been one of our greatest joys. We feel blessed every single day by that little girl. She has brought so much happiness into our lives. We are eternally grateful to you, Lynnie," Ron said, placing his hand on his heart.

The porch was silent, and then Lynne looked at them both sadly. "Over the past few months, since David has been out of prison, I've wondered if I did make the right decision for her—or if I was just being selfish. I knew keeping her would not be an option, for what are now obvious reasons. The question is, did I put her at risk by subconsciously wanting to keep her close to me? I promise you that was not my intention. It didn't even occur to me."

"You were right to give her to Betsy and Ron," Sam said. "What if someone else had adopted her and David found her. Who knows what would have happened then? You're also forgetting about the wonderful gift you have given to Melanie—the gift of Betsy and Ron as her parents."

Betsy looking intently said, "You did the right thing Lynne. We would not imagine our lives without her."

Ron, who had been pacing back and forth stopped and said, "You did what was best for all of us, Lynnie. We're not dealing with a normal human being. This man is evil. This is not your fault, nor is it Betsy's or mine. He is the cause of this. Not anyone else. He shouldn't have known about her. I still can't imagine how he found out."

Smitty weighed in next. "I know I don't know all of the background details and issues that are involved here, but I think he would have come to look for you, Lynne, with or without a child involved. He doesn't seem to understand the sheer magnitude of his wrongdoing. He should be ashamed and penitent, but he's not. He has no humanity. You're not dealing with a normal person here. You only have a few days to figure out how to handle this, and none of you should be placing blame on yourselves. We need to focus on Melanie's safety and happiness. I will do anything I can to help, and you know the rest of the shack girls feel the same way. We will do anything we can to help you."

"You're entirely right, Smitty, and we will probably need your help, especially if he comes back to the shack tomorrow," Ron said. "Betsy and I will make the decisions because we're Melanie's parents, but the clock is ticking. Speaking for myself, I could use all the advice and help you all can give. You can bet that Melanie is the only thing on David Hoffman's mind right now. He's focused on her—and we need to do the same."

Then Betsy, looked up at us with the eyes of a lion and said, "Melanie is our daughter, and we were prepared from the start to keep this information from her. I had begun to think we no longer had that choice, but now more than ever, I believe that was and is the right thing to do. We decided to protect this child from that man, and we will just have to figure out the best way to continue to make that happen. What we need is time. We can't get this resolved by noon tomorrow, that's for sure. We'll just have to keep her close to us, where we can protect her, until we figure it out. David Hoffman is going to have to come to terms with us, our timeline, and our decisions."

"He's not going to take to the idea of waiting. We'll all have to be on our toes," Smitty said.

"There has to be something we can do to stop him, but we need to remember that this son of a bitch is dangerous," Sam added.

"We all need to be careful and watchful, and protect each other," I said. "He frightens me, and I worry about what he might do."

"You could contact your attorney," Betsy suggested, "and also ask Officer Curtis what advice she might have about who to contact and what help might be available to people in a quandary like ours. I know we'll figure something out, even if it ultimately means we have to tell Melanie about her father—and maybe that is something we should do regardless of David Hoffman's threats. But I think we need to explore all our options first. And we need some time for that."

Smitty went over to Betsy and kissed her on the forehead. "We're here, and we'll do everything we can to help. Just call us."

Betsy got up and gave Smitty a hug. "I know, and I love you all for it."

CHAPTER 34

Summer 2018

THE NEXT MORNING, I went to the café in Melanie's place. The scenario had unfolded just as Betsy had predicted. At breakfast, Ron told Betsy he needed more help with the farm and wished he had someone to help him by driving the tractor. Melanie, overhearing this, immediately offered to help after she got off work from the café—at which point I jumped in and offered to fill in at the café so she could go help Ron first thing.

Melanie called Mr. Saunders, and he was fine with the idea of my taking her place for a week or so. And Josh—being Josh—bellowed loudly that it wasn't fair he was being excluded, and besides he had proved before that he could do the work. He demanded that he be allowed to work with Ron too. All was going according to plan.

Mr. Saunders showed me around the café, and soon everything fell into place—it felt just like my high school days. People coming into the café were surprised to see me, and several said they missed Melanie, but all went well and I was enjoying being there.

I'd been working about a couple of hours and was very busy with several customers when the door jingled and in walked David Hoffman. I felt an immediate sense of panic, and my stomach lurched as he looked at me. I could see he was surprised to see me as well. He smiled and said hello to Mr. Saunders, and they chatted like old friends. Then Mr. Saunders walked him over to me. It was all I could do not to run.

"Lynne, I want to introduce you to one of our best customers. This is Mr. Samuelson. He'll be sitting in your section at his regular table. He's one of Melanie's regulars."

I felt sick to my stomach. David was "one of Melanie's regulars"? How long had he known about Melanie, and how long had he been coming here? I could only assume that all this time David had been meeting with Melanie and "grooming" her. He was making her feel comfortable as he got ready to pounce. It took all of my strength to keep from reaching out and attacking him. I wanted to kill him. He was putting Melanie in danger and I wouldn't stand for that. David was a predator, and this morning I was his prey. He would show me no mercy, so I needed to be strong. I couldn't walk away and I couldn't avoid him. I had to face him head on, and I resolved to do it.

"It's nice to meet you," I said, trying to sound normal.

David extended his hand to shake mine, but I was holding a coffee pot in my right hand so I just nodded in acknowledgement as I said, "Let me show you to your table, Mr. Samuelson."

I walked David back to his table and waited for him to sit. "Would you like a cup of coffee?"

David, smiling, said through clenched teeth, "Where is my little Melanie this morning?"

I felt ill when I heard him say, "my little Melanie," so I had to force myself to focus and stay strong. I replied tonelessly, "She wasn't feeling well. I think she has the flu. We're all hoping she'll be well and back at work soon. What can I get you this morning?"

David said, not smiling now, "I better see her tomorrow when I come in."

"Just coffee then?" I asked.

"Bring me toast and two scrambled eggs with a glass of orange juice."

I started picking up his menu when he grabbed my arm and squeezed it tightly. "I better see her tomorrow," he hissed with a clear threat in his voice.

"Or what?" I said calmly.

At that moment, Mr. Saunders approached us. "How's it going here?"

This timely interruption gave me an opportunity to leave. While David and Mr. Saunders made small talk, I continued waiting on my other tables, dreading going back to his. I avoided looking at him and I was grateful that the café was busy. I'd have been very frightened if we'd been alone, because I knew he was beyond angry and capable of anything.

When David's order was ready I brought it to his table and said, "Here you go, Mr. Hoffman," when I realized I should have said Samuelson—"or should I say Samuelson? Sorry about that. May I top off your coffee for you?"

"You tell your sister that Melanie better be here tomorrow."

"Oh, Mr. Samuelson"—I enjoyed jerking him around by calling him by his fake name—"she'd like nothing better than for Melanie to be well, but sometimes these things take time, you know."

"She better be here," he said, raising his voice, and Mr. Saunders looked up to see what was going on. Collecting himself now, David said in a loud, friendly voice so Mr. Saunders could hear, "That would be great. Thank you, Lynne."

I poured him another cup of coffee and walked away from his table. My knees were shaking, but I was determined not to let him get to me and to keep control of the situation. Within a few minutes, he'd eaten his breakfast and got up to leave. He walked past me brusquely without saying another word. When he went to pay Mr. Saunders at the cash register, I heard Mr. Saunders ask him with a note of concern in his voice, "Was everything alright this morning?"

"Just delicious, as always," David said with his phony charm.

CHAPTER 35

Summer 2018

A LITTLE BEFORE noon, just as he'd promised, David showed up at the shack. He got out of his car and just stood in front on the sidewalk. Sam and Callie were sitting on the porch sipping their cups of coffee. They'd been waiting for him.

"Good afternoon, ladies," he called out.

"Good afternoon to you too," Callie called back in a cheery voice.

Then they just watched each other silently for several seconds. Finally, David, irate when he realized they weren't going to get Betsy for him, called out in an angry, demanding voice, "Tell Betsy I'm here to talk with her."

Sam walked down the steps and said calmly, "Betsy is not here today. She's not feeling well."

As he came closer to Sam, his face became contorted with anger and it was clear he was not listening. "Tell her I'm here!"

"Are you hard of hearing?" Sam said, stepping closer to him in turn. "She's not here today."

David was heating up, and he was now only a few feet from Sam. Callie decided to draw his attention away from Sam. "She's not here! We can't make her materialize if she isn't here."

Clenching his fists tightly as he held them at his side, he glared at Callie. "You tell her to come out here right now, or I'll cause problems she will definitely not like."

"Are you threatening us?" Sam asked.

"I'm warning you."

Callie called out again, "You need to leave or I'll call the police."

"You won't do it. You want to keep this little secret . . . but go ahead! I would be more than happy to explain the whole story to the cops and anyone else who shows up to witness this sideshow."

Sam, standing only two arm-lengths away from him, said in a low, gravelly voice, "You won't get her no matter what, so feel free to do whatever you need to do."

At that, David grabbed Sam by the arm. "Listen, you old bitch. You tell Betsy she better be here tomorrow or I'll take matters into my own hands. There's nothing that will stop me. I want my daughter."

"Get your hands off her! Get your hands off her this minute, or I'll shoot you in the head," Callie said, pointing a gun at him.

"Shoot him, Callie. We can claim self-defense."

Smitty, hearing the shouting, came outside to see what was going on. "Let's all calm down," she said.

David dropped his hand, and Sam stepped away before breaking into a laugh. "You have fucked with the wrong 'old bitches.' Call the police, Callie."

David held up both hands and started backing away. "You better tell Betsy what I said." Then he walked off and got into his car.

Callie and Smitty raced down to Sam. "Are you okay?"

"I'll have a few bruises, but nothing worth worrying about," she said, rubbing her arm. "I don't like the idea of Betsy or Lynne alone at any time. Ron is sticking close to Melanie. A couple of us should be at the farm and at least one person at the café when Lynne is there."

Callie said, "Between all of us, we can make sure someone is there at all times to keep an eye on them. While Ron's busy with the farm work and keeping the kids close, we should watch to see who's coming and going. We'll have to be very careful though—we don't want to raise any red flags for Melanie and Josh. We could stay at the little house. That would give us a good vantage point to monitor any unusual goings-on at the big house. If we take turns we can make it work. I bet Jo would go to the café with Lynne."

"We'll have to work in twos," Callie added. "I don't want there to be even the slightest chance of him catching one of us alone. We know how violent he can be, and I think he's feeling rather desperate right now, which makes him even more dangerous. Had I not been here and had my gun, I think he might have really hurt you, Sam."

Smitty looked down at the gun in Callie's hand. "Sam and I know how to use a gun. Callie, you clearly know how to use a gun. I would like there to always be at least one person at the farm who knows how to handle a gun—and I think we should tell Betsy, Ron and Lynne that he was here today."

Sam said, "How long do you think we'll need to keep this up? The son of a bitch is not going to stop because of any court order."

They all stood silently, thinking about what she'd said.

"Well, we'll have to do it until we can come up with another solution," Smitty said flatly.

"I wish we could tell the police," Callie said. "He really scares me. I listened when Lynne told us about the attack and what he did to her, and that was hard to imagine; but today, when I saw how aggressive he was, it really sunk in. We'll have to be very careful."

"I'll stop by the farm and talk with Betsy and Ron tonight to see what the attorney has been able to do and to get a sense of what their plans are," Smitty said. "I'll call you two to let you know what I find out. I'll also fill in Jo and Kellan about what's going on."

"What about Lynne?" Sam asked.

"I'll call her," Smitty said.

CHAPTER 36

Summer 2018

AS SHE LAY on her bed, Betsy cradled the phone on her chest and let her head drop back while letting out a huge cry of relief. The attorney had just called to tell her that he'd been successful in getting Lynne's order of protection expanded to include her family. David was not allowed near any of them—especially Melanie. She knew it was only a minor victory, but it was something. She also knew David wouldn't take this news well; it might make him feel like he was being pushed into a corner. And when an animal is cornered, it is even more dangerous.

It would be so much easier if they could simply tell everyone the truth about David Hoffman. No one knew the truth about him and what he had done. She hated knowing he was lingering around town. All David had to do was confide in someone, tell them he was Melanie's father. That he was trying to connect with his daughter, who'd been deliberately concealed from him and given away to someone else without his knowledge and consent—that he was the victim. It would be all over town and there would be no concealing it. Theirs was a small town—word would get back to Melanie.

Just then there was a knock at the bedroom door. "Who is it?" she asked.

"Hey, it's me," Callie said as she entered the room. "Are you okay?"

Betsy nodded and smiled. "Yes, the order of protection came through."

"Well, that's good news. Isn't it?" Callie said optimistically.

"Yeah, but I'm not sure it means anything."

"You know we're here to help you, right?"

"Yes, but I need eyes and ears in every direction. I just can't predict what he's going to do."

"Well, you may have more eyes and ears than you know about," she said, smiling. "We'll keep out of sight so Melanie and Josh don't see us around; but you should know that at least one of us will always be nearby if you need anything until this thing is resolved."

"Oh Callie, you guys are great—but you can't do that forever and this guy is not going to give up. I haven't been able to do anything other than stew over this whole mess, and I've come to the conclusion that, at some point, we're going to have to tell Melanie the whole story. That's really the only way to end this."

"Mom?" Melanie called, knocking on the door and coming in without waiting for an answer. "Oh, hi Callie. I'm sorry to interrupt," she said, walking over to Betsy and handing her an envelope. "This was sticking out of the mailbox. I saw it as we were coming in for lunch." Then when she realized Betsy was lying down, she added, "Are you okay, Mom? Why are you lying down?"

"I'm absolutely fine. I've been cleaning out some boxes in the basement, and it's very hard work," she said with a sigh. "I decided to take a quick break and lie down for a minute before you all came in for lunch."

"Well, it's hard work out there too," Melanie said, wiping her hand across her forehead.

"What are you doing?" Callie asked.

"I'm driving the tractor today. Dad says I'm pretty good at it, that I keep nice straight rows." Looking at Betsy she said, "We were going to make some lunch. Do either of you want anything?"

"No honey, I'm just fine. I need to get back to work myself," she said, sitting up on the edge of the bed and sliding her feet into her shoes.

"I could make you a cup of tea and you could talk to us while we eat. Would you like a cup of tea too, Callie?" Melanie offered.

"Your waitressing skills are paying off," Callie said. "I would love one."

"What's this?" Betsy asked, holding up the envelope.

"I don't know. It was just hanging out of the mailbox."

Betsy slid her finger along the edge of the envelope, pulled out the letter and started reading it. As she did, her face grew more and more pale.

"Are you okay, Betsy?" Callie asked. "You suddenly look very pale."

"Yes," Betsy said, putting the letter face down on her lap. "I think I just sat up too quickly."

Melanie asked, "Who's the letter from?"

Pausing for a second and then stumbling over her words, Betsy said, "Oh, uh, it's just a note from Mrs. Fletcher. She'd like me to . . . she wants to commission me to do a painting of the landscape around their pond."

"Well, what a wonderful opportunity. I bet she'll pay well too," Callie said.

"Congrats, Mom, that's great! Come down when you're ready. I'll put the tea out on the porch for the two of you," Melanie said. "And I'll bring the sandwiches out as soon as they're ready. We can talk while we eat."

Callie and Betsy walked downstairs and out onto the porch. Seating herself on the porch swing next to Betsy, Callie said, "What a beautiful young woman your Melanie is, Betsy."

Betsy didn't answer. She handed Callie the letter and sat back, letting the porch swing sway as she closed her eyes. Meanwhile, Callie read the letter.

You can pretend like you are in control, but as you can see you are not. If I can get this to you, I can get to Melanie too. It is only a matter of time.

"Oh Betsy, he's not going to give up, is he? What do you think he'll do if you don't tell her?"

"No, he's not going to give up. I don't know what he will do, but he is dangerous. At the very least, he could tell someone else, someone who knows Melanie well, and he can fill his story with lies. And because she won't know the truth about David and what he did to Lynne, Melanie will be confused as to why we lied to her and why Lynne gave her up for adoption. She won't know that she did this for her. We have to tell her—and we have to do it so she knows we did everything the way we did because we love her. There's no other way." Betsy sounded heartbroken.

"Oh Betsy, there has to be another way. Don't give up yet. We just need a little more time to think about what to do, and with Melanie working with Ron every day, we still have some time," said Callie.

"He could just as easily have written the letter to Melanie, and I wouldn't even know she'd gotten it. Hell, he might even have her cell phone number and could call her. He can get to her if he wants to. We need to prepare her for that. It's not fair for her to receive this news from anyone other than me or Ron."

They'd been sitting, holding their cups of tea, neither taking a single sip, when Ron and Josh came over from the barn.

"How are my favorite girls doing?" Ron asked as he sat down next to Betsy on the swing.

"Hey Mom," Josh said as he ran into the house past Betsy and Callie.

"You didn't say hello to Callie, Josh," Betsy called after him.

"I need to go to the bathroom," he yelled from down the hall.

Shaking her head, Betsy handed the letter to Ron. He read it, and when he was done, he tore it up. As he got up from the swing, he said, "Callie, would you like to join us for lunch? I believe Melanie is making tuna fish sandwiches—you won't find a better tuna sandwich anywhere!"

Betsy sat looking at him. "What do you think about the letter?"

"What letter?" he asked.

Surprised by his response and understanding the two of them needed some private time to discuss it, Callie replied, "No, but thanks, Ron. I'll take a rain check. I need to get back to work." Then she stood up and headed down the porch steps toward the little house.

"Ron?" Betsy started.

"I'm not going to talk about it," Ron said, sitting down on the swing next to her. "There is no letter. There is no David. There is only my little family, today."

CHAPTER 37

Summer 2018

"COME ON," SAM said. "Let's go outside and get some fresh air."

Smitty put a damp towel over the piece she was working on and washed her hands. The two women went out to the front porch and positioned the chairs so they could get some sun.

They'd decided to take a break from their work since they'd been unsuccessful at getting anything accomplished. Their attention was focused on what to do about David, now that the situation was escalating. The day before, Callie told all the shack girls about the letter and his ongoing threat.

"Sam, how are we going to resolve this problem?" Smitty asked. "I can't get any of my pieces completed. I just can't get my head into my work. How are we going to fix this? I know the decision isn't ours, but I can't help but think there must be a way we can stop him. There must be something we can do. Nobody should bend to his demands. He is a violent criminal who is holding us all hostage. He believes he has Lynne, Betsy, and Ron cornered."

Sam looked thoughtful and then said with uncharacteristic calm, "Well, I don't think there's any other legal measure to be taken that can stop him. He doesn't respect the law. He'll just continue until he gets what he wants—regardless."

Just then, a car drove up and parked. Sam put her hand up to her eyes to shield them from the glare of the sun to see who it was. She watched as the door opened and David stepped out. Looking at Smitty, she said, "Speak of the devil!"

David started up the path to the shack when Sam said, "You better not come any closer."

David stopped and held up his hands. "Hey, I'm not here to cause any problems. I just want you to pass along a message to Lynne and Betsy."

"You have nothing to say that they want to hear. What does it take for you to get the message that you should go away?" Sam asked. "There are multiple restraining orders against you, and we are not your messengers. You should go away, David. This ongoing effort to work around the law is only going to result in more extreme legal action being taken against you."

"You can't keep harassing Lynne, Betsy, and Ron—or even us," Smitty added with conviction.

The two women watched as the expression on his face changed from phony friendly to one of extreme anger. It was as if he'd become possessed. He glared at them fiercely as he continued to walk towards them.

Smitty said again, "You need to stop right now!"

Very calmly, Sam pulled a handgun out from under her work apron. "You are trespassing and we've asked you politely to leave. If you don't leave, I'll have to shoot you." She paused for a beat. "On second thought, I am so fucking sick of you and the problems you've caused that I'd like a reason to shoot you." Her face shone with determination.

David stopped, holding his hands up again. "You wouldn't shoot an unarmed man," he said.

"How do I know you're unarmed? You've been harassing us. You're a convicted felon—convicted of rape and assault. You're a perceived threat, and I'm simply defending myself," she said, stepping off the porch and walking toward him. "We're tired of you and your constant threats to us and our friends. You have no right to come here and claim the life of a child—a victim of your vicious act of violence. You shattered Lynne's life and now you're threatening to ruin Melanie's life, not to mention the havoc you've created for Betsy and Ron. You need to leave and leave for good!"

Sam stood only a few feet away from David, and was seething with anger.

Smitty called out, "Be careful, Sam. Don't get any closer to him. David, get back in your car and leave."

At that moment, Sam turned her head to look at Smitty, and as she did, David lunged at her, grabbing the gun. In one quick move, he backhanded Sam across the face and knocked her down.

"You stupid bitch. I've taken all I'm going to take from you." He stepped back and pointed the gun at her.

Sam said, "Go ahead, shoot me. They'll put you back in prison, and we'll be rid of you. As long as you're locked away, I'm happy."

At that moment, Sam's old truck came barreling over the sidewalk and into the yard. It ran right over David, narrowly missing Sam.

Smitty, who'd been descending the porch stairs to come to Sam's aid, froze in place, momentarily stunned. She watched the truck come to a stop, back up, and run over David again. She gasped and screamed, "Oh, my God!"

Sam had rolled away across the grass when she saw the truck coming; and as soon as she was out of range, she sat up and watched the macabre scene unfold in front of her disbelieving eyes. She just sat there holding the corner of her smock to the side of her head where David had hit her, dumbstruck.

"Oh, my God!" Smitty whispered under her breath, as she reached Sam.

The door to the truck opened slowly, and Kellan stepped out. Hanging on to the side of the hood for support, she walked to where David's body lay motionless and looked down at it.

Smitty helped Sam to her feet, and together they approached Kellan. All three women stood together in silence, looking down at the mangled mass that was once a man.

"Are you two alright?" Kellan asked. "Are *you* alright?" she asked again, this time addressing only Sam.

"Yes, we're alright," Sam said, looking down at the body as blood trickled down her cheek. Smitty took off her smock and dabbed at the blood on Sam's face. "I'm good," Sam said, batting Smitty's hand away. "What about him?" she asked, pointing to David.

"Do you think he's still alive?" Kellan asked.

"I hope not. It would be tough to try to put that piece of shit back together." Sam said, looking down at what was left of him.

"I just didn't know what to do," Kellan explained. "I saw him knock you down and then stand over you pointing a gun at you. I didn't know what to do, so I . . . I just hit him with the truck." She paused for a moment as reality seemed to finally sink in. "Oh, my God! What have I done?" she said in alarm.

"It was my gun. I'd been about to shoot him, but he got it away from me," Sam said. "I took my eyes off him for a second, and it nearly cost me my life. Then you came along and saved me," Sam said with a grateful smile on her face.

All three women stood transfixed, still looking at the ground and what used to be David, none of them saying a word for a minute or two.

Kellan, feeling suddenly lightheaded said, "I think I need to sit down."

Smitty came to her side and helped her up the porch steps.

"I've just killed someone, and I did it deliberately. Not just once but twice! What am I going to do?" Kellan said with terror in her voice.

"What are you going to do about what?" Sam asked.

"About him, of course," Kellan said pointing to David and then looking at Sam like she was crazy. "I just killed him." Hands trembling she pulled her phone out of her pocket and started to dial 911.

"Stop!" shouted Sam.

"We have to call the police," Kellan said.

"Let's think about this first," Sam said.

"Yes, Sam's right," Smitty said. "We need to think about the right way to approach this."

"Do you think we should check to see if he's still alive?" Kellan asked.

"I don't see how that's possible," Smitty said.

"If he's alive, I'll drive over him again," Sam said firmly.

Smitty knelt down next to David's body. She put three fingers to his neck for several seconds. Then she stood up and said softly, "He *is* dead."

Sam smiled, and in a very cheery voice, she said to Kellan, "You did good, girl!"

Both Kellan and Smitty looked at her, stunned.

"We better get this mess out of here before someone sees it," Sam said.

"What do you mean? Where would we take him?" Kellan asked, clearly confused as she watched Smitty disappear around the corner of the shack. She and Sam heard the door to the old garden shed squeak open, and a few seconds later Smitty came back with a bundle of gloves and a tarp in her hands.

"Let's drag him over to the shed for now. We can figure out what to do next once he's out of sight."

The three women struggled to roll him onto the tarp. He was heavier than they expected. once they covered up his body, they sat down on the porch steps to catch their breath.

"He's a big guy," Smitty remarked.

"Oh, and let's not forget to take his wallet, phone, keys, and anything else that could identify him," Sam said.

"What?" Kellan asked. "I'm not sure I'm okay with this. I can't just kill someone and walk away. We need to call the police," she said, this time more urgently.

Smitty countered, "We need some time to think about the repercussions of what's happened here. We don't want to act too quickly and leave ourselves no options. I'm sorry to say this, but what's happened here has given us options, options we didn't have until a few minutes ago, and we need to be careful and smart about how we use them."

Kellan nodded her head and knelt down next to the body, while Smitty and Sam uncovered David and rolled him from side to side, checking all his pockets and retrieving his keys, wallet, and cell phone. They wrapped up his body again and dragged it into the shed, then locked the door.

After taking off their gloves and washing their arms and hands thoroughly with the garden hose, the three women stood together.

Kellan said softly, "I can't believe what just happened. A few minutes ago I was driving back to the shack with some new brushes I just bought. Shopping for new brushes is one of my most favorite things to do—I love having new brushes," she said with a sad smile on her face. "Within a few seconds, I've gone from being so happy and content with life to this—I've become a murderer." Tears ran down her face. "Don't you think we should call the police?" she said, pleading with them now.

"I'm still not sure that's the right thing to do," Smitty said gently. "We don't want Melanie to ever find out about him, and if he just goes away, then Melanie is spared. Melanie won't have to find out about him or what he did to Lynne. If we call the police, there will be an investigation, the press will get involved, people will talk, and we'll be back to where we were before. If he just goes away, then no one needs to know."

The three women stood looking at the ground where David's body had been. There was a long smear of blood that ran from there to the shed.

"I'll get the hose and wash this blood into the soil," Smitty offered.

"In the meantime, Kellan, come sit on the front step, and I'll move the truck," Sam said. Kellan sat down slowly and started shaking.

"Are you cold?" Sam asked.

"No, I'm not cold," Kellan said, nearly whispering. "I think I'm in shock."

"Well, you just sit there and rest. I'll be back in a few minutes," Sam said.

As the truck backed away, Smitty came around the side of the shack with the hose. Everything seemed so calm and peaceful. It was a beautiful summer day. The birds were chirping, the sun was shining, and Smitty stood there calmly, casually watering the grass. Luckily, the shack wasn't located in the heart of town, so it was relatively secluded. There were no neighbors and no cars had passed. It was as if nothing had happened.

About thirty minutes later, Sam returned. She'd taken the truck to the car wash and cleaned off the remnants of David. She parked it in front of the shack and went up to Kellan. She sat down next to her and put her arm around her shoulders. "Are you doing okay?" she asked.

Kellan shook her head no and didn't speak at first. Then she said, "What are we going to do about him?"

"I don't know yet, but we'll think of something," Sam said looking at Smitty.

"Why don't you call Callie and Jo and ask them to come here?" Smitty suggested to Sam while she continued watering the grass. "This grass still looks a bit dry. I think I'll set up the sprinkler."

CHAPTER 38

Summer 2018

WITHIN THE HOUR, Jo and Callie pulled up. Sam, Smitty, and Kellan were still sitting on the porch with the sprinkler running on the lawn.

"What's going on? No one's watching the big house," Jo said with concern.

"Something's happened that means we don't need to watch the big house anymore," Smitty said, before telling them about David's recent fate.

Jo stood silently for several minutes with a glazed look on her face, while Callie started pacing back and forth along the edge of the porch. Finally she said, "Good. The problem with this guy has finally come to an end. We don't have to worry about him anymore."

"Yeah, but what are we going to do about his body?" Jo asked.

Uncharacteristically, Callie took charge and said matter-of-factly, "I have an idea. We have a meat locker outside of town where we receive entire sides of beef and whole pigs. We hang them there until we're ready to butcher them for the store."

"We can't just leave him in there. Someone will find him," Jo said in dismay.

"No one comes to the locker but Mike. We can put the body in there; and as long as we take him out before Saturday, we're good. Mike goes there on Wednesday and Saturday mornings. In the meantime, we can decide what to do with him."

Everyone just stood there, not sure about what to say, until Sam said, "Are you sure Mike won't go in there between now and Saturday?"

"Yes, I'm sure," she said. "He takes deliveries on Wednesdays. He loads what he needs for Thursday and Friday in our refrigeration truck and takes it to the store. He doesn't come back to pull more meat from the locker again until early Saturday morning. If we put the body in there today, we can firm him up, so to speak, so he won't make a mess." She paused and then suggested, "What do you think if we bring him back to the shack on Friday and feed him to the glass furnace?" She asked glancing around for approbation from the group, thinking she'd hit upon the perfect solution.

All of them, even Kellan, who'd been sitting motionless with her head in her hands, looked up at Callie in disbelief.

When she realized that everyone was staring at her, Callie said, "What? He is just a hunk of meat—and rotten meat at that. It's perfect!"

Finally Smitty spoke. "If anyone here is not okay with what's going on here, don't feel like you have to be involved. You can walk away right now."

"Well, speaking for myself, I'm in. I think Callie's plan is brilliant," Sam said.

"Wait . . . I don't think it's fair for all of you to take this on," Kellan said. "This is my fault and none of you need to be involved."

"No, you're wrong about that," Smitty said. "What would have happened if you hadn't arrived when you did? And what will happen if we don't get rid of him? The police will get involved and there will be an investigation, even if you confess. Everyone in town will find out what happened to him, to Lynne sixteen years ago, and most importantly, Melanie will have a burden to carry for the rest of her life. She'll learn that her mother was brutally raped by her father. She'll learn that her biological mother is Lynne. And that her father was a psychopath—not our wonderful Ron.

"If *we* hadn't killed him . . . well, I believe he wouldn't have stopped. First, Sam would be dead, or at least shot, and Melanie would never be safe.

He might even have tried to kidnap her. I've given this a lot of thought over the past several days. He didn't care about any laws or restraining orders. He didn't care who he hurt to get what he wanted. We just don't know what other horrible things he would have done. I'm convinced that his death is a good thing, and that concealing his death is also the right thing. No one needs to know anything about this."

After catching her breath, Smitty continued. "Kellan, I'd be happy to say that I'm the one who hit him and drove over him. I would be pleased to take credit for that. You can walk away from all of this and no one will think twice about it. That goes for all of you. No one needs to be involved. I would just ask that you not tell anyone; and if someone finds out, that you'll let me take the credit for killing him."

Sam reached over and took Smitty's hand and squeezed it.

"I want credit for concealing his body in the meat locker and for cutting him up. I'm in," Callie said.

"I'll get rid of his car," Jo said. "I'm in."

Kellan, with tear-streaked cheeks, looked at the four women. "It appears I had nothing to do with it—I'm definitely in."

All the shack girls laughed—although a bit uncomfortably considering the circumstances.

Looking at Jo, Sam said, "Let's grab another two sets of gloves, and you and I can figure out what to do about the car."

"We'll get his body wrapped up and ready to take to the meat locker," Callie said. "Then, when you two get back, we'll all take him over there and leave him until Friday."

Putting on her gloves, Sam said, "Come on, Jo, let's get rid of this car."

The two walked over to David's vehicle, looked around inside, and then opened the trunk, where they found a suitcase.

"What do you think we should do with this?" Jo asked.

"Well, for now let's take it out and put it in the shed with his body."

"Let's put it into a large garbage bag first," Smitty suggested.

After Smitty brought her the bag, Jo put the suitcase into it and left it in the shed. She found another unused tarp in the shed and brought it over to the car, where she carefully draped it over the driver's seat.

"Where do you think we should take this?" Jo asked.

"How about we drive it down by the river and leave it there? We wouldn't have to drive through town, so we probably wouldn't be seen," Sam said.

As Jo started the car, the other three women watched her and Smitty gave her a thumbs-up as she pulled away from the shack. Sam followed closely behind in Smitty's car.

Smitty, Kellan, and Callie wrapped David's body in another heavy-duty tarp they'd found in the shed, and tied it in place with rope. There was a lot of blood on the floor of the shed.

"What do we do about the blood?" Kellan asked. "I could get some rags and clean it up."

"I'll help you, but let's get the body taken care of first," Smitty said, patting Kellan on the shoulder affectionately. It was clear that Kellan was still having trouble dealing with the situation. Smitty added, "Kellan, if you don't feel like we're doing the right thing, we can stop right now and call the police. It's your call. But let me assure you that I'll say I was the one who ran over him and that I did it deliberately. This is not your fault."

"I know, and I understand why you're all getting involved in this. I don't want to call the police—I just can't believe what's happening is all. I support what we're doing and I'm good with it."

"Okay then, let's get this bundle into the back of the truck," Smitty said.

The three women dragged his body to the truck and struggled to load him into the back. Afterward, they stood silently and looked at the bundle for a few seconds until Callie said, "All right, let's put him in cold storage."

Smitty drove, and Callie—sitting in the middle—took Kellan's hand in hers and said quietly, "This ordeal will soon be over, and it couldn't have turned out better." Kellan didn't say a word, but tears rolled down her cheeks. "We all are partners in this," Callie added as she squeezed Kellan's hand.

As they approached the meat locker, Callie dug into her purse and pulled out a huge ring of keys. After searching through all of them she said at last, "Here it is," holding the locker key up in the air. "I have it!" She unlocked the door as Smitty backed the truck up as close to the door as possible. The three women dragged the body toward the back of the truck. While Sam kept watch, they started lowering him to the ground. Smitty, struggling to keep her grip let go of the tarp and he dropped with a thud. The two women looked at her, and she shrugged her shoulders saying, "He *is* heavy." Then without another word, the three of them dragged the body across the floor of the locker to a corner in the back behind several cases of sausages.

"Wow, he *is* heavy," Callie said. "I'm used to hauling heavy hunks of meat, but he's a challenge. We may want to cut him up before we try to do this again." Smitty looked alarmed at this remark, and Kellan gasped. Callie continued matter-of-factly, "Well, we'll have to cut him up if we want to get him into the glass furnace, and it'll be easier to cut him up here using the saws we use for the meat."

Smitty, looking dazed at the mere suggestion, said, "Of course, you're right," while Kellan simply nodded in agreement.

Within seconds, they'd locked the door to the meat locker and were in the truck on their way back to the shack.

CHAPTER 39

Summer 2018

WHEN THEY PULLED up, Smitty said, "I don't know about you two, but I need a good stiff drink."

"Amen," Callie said, with Kellan echoing her.

When Sam and Jo returned, they found the three women sitting on the front porch with several bottles of liquor close at hand.

"How did it go?" Callie asked.

"I think it went fine, but we'll have to see," Jo said cautiously. "We parked the car on the service road next to the river. We're hoping it looks like he stopped at the river to fish or hike, since who knows what he was up to. I threw the keys in the river. We'll need to burn the tarp, of course. We wore gloves the entire time. No one touched his car or keys except Jo and me—am I right?"

Everyone nodded.

"There were no cars that passed us. It helps that this didn't happen on a weekend when there would have been more traffic," Jo said, sounding relieved.

"Come sit down and have a drink," Smitty said.

"You won't have to ask me twice," Jo said quietly.

"Are you okay?" Callie asked.

"I'm just thinking about what's happened over the last few hours. This is a lot to take in. I want to be sure we're covering our tracks and haven't overlooked any significant details that could trip us up later. I don't question that what we've done is the right thing. I just want to be sure we're not leaving any loose ends, since we don't want this plan to unravel."

"Sam, what do you think about burning the body in the glass furnace?" Smitty asked.

"Funny you should ask that. I was just thinking about the same thing," she replied. "You know, the glass furnace was originally in a crematorium."

Jo, Kellan, and Callie just looked at her questioningly, until Jo said, "What?"

"Yeah. Betsy's father found it for me. We bought it from a crematorium in Chicago almost twenty years ago. He picked it up and drove it back here, then helped me retrofit it. It's much smaller now. I'm wishing we'd left it like it was. We'll have to do make sure we can fit him in there."

"We have a good saw at the locker, and it won't take much time," Callie said, looking pleased with her solution. The others, including Sam, looked at her, concerned. "What's the problem?" Callie said. "I've said it before and I'll say it again—he's just a hunk of meat—and rotten meat at that."

Kellan sat and looked out at the lawn, as the sprinkler continued to sputter across the grass. Slowly she said, "If we haven't covered up everything, and evidence is found, I'll confess to the murder."

"No, I've already claimed that honor," Smitty said. "And besides, this was self-defense. Don't forget that he knocked Sam to the ground and might have killed her had 'I' not come along and saved her. Speaking of which, how is your eye, Sam?"

"It's fine," she said, although her eye was very swollen and starting to turn blue.

"We should get some ice on it," Smitty suggested. "I'm sorry we didn't take care of it sooner."

"We had other things on our minds. It'll be fine," Sam insisted.

Smitty got up and went inside to get a bag of ice.

"This man has a criminal record for his brutal attacks. I'm certain 'we' saved Sam's life. And now, 'we' are saving Lynne's and her family's lives as well," Callie pointed out.

"We've all agreed to share equal responsibility for what's happened because we believe we've done a good thing—the right thing," Jo said, extending her hand to the rest of the women, who quickly put their hands on hers, with Kellan adding hers last.

"All for one and one for all!" Jo exclaimed, and they all echoed her.

"Well, I don't know about you guys, but I'm exhausted. I'm heading home to bed," Sam said, holding the bag of ice to her head.

"Wait for me—I'll ride with you," Kellan said.

"I better go too, or Mike will become concerned. It's late for me to still be out, and I'm working in the shop in the morning," Callie said. "We should plan to meet early on Friday to pull him out of cold storage—agreed?"

Kellan grimaced at the thought. "I can be here early."

"Me too," Jo said.

"Why don't we all meet here at eight o'clock so we can go over together to pick him up?" Sam said.

"One thing we haven't discussed is what to tell Lynne and Betsy," Smitty said.

"Well, I suggest we not tell them anything until after we've disposed of the body," Jo said. "Hopefully by then everything will be neatly wrapped up; and if something goes wrong beforehand, they won't know anything about this."

After the others agreed, they all stood up as if they'd just run a marathon—shoulders slumped, faces exhausted.

"Don't any one of you forget that what's happened here today is a good thing," Smitty said. "Don't doubt that for a minute. While what we've done isn't legal, it's still a form of justice. There was no legal remedy that would have solved the problem without leaving devastation in its wake. I'm proud of us," she finished, smiling at the other shack girls.

CHAPTER 40

Summer 2018

AT BREAKFAST THE next morning, Smitty asked, "How did you two sleep last night?"

"I didn't," Sam responded. "I tossed and turned all night. Once I start worrying, I can't sleep, and because I can't sleep, my worries become distorted and bigger than they should be. I'm thinking of taking a sleeping pill tonight just so I can sleep and regain a clear perspective."

"That surprises me," Smitty said sarcastically. "I would have thought you'd sleep rather soundly. How about you, Kellan?"

"I slept pretty well. I know that what we've done is the right thing. I just want everyone else to know that too. In particular, if we are ever found out, I want the police to understand what we understand, that there was no other way. I want them to look at the options and see that within the confines of our legal system there was no other way," Kellan said as she sat down with her cup of coffee. "I'm hoping they never find out about it, but if they do, I want to be sure they know why we did what we did. I'll be glad to get to work at the shack this morning. I need to focus on something else for a while."

Smitty and Sam agreed it would be good to have a positive distraction, and they all had projects they were working on, including several commissions. They drove over to the shack in relative silence. The air was crisp and clear for an early summer day, and they enjoyed the peaceful surroundings.

Once they were inside, they quickly got to work, and soon the sounds of the glass furnace and music filled the space.

After several hours, Sam wandered outside to take a break. A few minutes later, she came back in and announced, "Look who I found outside," indicating Officer Burkett, who'd followed her in. Smitty and Kellan stuck their heads out of their studios.

"Well, hello, Bob," Smitty called as she wiped her hands on her apron and tried to make her voice sound normal while a feeling of panic rose inside her.

Kellan was attempting to walk towards the back door when Smitty grabbed the back of her smock to hold her in place. "To what do we owe this honor?"

"I just thought I ought to check in on you ladies," he said, which despite his casual manner was clearly a ruse.

"Well Bob, I don't recall ever seeing you at our place before. Is there something happening we should know about?" Sam asked.

"Well no, not really," he said.

"How about a cup of coffee as long as you're here?" Sam asked.

"That would be great, Sam. Thank you," he said. "I don't think I've met this young lady before. Are you new here?" he asked, looking at Kellan.

"Oh, this is Kellan, our newest addition. She's been here a few months now. She's a very talented painter," Smitty said smiling at Kellan while letting go of her smock. "Maybe you should show Bob some of your work," she suggested.

Kellan took a step back, so Smitty nudged her forward towards her studio.

"Nice to meet you," she said to Bob in a faltering voice as she extended a shaky hand.

"Where did you come from?" he asked.

"Oh here and there," she said. "I really don't have much to show you," she said as she stepped back into her studio. "In fact, I need to get back to work, but it was nice to meet you." Once inside, she shut the door.

"She's very shy," Smitty explained. "She's still getting settled here, but she's doing very well. She lives with Sam and me at the moment, but she'll soon be moving out to Betsy and Ron's farm to live with Jo in the little house."

"Speaking of whom, where is Jo?" he asked.

"She's on her way here," Smitty replied.

"So is everyone here today?"

"Not quite yet, why do you ask?"

"Just curious. How many women work here?"

"There are seven of us if you include Lynne. But she's moving back to Chicago now that Betsy seems to be doing so much better. She only comes here every once in a while," Sam said.

Sam handed an empty cup to Officer Burkett and was preparing to pour coffee into it when he nonchalantly asked, "Have you seen any strange men around?"

On hearing the question, Sam spilled the hot beverage on his hand. He pulled his hand away hastily, shaking off the hot liquid. "Damn! That's hot!" he cried out.

"If you'd held your hand still, that wouldn't have happened," Sam said. "You baby—I hardly spilled any on you."

"But it's *very* hot," he said, sounding annoyed at her blasé attitude.

"What? Are you hunting for someone? Should we be worried?" Smitty asked, getting the conversation back on track.

"Well, hunting may be the wrong word. But we are keeping an eye out for someone," he said.

"What does this man look like? What did he do?" Sam asked.

Officer Burkett didn't answer—he was rubbing his sore hand—so Sam asked again, "What did he do?"

"Should we be worried?" Smitty repeated.

"Do you have a photo of him?" Sam asked.

"Well, yes," he said fumbling in his pocket. Before handing the image to Sam. He's a little over six feet in height, dark brown hair, blue eyes, and he's in his early forties." He paused and asked with a tone of concern, "Do you often see strange men out here?"

"Well, you're here—one more strange man than we were expecting. Should we be worried about you?" Sam snapped back passing the photo on to Smitty.

"We are actually pretty secluded out here," Smitty said. "We're just off the beaten track enough so that anything unusual typically registers with us. Why are you looking for him?"

"I didn't mean to alarm you. I just wanted to alert you all to keep an eye out for anything unusual—especially because you're out here and removed from town, you should be extra careful. I just wanted to let you know," Officer Birkett said.

"Does that mean you'll arrest the guy if you find him?" Sam asked.

"Well, no, but we want to know where he is."

Starting to become angry she said, "This is bullshit. If you know there's someone who's a problem roaming around in public, and you feel compelled to warn us about him, but aren't going to do anything about him, what's the point in that—other than to scare us?"

Wanting to defuse the situation, Smitty went over to Officer Burkett, took his arm, and calmly guided him toward the front door of the shack. Sam watched them silently, but inside she was seething, amazed that Smitty could keep her cool and chat amiably with Officer Burkett as she saw him out.

As he lingered at the door, Officer Burkett called out, "Well, thank you for the coffee, ladies. Please let me know if you see anyone who matches that description."

"Yeah, a fucking lot of good that'll do," Sam yelled out to him.

"We will be watchful, Bob. Thanks to you we'll certainly be on our toes. And we'll call you if we see anything unusual," Smitty said.

At that very moment, Jo came in through the back door, looking very anxious. "What's that police car doing outside?" she yelled, before she spotted Burkett on his way out. "Oh, hello!" she said in surprise.

"Oh Jo, you'll like this. Bob here was just telling us that there's a strange man lurking about. He won't tell us who he is or what he's done. He just wants us to keep an eye out for him. Oh, and this is good . . . he also tells us he won't do anything about him if we do see him lurking about. He just wants to know if we do. I guess this guy will have to kill one of us first!" Sam shouted sarcastically.

"Hello, Jo," Officer Burkett said, ignoring Sam. Then he walked out the front door.

Smitty accompanied him onto the porch, while Jo and Sam crept soundlessly along the hallway to the front door and waited for her. They both stepped back as the door opened and she came back inside. "Well, that was a bit scary," Smitty sighed.

"Scary because of the unknown man lurking about, scary because Sam lost her mind, or scary because you could see yourself behind bars?" Jo said.

"I would glean from his visit that he does know something about David," Smitty said calmly. "But he doesn't know that we know."

"He doesn't know we know!" Jo repeated, sounding quite excited.

"And we need to keep it that way," Smitty said firmly.

"Is he gone?" Kellan called through her door.

"Yes, he's gone," Smitty said.

Slowly the door opened and Kellan stepped out, her face red from crying. "I was so scared he knew what had happened and was here for us."

"No, he doesn't know what happened. That said, we still need to be careful and get this situation wrapped up as soon as possible," Smitty said.

"I'd like to get rid of that suitcase of his before it's found. What should we do with it?" Sam asked.

"Let's burn it with the body," Jo said. "But before we do, Callie wants to go through it. She'd like to have a couple of his shirts."

"What? What do you mean she wants a couple of his shirts?" Sam asked.

"I think she wants to incorporate them into one of her pieces. Since she mentioned that idea to me, I've been wondering if there's something I would want, but I haven't figured that out yet."

"It's funny you should say that," Smitty said. "I was thinking about using some of his ashes in my glazes for a few of the pieces I'm working on."

"Why would you want anything to help you remember him—or God forbid—remember what happened to him?" Kellan asked in amazement.

"Well, this is a significant event in our lives. I want something that memorializes our courage and our commitment to each other, Betsy, Ron, Lynnie, and the kids," Smitty said. "I'm not proud of this situation, but I'm not ashamed of it either—and this is a critical moment. I want to commemorate it."

"Perhaps I could take some of his hair and make some brushes. I could paint something with them that reminds me of us," Kellan said thoughtfully. "I acted on impulse, and I know full well that none of you had to get involved in what I did. At the moment I hit him, I didn't even think about Lynne, Betsy, or Melanie. I was just concerned for Sam. Now, what I did has a larger meaning for me, and I want you to know that I love you all."

CHAPTER 41

Summer 2018

JO WENT OVER to the shed, and came back—with gloves on—carrying the suitcase. She placed it on a large plastic garbage bag in the middle of the floor in Smitty's studio. Just then, Callie entered the room. "What's going on?" she said in a horrified tone. "Why is that suitcase there?"

"We decided we need to get rid of it," Jo said, as she was opening it.

"You just missed the excitement," Smitty said to Callie. "Bob Burkett was just here."

"Bob? Officer Bob? Why?"

"He was here to warn us about a strange man who might be lurking about town, although he was quite clear that he wouldn't be able to do anything about him. He just wanted us to know about him. What a joke!" Sam said with a scowl.

"Well, no fear of that. We took care of him," Callie remarked, while donning some gloves and kneeling on the floor next to Jo. Together, they carefully sifted through the contents of the suitcase. After a few minutes, Callie had settled on a handful of shirts, laying them neatly in a pile on the bag. Then she got up and went down the hall to her studio where she grabbed a pair of scissors. When she came back, she started cutting up the shirts into large squares of fabric.

It was Jo's turn next. After peering into the suitcase, she rummaged through his shaving kit and setting that aside, took a pair of leather shoes. "I could cut the leather into something for one of my pieces," she said, taking out one of the shoes and leaving it on top of the bag. Then she retrieved a heavy-duty utility knife from her studio and cut the shoe apart.

"Did you see a belt in there?" Sam asked.

"Yes, here's one," Jo said, handing it to Sam.

"I could probably use this in something." She sat down next to Jo and separated the outer part of the belt from the lining and buckle. "Once you get what you want out of the suitcase, I'll take a torch to it. I have one in my studio," Sam said.

Minutes later, Sam, wearing a respirator mask, was standing over the suitcase in the middle of the studio—the door and windows wide open—using the blowtorch to melt the nylon fabric and plastic pieces.

When she noticed some interesting shapes forming from the melting mass, Jo asked if she could use the torch. "There may be something here I can work with," she said.

"Okay," Sam said, handing the torch and mask over to Jo. Sam smiled as she watched Jo work with the torch, skillfully melting and sorting the bits and pieces of what used to be the suitcase. Soon what was left of it was completely unrecognizable.

CHAPTER 42

Summer 2018

EARLY FRIDAY MORNING, Callie arrived at the studio and asked in a cheery voice, "Is everyone ready to get this done? I think we'll need at least three of us."

"I think we should all go," Smitty said. "Unless someone doesn't feel like they can."

"I'll go," Kellan said. "Jo, will you drive your car? I could ride with you."

"You bet," she said.

Soon Jo and Kellan, who were in Jo's car, and Smitty, Sam, and Callie, who went in Sam's truck, were on their way to the meat locker.

SAM BACKED UP the truck directly in front of the locker, but Jo decided to park her car down the street to keep from drawing attention to them. She and Kellan walked over to the locker and met the other three women inside. There in the back, past a huge hanging carcass of meat, next to the boxes of sausage, frozen stiff as a board, was David, wrapped up tightly in the tarps. It took several minutes of shifting, shoving, and lifting before they were able to drag him out to the table near the meat saw.

They took a break for a few minutes—their chests heaving from the struggle. After catching her breath and looking pale, Kellan said, "Maybe I should go outside to be sure no one comes in—just in case."

"Why don't you go with her, Jo," Smitty said. "We can handle this, and you can tell us if you see anything, or stop anyone from coming in."

Within seconds of Kellan and Jo going outside, Smitty, Sam, and Callie could hear them speaking with someone.

"Shit!" Sam whispered.

"Quick! Drag him back," Callie whispered.

The three women frantically dragged him back into the corner, when the door suddenly opened, and two men stepped inside. "Hey ladies," one of them said while approaching Smitty and holding his hand up to give her a high five. "Congratulations! We hear you all hit a deer yesterday with your truck. What luck!"

"Yeah, what luck," Smitty repeated dully, while trying to look excited.

The other man sidled up next to the first. "We know a great butcher if you need one."

Callie, cool and calm, said, "We're going to do the butchering ourselves. Most of it will be made into sausage. I have a great recipe I plan to use."

"What are you guys doing here?" Sam asked.

"Mike butchered a side of beef for us, and we're splitting it up. He gave us the keys and told us to come over and pick it up ourselves," the first man said, pointing to a couple of boxes piled up next to the door.

"Oh well, that was nice of him," Callie said.

"Do you need some help getting the deer into your truck? We'd be happy to help you," said the other man.

"No, but thanks anyway. We're going to do most of the butchering here. So I think we're good," Sam replied hastily.

Jo and Kellan came back in and stood awkwardly by the door, while Callie and Sam chatted with the men as they loaded up their truck.

"We'd be glad to help you," the first man offered again.

"No problem," Callie said.

"We're going to make a celebration of it," Sam said, pulling a bottle of whiskey from her coat.

"Way to go!" the second man said.

Callie and Sam stood outside until the two men were gone from sight. When they went back inside, Sam said, "Shit! Shit! Shit! That was close."

"Everything okay in here?" Callie asked.

"I think I might have frostbite," Jo said.

"Well, let's get this done so we can get out of here," Callie said.

Kellan and Jo resumed their posts outside to watch for any other potential intruders.

"I think I may be having a heart attack," Kellan said, sounding alarmed. "My heart is going to pound right out of my chest."

Jo smiled back at her. "I know, mine is going crazy too. I think I'll be rather jumpy for a while until we get past this. I keep telling myself that if I can get through today, it'll be smooth sailing from now on."

"From your mouth to God's ear," Kellan said. "Although I'm guessing God is probably pissed at us."

"Nah, I think he understands what we did and why. I think he's on our side," she said reassuringly. "I'm going to run inside for a second to see how things are going." Kellan could hear Smitty yell, "Who is it?" in a strained voice as the door closed behind Jo.

She returned quickly. "They're almost done in there. We got the better job, by the way."

"No doubt about it," Kellan said.

"Let's drop the tailgate," Jo suggested. "I think they're about ready for us to help them carry out the bundles."

"Bundles?"

"Yeah, they have him bundled up like pieces of meat, all ready to go straight into the glass furnace when we get back to the shack."

"What would we have done without Callie and all of her resources?" Kellan asked.

"This is a resourceful group, so I'm sure we would have thought of something," Jo said as she dropped the tailgate of the truck. Then she reached over and patted Kellan's hand. "I'm so relieved to know he won't be coming back to hurt any of us again."

Suddenly, the door to the locker opened and Sam emerged with a bundle in her hands.

"Are you ready for some help?" Jo asked.

"Yep," Sam said as she unloaded her bundle into the truck. Then she went back inside and the door closed behind her.

Jo hopped down and went inside after her. It took a few trips, but finally they succeeded in getting all of David into the back of the truck and closed the tailgate. Leaning against it, Smitty said, "Well, that's something I hope never to repeat in my lifetime."

Callie was the last one to emerge, and she locked the door behind her. "Let's go, ladies," she said as opened the door to the truck and climbed inside.

Smitty and Sam got in on either side of her, and Kellan and Jo waved at them as they walked back to their car. As the truck pulled away, Sam started to giggle, and soon Smitty and Callie joined in with bursts of nervous laughter.

"When I heard those guy's voices, I thought I was going to have a stroke," Smitty said.

"I think I peed my pants a bit," Sam said, causing the laughter to start up all over again. Then she added, "I have newfound admiration for you, Callie."

CHAPTER 43

Summer 2018

It was nearly noon when Lynne finished her shift at the café. "Mr. Saunders, do you need me for anything else before I leave for the day?" she asked.

"No, thank you, Lynne. I can't tell you how good it is to have you back," he said with a wink. "You're the best waitress I ever had."

"Well, I'm not sure that's true, but I will accept the compliment graciously," she said with a wink back. "See you tomorrow then."

She stood outside the café wondering where Jo was this morning. She had been coming into the café to keep an eye on her. She looked up and down the street without realizing that she was looking for David. She expected to see him everywhere she looked. She knew he was out there —but where? The stress of not knowing where he was or what he was up to was exhausting. It had been nearly a week since she'd last talked with him, and she knew he was angry and wouldn't just be sitting around waiting. He was plotting something.

She hoped that everything was alright at the farm. That was the worst part of working at the café—not being able to be at the farm with Betsy, even for those few hours. She knew Betsy and Ron were worried sick about the situation; and struggle as they might, they'd had no luck coming up with a good solution.

Lynne parked at the little house, and without dropping off her things, she went straight over to the big house. Betsy was at the kitchen counter, making lunch for Ron and the kids. She looked up and Lynne could see that she was exhausted. "You've not been sleeping, have you?" she said.

"Not very well. I keep thinking a solution will come to me, but I just don't see any alternatives and it makes me so very sad. I know Melanie is strong and has a good sense of self, but finding out about this would rock even the strongest person. I can't keep delaying what appears to be inevitable." Then changing the subject, Betsy asked, "When do you see Collin again?"

"Well, I don't know," she said. "He asked me to come to his house in town this weekend, but it's hard for me to go back there. There are too many bad memories."

"Have you told him that?"

"I don't want to keep using that as an excuse. If I were him—and since he doesn't know what's going on with David right now—I would be pretty tired of hearing about it. It has been nearly sixteen years, for God's sake!"

"Collin is a kind man, Lynne. I'm sure he would understand," Betsy replied. "Maybe you could go away someplace together for a few days—take a little vacation. You could use one, and you deserve one."

"Are you crazy? I couldn't go away with all this going on. No way! I will not leave you all until the situation with David has been resolved."

"Well, that could take a while. Who's over at the little house today? Do you know?" Betsy asked.

"No, I don't. I haven't seen anyone. They're pretty good at hiding out."

Just then Josh ran through the back door, yelling, "Hi Mom, hi Aunt Lynnie. I've gotta go to the bathroom!"

Both Betsy and Lynne burst out laughing, until Betsy said, "These long mornings out in the field are hard on his bladder.

"I would guess so," Lynne said, grinning broadly.

Ron and Melanie came in a few minutes later. Ron kissed Betsy on the forehead and said, "Hey, ladies. How's it going today?"

"Good. How about you?" Lynne said.

Interrupting, Melanie said, "How was the café this morning, Aunt Lynne? Do my customers miss me?"

Lynne's stomach fell as she thought for a moment about what that might mean. Was Melanie referring to David specifically or her customers in general? "It was pretty empty today," Lynne said. "Perhaps they do miss you, and they've decided to wait to come back when you do."

"Nah, they like you too, Aunt Lynnie. When I go back they'll probably be sad that you're not waiting on them anymore."

"How about some lunch?" Betsy asked, changing the subject. "I made lasagna today. How does that sound!"

"Yeah!" shouted Josh from down the hall.

"Didn't you shut the door?" Betsy yelled back.

"No time," he responded.

Betsy rolled her eyes and frowned at Ron.

"What? Why is this my fault? I can't help it if he won't go outside. He takes after you in that department," he said with a wink.

"Even I'll go outside," said Melanie. "It's too long to wait to come home."

"Let's not think about it," Betsy said as she put the food on the table.

"I'm going to head to the little house," Lynne told them.

"What? You're not going to eat lunch with us?" Ron asked.

"No, I ate a late breakfast at the café. I think I'm gaining weight. It's too hard to resist those fresh cinnamon rolls so early in the morning. Warm, soft, delicious!" Lynne said, as she left the kitchen and closed the door behind her. As she walked slowly over to the little house, she thought how much she would miss all this.

When she entered the kitchen of the little house, she was surprised to find no one inside. Picking up her cell phone, she called Jo.

"Hey, Lynne. Where are you?" Jo asked without saying hello.

"I'm at the little house. Where is everyone?"

"Ah . . . well, we're working on a project together," she responded.

Confused, she asked, "Isn't anyone watching the big house?"

"Well, ah . . ." Jo hesitated, and then Smitty's voice came on the phone. "Hi, Lynne. We had an unexpected problem to deal with, and as a result the schedule got messed up this morning. Can you stay there for a while?" she asked.

"Yes, I can stay here. Are you all okay?" Lynne said.

"Yes, but we'll need to explain it to you later."

"Okay," she said, hanging up the phone. She started thinking about what could possibly be going on, and hoped it had nothing to do with David. She knew her friends wouldn't leave Betsy, Ron, and the kids unattended unless something was very wrong. She started imagining all kinds of scenarios before telling herself to stop and wait for the explanation. If Smitty said they were all okay, she should believe her.

CHAPTER 44

Summer 2018

OFFICER BURKETT WAS driving down the old service road by the river when he passed a parked car. He figured someone must be fishing nearby, but decided to pull up behind the vehicle and investigate anyway. He walked up alongside the car and saw no one inside. So he went down to the river's edge and looked up and down the banks, but there was no one around. "Well, they must have gone for a hike," he said aloud as he got back into his car. He quickly ran the license plate number, which told him the car was a rental. *Must be some folks on vacation*, he thought, and then drove on into town.

Bob Burkett had been a police officer for more than twenty years. There wasn't a lot of criminal activity that went on in this sleepy little town, and he liked it that way. This problem with David Hoffman had him on edge. He was caught in the uncomfortable position of waiting for something to happen. He would at least like to talk with the guy and let him know he was keeping an eye on him and didn't like him hanging around. But so far, he hadn't been able to meet up with him and hadn't even been able to find anyone by that name in town.

Bob was a few years older than Ron and had known him his entire life, because Ron and his younger brother were close friends. So he'd been taken by surprise when he received notification from the court that there was a restraining order on David Hoffman that prohibited him from going anywhere near Lynne Parker. And then a few weeks later, another restraining order to keep Hoffman from going anywhere near the Parkers' farm as well as Ron, Betsy, and the kids. He'd done a little sleuthing and found out that this guy had severely beaten and raped Lynne nearly sixteen years ago, and he didn't like the fact that this guy was hanging around now. Nothing good could come of it. So he wanted David out of town, and while he couldn't force him to leave, he could make him aware of this fact, and make his stay as uncomfortable as possible. But since he hadn't been able to find him to speak with him, he would have to just keep his eyes and ears open for the moment when he might materialize.

Officer Burkett sat down at his desk and logged onto his computer. He searched for the rental car company's phone number, then called to ask who'd rented the car he'd spotted down by the river.

"David Hoffman," the man on the other end of the phone replied.

"Thank you," he said and hung up. This could be his chance, he thought. And he drove back to the river to wait.

CHAPTER 45

Summer 2018

CALLIE AND SAM were at the shack, sitting outside on the porch. It had been a very long afternoon, and they still weren't finished putting the bundles into the furnace. Kellan and Jo had retreated to their studios, but no one was getting any work done. The events of the day were wearing on everyone, and until the last bundle was inside the furnace, no one could relax. It was now just a matter of waiting for the furnace to do its work.

Smitty came out onto the porch with three glasses of wine. "How about a drink?" she asked.

"Thank you, I'd love one," Callie said.

After Smitty handed her a glass, she touched Callie's shoulder. "You were magnificent today. We could never have done this without you."

"I'm just sorry it was so hard on Kellan and Jo."

"I don't know that it was harder on them than on any of the rest of us. It's been an exhausting day, but we all know we did the right thing," Smitty said.

"Hell. We should be celebrating. It's over!" Sam said loudly. "This whole fucking problem with him is over! Melanie is safe from him. Lynne can go back to her life without always having to look over her shoulder. And Betsy and Ron can raise their family without worrying that a violent crazy man is lurking around the corner. It's over!" she repeated gleefully.

Kellan came out to join them. "Hey, where's mine?" she asked. "I could use a drink."

"Wait right here. I'll get you one," Smitty said, as she went back to her studio to get two more glasses and a couple more bottles of wine. On the way back, she stopped and knocked on Jo's door. "May I come in?" she asked.

"Sure. Come in," Jo called out.

Smitty opened the door, and saw that Jo was laying out some things on her workbench and studying them.

"What are you doing?" Smitty asked.

"Well, I'm considering what to do with the pieces I kept to memorialize this past week," she said. "The week has been so hard physically and emotionally, and I have so many ideas running through my head—I want to catch some of them while they're still fresh. I've decided to make a few pieces using what I saved from David. I think I'll sell most of them, and put the money into an account for Melanie's college tuition. What do you think? I know what we did is right, but I want something tangible that will benefit Melanie directly."

"I think that's a fantastic idea. Have you told the others?"

"No, but I will."

Holding up the bottles of wine, Smitty said, "We're out on the porch drinking wine whenever you're ready."

About thirty minutes later, Jo came out and Smitty poured her a glass. All five of them raised their glasses and toasted each other.

Sitting on the top step, Jo said, "What are we going to tell Lynne, Betsy, and Ron?"

"Well, I've been giving that a lot of thought," Smitty said. "I think we'll have to tell them the truth."

"Really?" Kellan said sounding surprised.

"If we don't tell them, they'll continue to worry about him. They will likely tell Melanie about him, and then she'll wonder for the rest of her life what happened to him. I think our only option is to tell them that he's dead," Smitty said.

"Well, we certainly don't have to tell them all the details—just that he's dead," Sam said. "We don't need to tell them any more than that."

"Lynne called and wanted to know why no one was at the farm. I told her we were dealing with something, and that we would be there soon and explain. Does anyone else have a different opinion?" Jo asked.

"Does anyone need more time to think about this?" Smitty asked.

"No," they all replied in unison.

Jo added, "I think it's the right thing to tell them he's gone for good, and I agree we shouldn't give them any details. If something goes south, it'll be much better for them if they don't know."

CHAPTER 46

Summer 2018

SMITTY, SAM, AND Kellan drove over to the farm in the truck, and Callie and Jo followed behind in Jo's car. They'd decided it would be best to tell Lynne first. Jo entered the little house and the rest of the shack girls followed behind her.

"Hey, Lynne," Jo said.

"Hey. Are you guys all alright? I was worried something had happened to one of you." Then looking at Sam she said, "What happened to your eye?"

"Well, funny thing," she said stammering, "I walked into the corner of the door on my way to the bathroom."

"You must have been walking pretty quickly. That is quite the bruise. Are you okay?"

"Yeah, I'm great. We are all great," Sam said with a reassuring smile. "We've never been better."

Lynne looked at each of them and raised an eyebrow. "Well, if that's the case, why do you all look so exhausted? What's going on?"

Smitty walked over to the couch. "Why don't we all sit down?"

When Lynne was sitting, Smitty said bluntly, "David is gone."

"What do you mean he's gone? Where did he go and how do you know that?"

"He's gone for good," Kellan said.

"What do you mean 'he's gone for good?'" Lynne asked.

"He's gone and he's not coming back," Sam said to stop the volley of questions.

Each of the women looked at Lynne, and she could see from their faces that what they were telling her was true.

"He's dead?" she asked slowly.

"He's dead," Jo said, with Kellan, Smitty, and Callie nodding solemnly in agreement.

Lynne sat quietly for a few minutes. "But how? And how do you know?"

"It doesn't matter," Smitty said. "We decided to tell you about it so you wouldn't worry about him anymore—and we also decided it's better not to tell you how we know. But we do know for certain that he's dead—and because you know us and trust us as you do, hearing this from us should put your mind at rest."

"Well, I don't think it's enough. I want to know and I deserve to know what's happened."

"Holy shit!" shouted Sam. "It's over and we're sure he's dead. That's all that matters!"

Now Lynne felt like she'd gone too far. "I'm not accusing anyone—and believe me, I'm glad to hear this news—but I worry that one or all of you might be in trouble."

"We're not in trouble, and we don't anticipate being in trouble; and we think it's better that you don't know any more than that," Smitty said, trying to calm her.

"Okay. I can accept that he's dead, but I still don't want any of you to be responsible for something that was my fault. I should be the one responsible for this, not all of you. After all, without me, none of you would have been involved in the first place."

"No—in fact it's not your fault. It's *his* fault, and the fact that he's gone is also his fault. We believe what's happened is for the best, and you need to believe that too," Callie said.

"But I have so many questions," Lynne said. "It's a lot to take in."

"Yes, it is, and I'm not sure we've fully processed it all ourselves," Jo said.

"Where's his body?" Lynne asked.

"He's gone," Sam repeated. "You don't need to worry about anything else."

"Okay," Lynne said softly, while still freaking out and feeling a wave of relief at the same time. And then she couldn't hold back deep, gasping, sobs.

Smitty sat down next to her and held her, Lynne let it all pour out.

"I am so glad that he's gone," Lynne she said when she had her voice back. "I don't know what happened, or how it happened, but I know that I love you all so much. I can't tell you the relief I feel, or how grateful I am for the weight that has just been lifted off of me, Melanie, Ron, and Betsy."

"Oh, honey," Jo said.

"We love you too," Kellan murmured.

Just then a car pulled up to the front of the little house. Kellan leaned over to look out the window. "It's Collin," she said in surprise.

"Were you expecting him?" Jo asked.

"No. No, I wasn't expecting him. What should I do?" Lynne said, hastily wiping her eyes.

"Go pull yourself together while we keep him entertained," Callie said.

Lynne got up and ran up the stairs as Sam opened the door. "Well, look who's here," she said.

"Hello Sam, how are you?"

"I am damn fine, Collin. How are you?"

"Well, I'm not sure I'm damn fine, but I'm pretty good."

"Good to hear, good to hear," Sam said, closing the door behind him.

When he looked around the room and saw all the shack girls, he said, "Well . . . uh, I'm sorry. It appears I may be interrupting something."

"No. We just walked in. We were at the shack all day and just decided to check in on Lynne and Betsy. Lynne is upstairs freshening up. She'll be down in just a minute," Smitty said.

"What have you all been up to today?" he asked, feeling more at ease.

"Well, I've been running the glass furnace all day. I had to clean up a mess and put things back in order," Sam said matter-of-factly.

"Actually, we've all been doing some cleaning up at the shack," Callie said.

"What have you been up to today?" Jo asked Collin, trying to redirect the conversation.

"Well, I was at the dairy all day and decided to come by and see if Lynne would like to have dinner with me."

"You could have called first," Sam pointed out.

"Well, yes. I could have called, but I didn't. Did I do something wrong? I still feel like I'm interrupting something here." He was feeling uncomfortable again.

"No, don't be silly," Callie said. "You should know by now that you need to ignore Sam. She likes to be difficult."

Lynne came down the stairs just then. "Why should he ignore Sam?" she said anxiously.

"Because I'm being my usual difficult self," she said, looking accusingly at Callie.

"Hi," he said as he kissed her. "I'm sorry. I should have called first. I just thought I'd stop to see if you'd like to have dinner with me."

"Well . . ." she started to answer when Smitty interrupted her. "Well, I'm sure she would love to. We were on our way out anyway. We'll come by tomorrow, Lynne, and perhaps you and Betsy would find some time to talk with us—okay?"

"But don't you want to talk with her now?" Lynne asked, looking concerned.

"No, it can wait until morning, but we shouldn't wait too long," Callie said.

"Okay, then—you two go and have a great time tonight. We'll come back in the morning," Callie said as she followed the women out the door.

"Alright, I'll see you all then," Lynne said behind them.

Collin took her hand and they were out the door. "Are you okay with this, Lynne? I feel like I just interrupted something important, and I didn't even give you an opportunity to tell me if you had other plans for tonight."

Lynne squeezed his hand and stood on her toes to whisper in his ear, "I'm happy you came, and I would love to go to dinner with you," before she kissed him on the cheek. Still, her head was swimming with a multitude of questions for the shack girls.

CHAPTER 47

Summer 2018

As THEY DROVE to the restaurant, Collin told her about his day at the dairy, but Lynne's mind kept wandering back to the shack girls and David.

"Where would you like to go for dinner?" Collin asked.

But Lynne was silent, lost in her thoughts.

"Lynne? Are you there?" Collin said, squeezing her thigh to get her attention.

"I'm sorry, Collin. What did you say?" Lynne said, feeling embarrassed. When he repeated the question, she said, "Oh, you pick. I'm good with whatever you want."

"Okay, how about spiders and moths for dinner?"

"What?" she replied, sounding bewildered.

"Well, if you don't care, then let's have those for dinner."

"Okay, I get it. How about Mexican tonight?"

"Perfect," he said, looking at her with a furrowed brow. "Are you sure you're up for this?"

"You know, I'm trying to calm my mind. It's whirling with a million things, and I need you to help bring me back to reality. Would you pull over for a second?"

Collin, looking concerned, pulled the truck over to the side of the road. "What is it, Lynne?"

She scooted over and reached down to the side of his seat and pushed the button so the seat went as far back as it could go. Then she pulled herself up onto his lap and grabbed his face in her hands and kissed him with every ounce of passion she had. When she was done kissing him, she pulled back far enough so she could see his face. "Now you kiss me."

"You don't have to ask twice," he said, pulling her in tight against his chest. It was a long, strong but tender kiss. "How was that?"

"Well, I think you can do better. If you want to knock what's in my head out of the way, you're going to have to do better than that."

He gently pushed her off his lap, opened the driver-side door, stepped out, and then slid her off the seat, holding her against him as she laughed and clung to his chest.

"I needed more room to move," Collin said.

"Go for it," she said with a sly, encouraging smile.

Then he stood her against the truck, and taking her head in his hands, he kissed her again. This time it was less tender. He stepped back and looked down at her. She stood there with her eyes closed and her hands pressed against the side of the truck to hold herself up.

"Much better. What do you say to having dinner later?" Lynne said with a mischievous grin on her face.

"What did you have in mind?"

"How about we check into the inn instead?"

Collin looked confused for a brief second and then caught on. A big smile formed on his face.

COLLIN OPENED THE door and Lynne stepped inside. Before she could even say a word, he pulled her in close and kissed her. "You know how long I've waited for you?"

"Ah, maybe fifteen or sixteen years?"

"Actually, since the day I moved into my house. I saw your car pull into your driveway, and then you walked out to the curb to pick up the newspaper. You had on this black skirt and white blouse. I remember your beautiful brown hair pulled back in a ponytail and the red lipstick you were wearing. You looked so professional. I wanted to introduce myself, but I knew you were out of my league."

"What? That's crazy talk," she said, looking him squarely in the eyes. "You're one of the best things to ever happen to me," she added, and then she kissed him.

She giggled as he picked her up and put her on the bed. They took their time kissing and slowly undressing each other before Collin paused and pushed his body up so he could see her whole face. "I love you, Lynne. I want you to know that."

Lynne didn't say a word, but her eyes filled with tears.

Collin suddenly looked sad and he asked with concern, "Are you okay, honey? Is this too much for you?"

"Yes, this is too much for me. My heart is so full it has just burst. I can't contain all of the love and happiness I'm feeling, and it has to come out somewhere."

He dropped to his elbows and using his fingertips, he gently wiped away the tears that trickled down the sides of her face. "I didn't mean to burst your heart," he said softly. "I just want to love you and be loved by you, that's all."

"You are loved by me, body and soul," Lynne said.

Collin made love to her, and she made love to him. She had never felt like this with anyone before. She was completely open and vulnerable and gave all of herself to him. She'd kept herself from having a real relationship with anyone since the attack—and since letting Collin go nearly sixteen years ago. She hadn't been sure she was capable of having a real relationship because she'd been so broken and damaged. But here she was, making love with Collin and savoring every second and every emotion she was experiencing—and it was more wonderful than she'd ever dreamed it could be.

Collin held her in his arms, tight against his chest as more tears flowed. Every once in a while he would look down at her and pull her closer to him. He didn't know what she knew, that David was gone and she was free; but he knew that she needed to feel safe and know that he loved her.

They made love twice more that night, and each time was more tender and blissful than the last. Lynne woke first in the morning and she rolled over to face him, leaning on her elbow, face cupped in her hand, so she could look down at him. She ran her finger across his eyebrows and down the side of his cheek to his jaw. Collin slowly opened his eyes and looked at her.

"Hey," he said.

"Hey back," she replied.

He ran his hand up her thigh to the soft, tender skin along her breast and rocked her close enough to kiss him. "Are you okay?" he asked.

"No, I'm not okay. I'll never be okay again," she said with a grin.

His beautiful green eyes crinkled at the corners and his smile lit up the room. "Good," he said with satisfaction.

"I don't want this to end, Collin, but I need to get back to Betsy's. The shack girls are going to meet me there this morning. Plus, I'm starving, so you'll have to feed me something before I go. And Mexican will not do."

"How about we go downstairs and I buy you a huge stack of pancakes, and you eat the whole thing before I take you home?"

"May I have whipped cream and strawberries on them?"

"You may have whatever you want."

As they pulled up to the farm, Collin said, "Dinner was great last night. I'll have to stop by and take you out again."

"You better," Lynne said, leaning over to kiss him again. "You better stop by soon!"

CHAPTER 48

Summer 2018

WHEN LYNNE ENTERED the kitchen of the big house, Betsy and Ron were sitting at the table sipping coffee and chatting with each other.

"Hi guys," Lynne said as she came in.

"Where have you been?" Betsy asked. "I walked over to talk to you last night, but Jo said you'd gone to dinner with Collin."

"Never mind," Ron said, noticing the grin on Lynne's face. "I may not know where you've been, but I can tell by the look on your face what you've been up to. Congratulations!"

"What?" Betsy said, standing up and taking Lynne by the shoulders. "What have you been up to, missy?"

"Nothing," Lynne said innocently, her eyes downcast, but still grinning. "I've not been up to anything."

"Liar! You are a liar!" Betsy said as she squeezed Lynne. "He is pretty great, you know."

"Yes, he is," Lynne said back.

Just then, there was a knock on the back door and the shack girls walked in.

"Wow, to what do we owe this honor?" Ron asked. "We have the full crew here this morning."

"Where are the kids?" Smitty asked.

"They're playing video games in Josh's room. Why?" Betsy asked with concern.

"We have some news," Callie said.

"We have some fucking great news," Sam added.

"Well, let's hear it," Betsy said as Smitty, Callie, and Jo pulled up chairs, and Sam and Kellan stood behind them.

"You don't have to worry about David anymore," Smitty said firmly. "He's gone."

"What do you mean he's gone?" Ron asked. "Gone where?"

"He's gone someplace he won't be coming back from," Callie said.

"What do you mean 'he's gone someplace he won't be coming back from?'" Betsy parroted.

"Ding dong the witch is gone. The wicked wicked witch is gone," Sam said in a singsong.

"He's dead?" Betsy asked, sounding horrified.

"We know with certainty that he's gone, and we're not going to tell you more than that. If someone comes around asking about him, you can honestly tell them you don't know. But we had to tell you that he's gone—really gone and not coming back—or you'd continue to look over your shoulder for the rest of your lives," Sam said.

"I can't just leave it at that. What have you done?" Betsy asked angrily.

Ron looked over at her and said, "Betsy, I don't want to know. All I need to know is that he's gone. I don't care where or how." Then he walked over to Sam and gave her a big hug. "I don't know what to say other than we are eternally grateful," he said as he tried to choke back his tears.

When she saw his eyes well up, Betsy got up and took him in her arms, and the two of them cried for several minutes. Lynne and the shack girls looked on silently, wiping away their own tears.

"I needed this," Kellan said.

Jo squeezed her hand and said, "We are free."

CHAPTER 49

Summer 2018

AS THE BEAUTIFUL weeks of summer went by, Josh continued to go out into the fields with Ron. Betsy was amazed, since she'd fully expected him to lose interest any minute and whine about having to help with the work. But miraculously he did not. The two of them would head out at the first light of dawn and work the whole day together. And it did her heart good to see it bringing them closer.

Betsy and Lynne dropped Melanie off at the café every morning on their way to the shack—although most days it was Melanie who drove them. Once there, Melanie loaded them up with fresh hot coffee for all the shack girls, and Lynne and Betsy would arrive at the shack and stop by each studio, coffee in hand.

Betsy would head to her studio to paint, while Lynne would go to hers to work on the projects Margie had assigned her. At midmorning she would take a break and sit out on the porch. She could see far down the road towards town and also in the other direction, leading to farms and the open road. She was relatively remote from all the activity going on inside, but still close enough so that she could hear the glass furnace running and music emanating from each studio, reflecting to some extent the personality of the artist who'd selected it. And she would often hear their laughter. She would so miss the sound of their laughter.

Today she watched a police car come down the road from town toward the shack. But instead of driving past, it stopped. Officer Burkett got out of his car and approached.

"Good morning, Bob. To what do we owe this pleasure?" Lynne asked.

"Good morning, Lynne. How are you?" he replied.

"I'm good. It's a beautiful day."

"Yes, it is," he said, removing his hat and sitting down next to her. "This is a great place to sit. You can see everything from here," he remarked.

"I know. It is pretty great, isn't it?"

"Who's here today?" he asked.

"Everyone's here. They're all working away inside. So, what can I do for you?"

"Nothing. I was just driving by and decided to stop and see how you all were doing."

"Well, that's very nice of you."

"You're aware of the fact I've been looking for David Hoffman, right?"

Lynne's throat tightened. "What?" she said. "Why would you be looking for him?"

"Well, as you know, there are two orders of protection against him. I was just wondering if you've seen or heard from him recently, in spite of the orders."

"Well, no, actually. I haven't seen him in several months."

"When was the last time you saw him?"

"Well . . . uh, I guess it was just after school got out. I saw him at the café."

"Did you know he was using a false name?"

"I heard that."

"Who told you that?"

"Why are you asking me these questions?" she asked, becoming increasingly concerned. "Have you seen him?"

"No, I haven't seen him and I am surprised. I'm just wondering why no one has seen him. How did you know he was using a false name?"

"Well, Mr. Saunders introduced me to him at the café. He referred to him as David Samuelson."

"So you think he had been going to the café to see Melanie? I guess I should preface that question by revealing the fact that I know you're Melanie's birth mother and that David Hoffman believes he is her birth father."

Lynne looked down at her hands. "Who else knows that? Do you know what he did to me?"

"Yes—and no one else knows. I've had several long conversations with an Officer Curtis, in Chicago, about this case. She is quite the advocate for you, you know. She is the one who contacted me about each of the orders of protection. She has made it quite clear that this was a confidential matter. In fact, I had to do quite a lot of digging to find out the story myself. I wanted to know the story behind why you took out an order of protection against him, and why there was a second one for Ron, Betsy, and the kids. I thought it was important to know what this guy was up to and why."

"So you know what he did to me too?"

"Yes, I read the file, and I've had several conversations with an Officer Curtis—who I understand handled your case. I'm very sorry about what happened to you, Lynne. It was a very brutal attack. Officer Curtis was deeply affected by it, and she has emphasized repeatedly how hard they'd worked to keep everything about your case confidential. It became personal for her, and she was very reluctant to tell me anything. I promised her I, too, would protect you and your privacy."

Lynne, keeping her eyes down, smiled. "She was a great help to me during a very difficult time."

"So when did you find out he was out of prison?"

"The day he showed up here several months ago and started threatening me." She paused and then added, "I was so surprised to see him. I had naively thought he would get out of prison and go on with his life and let me go on with mine. But he didn't. I got the order of protection because I had to do something to keep him from coming around and intimidating me. And then when he started bothering Melanie too, well, that was just too much," she said with a deep sigh.

"Melanie doesn't know about any of this. She doesn't know who her birth mother and father are, and certainly doesn't know anything about the backstory involving David." And then she added in a pleading tone of voice, "And we don't ever want her to find out."

Officer Burkett looked at her sadly. "Oh, please let me be clear—it's not my intention to tell her or anyone else about this. I just wanted to know more about David's history so I'd have a better idea of what I should be looking out for."

Lynne nodded her understanding. "You know, he started showing up at the café and talking to Melanie. He was grooming her—just like a child molester does," she said angrily. "He can be very charming when he wants something. She never knew or suspected anything about what was really going on. Just like I never knew or suspected. That's when Betsy and Ron requested the order of protection and decided to keep both Melanie and Josh at home. Did you know that he wrote a threatening note to Betsy?"

Bob shook his head no.

"He put it into the mailbox at the farm—no postage—just put it directly into the box. Melanie was the one who found the note. Thank God she didn't open it," Lynne said.

"No, I didn't know about that."

"Do you know how frightening that was to us? He did it to show us that he could do what he wanted and that no one could stop him."

"Do you think Betsy or Ron know where he might be?"

"No, I don't think they do."

"I noticed that Melanie is back at the café. Do they think it's safe for her now?"

Lynne was caught on that one. She didn't have a good answer. "No, I don't think she's safe, but what can we do? We can't keep her locked up forever. David demonstrated, by virtue of that note, that if he wants to get to her he can—and we won't be able to stop him, and there are no laws that will stop him either."

"You think he will violate the order of protection? Do you understand that I am here to enforce it?" he said.

"Yes, I understand that, but you can't be everywhere, and you don't even know where he is," she said angrily.

After a brief pause, she continued, "Fortunately, Melanie is a smart girl and knows that I love her and that her parents love her more than life itself. I may have given birth to her, but Betsy and Ron are her parents and always will be. David can't take that away from her. All we can do is provide the best possible support system for her and teach her the skills to keep her safe. There is not a lot more we can do. She's nearly sixteen years old, which makes her a young woman."

"Maybe David is dead, and you won't have to worry about him anymore."

Hearing that, Lynne gasped like the wind had been knocked out of her. Gathering all the courage she could muster she said, "What do you mean? Do you think he's dead?"

"Well, it would appear something has happened to him, since he's never come back for his car."

"What do you mean?"

"His rental car was found outside of town, down by the river on the service road. It was there for more than a week, and when he didn't come back for it, I had it impounded. Apparently it was wiped down. There were no fingerprints—including his—anywhere on the vehicle."

Then Lynne's heart stopped. "What are you saying?"

"Well, I don't know. I think it's odd that he didn't come back for it, and that the car had been wiped clean. I just wondered if you'd seen him or knew anything about it."

"Well, no, I didn't know any of that," she said firmly. "I haven't seen him. And based on my previous experience with him, he certainly could have wiped it down himself. He didn't leave any fingerprints in my apartment, even after leaving devastating physical evidence on my body."

"Well, it is a possibility he did it himself, and I'm looking into that," Officer Burkett said calmly. "Right now, he's officially considered a missing person who is actively being sought," he said with a new note of authority in his voice. "Do the women from the shack know about your connection to David Hoffman?" he asked.

Lynne sat for several seconds trying to think about what she should say and decided to tell him the truth. "Yes, they know about him," she said softly. "He's been here at least twice, first to threaten me and then to threaten Betsy."

"Was there a reason you didn't report his visits to my office?"

"Well, we requested the orders of protection after those visits," Lynne said in an agitated tone. "I figured the court would tell whomever needed to know. Short of calling you myself, I'm not sure what else I could have done." Pausing and getting even more agitated, she continued, "And, now here you are, asking me if I know where he is. You don't instill a lot of confidence Bob."

"Why are you angry about this?"

"I'm tired of him. I'm tired of the whole situation, the impact he has had on my life, and now the life of my family. I've tried to keep what happened to me confidential; and more importantly, I didn't want anyone to know about Melanie. I've made a conscious decision not to tell anyone. You see, no one knew about the pregnancy until I went for my deposition—and somehow David found out. He showed up here and has turned our lives upside down. It's not personal, Bob."

"Okay," he said, getting up to go.

"Okay?" Lynne repeated. "What does 'okay' mean?"

"It means I got the answers to the questions I needed and now I'm leaving."

Lynne was angry now. "But what does that mean with respect to David? Where is he? Do you think something happened to him? I'd like to know."

"I have no answers for you, Lynne," he said calmly. "But I do get the feeling you know more than you're telling me."

"You're wrong about that—I don't know what happened to him," she said a bit too hastily.

Bob reached his hand inside his vest and slowly pulled out a thin paint brush and laid it in Lynne's lap. Leaning in and looking closely at her he said, "Lynne, I found this in David Hoffman's car. I'd like to know what happened to him and I think you all may know more than you're telling me. But let me be clear, my primary concern is for the safety of you, Ron, Betsy, the kids, and the ladies here at the shack." Then he stood up, put his hat back on his head, and tipping the brim to her said, "I wish you the best, Lynne."

She stood up, brush in hand, and watched as he walked over to his car and drove back towards town. Feeling overwhelmed, Lynne sat down and, for more than an hour, rolled the delicate little paint brush back and forth between her fingers trying to decide what to do. She recognized the brush immediately. It was one of the pair that Jo used to pin up her long, dark, hair.

Lynne had a lump in her throat as she contemplated what must have happened that had caused that brush to end up in David's car and what sacrifices had been made to protect her and Melanie. She debated whether she should tell the shack girls about what had just happened. She wanted to know what had transpired that day. Finally, she decided no, she wouldn't tell them. If Bob wanted to talk with them, he would, and for all she knew he may have already. But she didn't think so. He had handed her a prime piece of evidence and left it for her to decide what to do with it. She slid the brush into her purse and decided to let it all go. Regardless of what Bob knew or didn't know, the real threat was gone.

CHAPTER 50

Fall 2018

AUTUMN CAME TOO soon. The beautiful summer days had passed so quickly and now they were done. Lynne had been dreading the start of fall because it marked the time when she would move back to Chicago and leave behind her precious time with Betsy, Ron, the kids, and of course, the shack girls. She'd packed up what few belongings she had at the little house and put them in her car. Now it was time to say her good-byes.

She drove to the shack and stood outside, studying it. It really was nothing more than a shack, but it held such wonderful people and equally wonderful memories. She thought of her mother, sister, and the great women who filled that space.

She went upstairs to her office and sat down at the picnic table that served as her desk. She looked out the window at the rows of crops in the distant fields. She could hear Kellan across the hall and decided to head over to say good-bye. Kellan was working on a landscape painting that featured the shack as its focal point. Looking at it, Lynne said. "You've captured the true personality of this place. It looks almost beautiful."

"It *is* beautiful," Kellan said. "It's the place where I am most at home, and where my dearest friends are. It's also the place where I can be creative and express myself. I think this painting is turning out to be one of the best I've ever done. It reminds me of all of you, and I painted it using these special brushes."

"What's so special about those brushes?" Lynne asked, pointing to the bottle that held a dozen or more of them.

"Jo made them for me," she said.

"Really. I didn't know that Jo made brushes," Lynne said, as she picked them up and ran her thumb across the bristles. "They're unusually soft, and the handles are so smooth."

"Yes, she did a beautiful job for me."

"Are you going to sell this painting?"

"Yes, I already have a potential buyer in mind. He's been after me to do more rustic settings, and this is certainly that," she said, holding her hands out to indicate the sides of her studio.

Lynne gave Kellan a big hug. "I'm so glad you're one of us, and I'm also glad you're going to live with Jo. That way I know she won't be lonely after I'm gone. You two will be good for each other."

Kellan squeezed her back. "We'll miss having you here with us every day, Lynne, but we know we'll see you often. So please come see us as often as you can, okay?"

"I will," Lynne said as she left Kellan's studio and headed down the stairs to Callie's.

From outside the door, Lynne could hear the sound of Callie's huge quilting machine. "Hey Callie, what are you working on?" she asked as she knocked and opened the door.

"Hey Lynne, come in—I'm glad to see you. I'm making a wall quilt."

Lynne gazed at the work in progress. "I love how you've combined the colors. It's beautiful."

I wanted to create a scene. Something that would remind me of this summer."

"It's incredible. It looks like a photo of the farm. Is it the farm?"

"Yes, it is."

"Wow, the sky is incredible. How did you do it?"

"Well, I had some old shirts that were in different shades of blue, so the lighter tones were perfect for making clouds in the sky. Also, I had a wide variety of fabrics to work with, as well as a photo I used," she said, holding up a photo of the farm. "I think I'll enter it into the international show in Texas this year."

"I bet you'll do well. It really is beautiful."

"Are you getting ready to take off?" Callie asked.

"Yes. I have everything loaded in my car, but I wanted to stop by and say good-bye to everyone before I left."

"When will you be back?" she asked. "And when you're here, will you be sure to come by the shack?"

"Absolutely!"

"It'll be hard to come here every day and know we won't see you. But I'm so happy you're getting your life back. It's about time!" Callie exclaimed.

"It is about time—you're right. But I feel like a kid going away to school for the first time."

"You'll be fine." And Callie went over and wrapped her arms around Lynne as she added, "You'll be just fine."

Lynne went on to visit Jo's studio. She was working on an interesting mixed media piece that consisted of twigs, dried plants, bones, leather bits, rocks, and roughly woven grasses.

"Hello, Lynne. Are you here to say good-bye? I'm not sure I can take another one. It was hard enough on me this morning as I pulled away and saw you in my rearview mirror. My roommate has moved out, and I'm so going to miss her," she said with a pretend pout.

"I'll miss you too. This piece is really coming along well," Lynne remarked. "Was it commissioned?"

"Yeah. I think it's pretty interesting too."

"Are these bits of bone?"

"Yes, they are. Aren't they great?"

"Where did you find them?"

"Oh, I don't remember," Jo lied. "They really fit the piece though, don't they?" Then changing the subject, she said, "I have a friend who just opened a gallery in New York, and she asked me if I had anything unique I could send her. I think she might like it." She wiped her hands on her apron. "You headed down to see Smitty and Sam?"

"Yes," Lynne said, starting for the door.

"I'll go with you," Jo said.

The music coming from Sam's studio was loud, just as it always was. Sam liked to listen to seventies rock music when she was working—and the volume had to be loud to be heard over the sound of the glass furnace. It was going strong when they opened the door. Sam had her goggles on and was soaked with sweat.

"It must be two hundred degrees in here," Lynne yelled.

"On my God! You scared the shit out of me!" Sam yelled back, not stopping her work. She was holding a multicolored vase that had just come out of the furnace. She put her mouth to the blow hole and blew to inflate it, spreading the beautiful colors in ribbons around the sides.

"That's incredible, Sam," Lynne called out. "I don't think I've ever seen you produce anything like this before."

"You're damn right. And I'm going to sell a suite of these. Hey, did you change your mind about coming with us to Jackson Hole in a few weeks? We're working on Betsy. Smitty, Jo, Kellan, and Callie are going. Maybe if you come, she will too."

"Are you crazy? I will have just started my new job. I can't take off for the wild west after a week on the job!"

"Well, at least talk Betsy into going with us," Sam said, and went on with her work.

Jo gave Lynne a hug and said, "I'll let you have Smitty all to yourself. I love you, Lynne. I'm so glad we had the chance to live together. You're like a sister to me—and I'm so grateful to have you and Betsy in my life."

Lynne squeezed her back, and as they parted said, "I feel the same way about you."

When Lynne went into Smitty's studio, she saw her loading the kiln. "Hi, Smitty," Lynne said. "I just came to say my good-byes before I hit the road."

Smitty looked at her with big, sad eyes, "Oh Lynne, do you have to go? Who's going to share my studio with me after you're gone?"

"You should be glad you don't have to share it with anyone! Besides, you won't have me budging my pieces into your kiln all the time."

"I love your budging," she said with a frown.

Walking over to the shelf, Lynne touched several of the pieces that had unique glazes on them. "These are lovely. Are these new glazes? The pieces are exceptionally beautiful."

"Yes, as a matter of fact I refer to those as my 'relief' glazes," she said.

Not understanding, Lynne asked, "What do you mean, your 'relief' glazes?"

"Well, they form a relief on the surface of the piece, and I developed them this summer using special materials, including ash. For me, the word 'relief' captures the tactile and emotional experience of touching them."

"Relief," Lynne repeated, as she ran her fingers over the surface. "Relief is a very apt term for this glaze."

Wiping her hands on her apron, Smitty came over and gave Lynne a big hug. "I'm so sad to see you go, Lynne, but I know it's the best thing for you. You'll come see us often, won't you?"

"Yes. I bet I'm here every weekend. The kids will have track meets and other activities I want to see, and I also hope to spend some time with Collin at the dairy. I'll stop here on my way, coming or going."

"What are you going to do about your art?" Smitty asked.

"What art?" Lynne replied.

"You can't let your talent go to waste. Will you stop by and work on your art?"

"Only you would say that, Smitty," Lynne said with a smile. "I'll never forget our lovely time together these past few years. And while I'm sorry that Betsy had to suffer, I'm so grateful for my time here. I love you, Smitty. I love all of you shack girls."

Lynne walked out onto the porch and stood there for a few moments, just taking in the view up and down the road and out into the fields beyond. She knew that while she wouldn't be here physically every day, she would always be here emotionally—and more importantly, she would always be one of the shack girls.

The End